The Pleasu

Sara Sheridan was born i̶̶̶̶̶̶̶̶̶̶ studied English at Trinity College Dublin and then went on to live in Galway before returning to her native Scotland. She now lives in Edinburgh with her daughter, Molly. In 1999 she co-wrote a short film, *The Window Bed*, which won a Sky Movies award, and she is now working on her first feature-length screenplay, IOU. She was recently nominated for a Young Achievers of Scotland award.

Sara is the author of two previous novels, *Truth or Dare* and *Ma Polinski's Pockets*, and is currently writing her fourth novel, *The Love Squad*.

Praise for Sara Sheridan's previous novels:

'A thriller for a new generation . . . Sara Sheridan will go far'
Harpers & Queen

'It made me laugh out loud, but it also nearly reduced me to tears'
Sunday Express

'Darkly comic and compassionate'
Mike Ripley, Daily Telegraph

'Poignant, exhilarating, funny'
Time Out

'Written in a snappy, quick-witted style, this urban odyssey looks set to gain many admirers'
Edinburgh Evening News

'A revenger's tragedy crossed with a blithe and black picaresque road comedy . . . so well written you never notice the writing'
Glasgow Herald

'A thoughtful, passionate novel'
Daily Telegraph

Sara Sheridan

The Pleasure
Express

ARROW

Published by Arrow Books in 2000

1 3 5 7 9 10 8 6 4 2

Copyright © Sara Sheridan 2000

Sara Sheridan has asserted the right under the Copyright, Designs and
Patents Act, 1988 to be identified as the author of this work

First published in the United Kingdom in 2000 by Arrow

Arrow Books Limited
The Random House Group Limited
20 Vauxhall Bridge Road, London, SW1V 2SA

Random House Australia (Pty) Limited
20 Alfred Street, Milsons Point, Sydney,
New South Wales 2061, Australia

Random House New Zealand Limited
18 Poland Road, Glenfield
Auckland 10, New Zealand

Random House (Pty) Limited
Endulini, 5a Jubilee Road, Parktown 2193, South Africa

The Random House Group Limited Reg. No. 954009

www.randomhouse.co.uk

A CIP catalogue record for this book is available from the British Library

Papers used by Random House UK are
natural, recyclable products made from wood grown in
sustainable forests. The manufacturing processes conform to
the environmental regulations of the country of origin

ISBN 0 09 940978 X

Typeset by SX Composing DTP, Rayleigh, Essex
Printed and bound in Denmark by
Nørhaven A/S, Viborg

With many thanks to all the helpful people in Hong Kong who showed me around. This book is about greed, cowardice and corruption and for that reason I hesitate to dedicate it to anyone in particular, but special thanks are due to Lynne Drew, Kate Elton, Val Hoskins, Simon Trewin, Michael Swift, the Choos, the Dunbars and the Barleys. And also to the Scottish Arts Council who gave me a grant to visit Hong Kong to do additional research after my initial trip proved too short. Thanks.

Prologue
Ko: Revolution

Pain does lots of different things to you. Rosie had gone into shock. Her smooth skin was clammy and cold and she looked like she was going to throw up, holding on to her wrist in disbelief. I couldn't blame her. It seemed entirely out of place, there in her glamorous bedroom with the view of Hong Kong through the window and the luxurious silence of our house engulfing us, that Bobby should have broken her wrist. In cold blood.

I felt a mild panic consume me as I stroked Rosie's hair and told her that the doctor was coming. I had never before felt I would rather something had happened to me than to someone else, but Rosie was my best friend, and I wished that Bobby had snapped my wrist instead of hers. That's how difficult it was to see her in pain, her dark eyes glassy and her lips tight together, trying not to cry. The initial rush of adrenalin was subsiding, its anaesthetic draining away, and Rosie started to whimper.

'Bobby,' she whispered, 'I can't believe it.'

And suddenly it hit me that we had been thinking too small. Like us, Bobby was just working for someone else. Some man we'd never met.

1

'Hush now,' I murmured, worried at how pale Rosie had got. I checked my watch, hoping she wasn't going to pass out. The doctor couldn't be long.

'You ever know anyone who got killed?' Rosie asked me.

I lay down next to her and breathed in the scent of Opium on her pillow.

'No,' I said. 'My grandfather died, though. He killed himself.'

She didn't say anything, so I decided to keep talking. I thought the story might distract her and well, I hoped it would distract me too. I didn't want to think about the mess we were in. I didn't want to even consider the possibility of either of us getting killed.

'My grandfather used to gamble,' I continued. 'He was a risk-taker. An adventurer. He had travelled a lot. Fought in the war. We didn't see him all that much, he just used to get a bit drunk and lumber around at family parties. Used to say to us kids, "What have you got in life if you haven't got friends and freedom?" And he used to do card tricks, and tricks with boxes of matches and two pints. He used to make pennies appear and disappear. If you were ten he was amazingly charismatic.'

'How did he die?' Rosie asked.

I sat up on the bed. 'Well, he had a heart attack and the doctor sent him home. Told him to stay there for three weeks and just rest. No booze. No excitement. Grandad waited for the doctor to leave and then he got up, got dressed and got himself down to the local. He bought everyone a pint, tipped a whole lot of horses in the next day's races, was the life and soul of the party and at chucking-out time he came home, got into bed, had another heart attack and died.'

Rosie was silent for a moment or two. Then a tiny smile turned up the corners of her mouth.

'How did we get into a mess like this?' she asked.

And then we heard the doctor coming up the stairs.

Chapter One

Chia Jen: The Family

I wonder sometimes what might have happened if I had stayed in Coatross. I'd be married now. Married and broke. Heavily in debt to the bank over some poxy little house somewhere, struggling to afford to be able to furnish it. That's what the alternative was, though I never knew I'd get as far as I did. Never guessed I'd become a high-flier – one of the best in my field. Never knew I'd end up in Hong Kong. All I knew was that when an opportunity arose I had to grab hold of it. 'Kate,' I said to myself, 'you have to go forwards.' And the world opened up for me.

Coatross seems like it was a million years ago, a million miles away certainly, but of course there are some things I remember about Scotland. Some particular things which, for good or bad, formed me. I always liked arithmetic when I was at school, although of course I didn't tell anyone that. It would have totally blown the air of mystery which, by the age of twelve, I had carefully cultivated around myself. But there was just something irresistibly satisfying about those neat little columns of numbers which all added up perfectly. And now I'm a big girl, so to speak, I still get kind of a kick out of counting stuff up. I like a neat equation.

That's to say, by way of practical application, I get a kick out of totting up my money.

When I was twelve years old I got my first job helping out at the paper shop on Saturday and Sunday mornings. My father wouldn't allow me to get any kind of a weekday job at all. He considered school work too important, which now, in the light of how little it's ever, ever mattered in anything that I've done, just seems laughable. My dad was of the old school, the keep them down, don't let them aim too high because they'll only be disappointed fraternity; working on the production line all his life. My uncle used to say that Dad should have been promoted, but Dad didn't want that. Not for himself or for anyone else. He liked his place in the world, he liked the status quo. It gave him a sense of order which he didn't want disrupted by anything, certainly not by success or achievement at any rate. But he still thought school work was important. Not because an education might get you anywhere, but because it was the right thing to do. Good kids went to school and Dad, if nothing else, was always good. A good man who knew his place, born at least a century too late. So I spent a lot of my childhood playing along with him, hiding my ambitions and my dreams from the old man, because I knew from quite a young age, with absolute conviction, that I could do whatever I wanted, whatever I set my mind to. I only had to try.

At the weekend, once school was over, I was allowed to work and work started early, earlier than school ever began. I had to be at the paper shop by six. Most mornings it was dark and cold and I'd make myself a cheese sandwich and eat it as I walked along the pavement towards the yellow-lit shop window with the crumbs sticking to my green woollen gloves and my breath clouding up in front of me. Coatross was a small town and I knew everyone I delivered the paper to by name. And they knew me. Wee Kate Thompson from down the crescent. Not that they ever looked.

After my paper round Mr Shaw would make me a cup of instant hot chocolate to warm me up and then I'd restock the shelves and tidy out the back room, cut strips off all the unsold papers and, last of all, seal up the envelopes on the bills which were due to go out the following week. I took pride in that little job, I did all that useless stuff very carefully and I tried to be really neat. Really tidy. I got fifteen pounds a week for it, in cash, and I got the pick of the sweet counter. I saved every penny from there, and from my Sunday afternoon job, washing cars out in front of our house. That was two pounds a time, including rubbing on the wax afterwards. These days I'd tip a waiter all of what used to be my weekly wage, but I saved all of that money, earned pound by pound. I had a blue tin money box which I kept at the bottom of my wardrobe and I kept track of every penny because I knew I'd need it one day. I realized, I suppose, that I was only biding my time.

As I remember it, I was thirteen when I knew I was leaving for the big city. Not Edinburgh, where, much to my grandmother's delight, my cousin had gone and taken a job with one of the big insurance companies, calculating premiums over the phone. That just sounded like a glorified job at the newsagent's to me and I certainly wasn't up for that. No, I was heading south where the streets were wide and the lights burned brightly all night and I would never have to see the steaming grey roofs of Coatross again.

The summer I was thirteen Rhona Campbell's big sister got married and I was one of the bridesmaids. There were six of us – all at school together, and we'd played around as kids – and we went over to Perth in a hired coach and traipsed up the aisle in grey and pink taffeta. Afterwards there was a reception at a posh hotel, and left unsupervised we ran wild. Rhona and Annie got hold of a couple of bottles of Martini and we drank them as if they were wine and then legged it out the back of the marquee to sit in the last of the sunshine and giggle. Annie got sick and Rhona began to dance like a maniac.

I was bored so I wandered off on my own. The hotel had huge gardens and there was a river away down at the bottom, so I headed off to investigate, trailing my long grey skirt behind me. When I got down there, I found I wasn't alone.

'My name's Dean,' he said, and we shook hands rather solemnly.

Dean was in his early twenties, I suppose. To me he looked just like some kind of film actor. He was very, very glamorous in his dark suit and white shirt with no collar and when he spoke he had a Glasgow accent which made him sound as if he knew what he was talking about.

'You one of the bridesmaids?' he asked.

'Nah, just wearing the ballgown for kicks, you know.' Thirteen-year-olds have some lip on them.

Dean and I swigged something even stronger than Martini out of a bottle he had in his pocket, and we set to talking and well, we really did just talk. Or rather, he did. All about London, and how fantastic it was. About nightclubs and parties and earning lots of money. About the buzz of a capital city. About feeling international. He had a very assured air about him, quite different from anyone in my family, in fact quite different from anyone I knew.

'You,' he said, 'you're gorgeous. Wasted up here.

7

Wasted. Girl like you belongs somewhere, as amazing as you are. Girl like you.'

I was starry-eyed.

Later, when the coach took us back to Coatross, and I ambled upstairs to my bedroom, trying not to let on how much booze I had consumed, I decided that Dean was right. I didn't belong in Coatross and I never had.

'Going to go and live in London,' I mumbled to my mother, who didn't take the news too well. Maybe it was the alcohol on my breath.

'You're not going anywhere, young lady,' she said. 'You belong here. Isn't that right Hugh?'

And my father agreed with her.

'When I grow up, I mean,' I tried to explain, but my father leaned over to kiss me goodnight.

'You were born here, and here you'll stay, young lady, close to your family,' he said.

But I planned it every moment with a steady kind of calm, watching my emergence from the chrysalis with no wonder in my eyes. I was going. I was as good as gone. I was just biding my time until the very first opportunity to leave. I had a big map of the London Underground up on my wall and I used to lie on my bed and stare at it. I could tell you the best way to get from anywhere to anywhere else on that old tube map without even having to look. Hammersmith to Ladbroke Grove, Sloane Square to Elephant and Castle, Charing Cross to Pimlico.

The last day of school was my last day at home. The last I saw of Rhona Campbell and Annie, they were talking about Robbie Williams leaving Take That and heading down to the chippie for a bag of scraps. I didn't even say goodbye to them – by that time we were so obviously different there just didn't seem to be any point – and I just went home for the last time. I don't expect they thought I really meant it when I said goodbye. They probably had it in mind that I'd be back after the summer, with my tail between my legs and an application form for a job at the Riverside Works in my hand. The negotiations had been going on for weeks, until finally they had agreed to the inevitable and said that I could go, and in a way, I think me leaving was a bit of a relief. It had been quite uncomfortable for them seeing me grow up so much, seeing me independent and just waiting until school was over. I'd become a different person. And if they saw me now, well, they'd never recognize me and I reckon they're better off not knowing what happened. Not knowing the things I did. Trust me. I'm just a bad girl, I guess. A bad, bad girl. You don't know the half of it.

That last day of school, I rode the bus into Edinburgh in the evening and took the sleeper from Waverley, tossing in the little bunk bed in my excitement, disturbing the slumber of the middle-aged lady on the bottom mattress so that every ten minutes or so she'd complain. But I couldn't help it. I was so excited. I was just eighteen years old and off to the city I'd always dreamed of, with my life savings in a little leather pouch close to my heart and only adventure ahead of me. There were cheaper ways to get there of course, it cost a lot less on the overnight coach, but I had over two thousand hard-earned pounds on me in cash – untold riches in those days – and besides, I wanted to arrive in some kind of style. It was the beginning of my odyssey into the outside world and I wanted it to be just the way that I had imagined all those cold, low-lit nights I'd lain in my single bed at home and dreamed.

And I did the right thing. I knew it the moment I

stepped on to the platform at King's Cross and out into the early morning sunshine. London took my breath away with its myriad possibilities and I discarded Coatross. I let it go. I saw London's endless streams of potential, and I was ready for it. I remember laughing because I was just so delighted and then I put my bag on my back and I walked. That day I went everywhere just staring at the huge, regal buildings in the wide, majestic streets. There were so many people that I couldn't quite believe it. I must have looked bewildered by it all – a young Scottish face in the teeming crowd. A pretty girl from a very small town who wasn't going back. I walked through Charing Cross, Covent Garden, Soho, Leicester Square, Piccadilly Circus, Hyde Park, Sloane Street, Chelsea, all along the walkway by the river, and I remember thinking that at last all those names meant something to me.

After ten hours of wandering around I realized, with a delighted excitement, that I hadn't seen the same face twice. You don't know what a kick that gives you when you come from a small place and really belong in a large one. It all seemed so glamorous, so complex and bewildering and beautiful and I knew I'd found the right place for me. I'd walked around all day and just disappeared, and I kind of congratulated myself. I did belong there. I had, after all, known what I was doing.

After that I just had to find something that I was good at. I had enough money to last me for a while as long as I was careful, but of course I had to find myself a job. And, I thought, not just any old job. Not just some newsagenty, delivering paperish kind of a job. Nothing which would remind me of home. No, I had to find myself a vocation. I had to make my fortune. After all, there was no point in coming to the big city and serving in a burger bar. Waitressing, typing and selling things in a shop were out too, and I suppose that sounds really snobby but I had this vision of the way things were going to be and I was determined to stick with it. I knew that I was talented. I was positive about that. I wasn't sure exactly what I was talented at, but I was ambitious enough to wait it out and see what turned up. I'm a strong believer in instinct and my instincts told me that things would take off fast.

A Glasgow girl I got chatting to in the park told me about a squat in Kilburn and I settled down there. It was one of a row of three-storey brick houses which were all boarded up, and to get in you had to climb over the side gate and through a little window at the back. Not the most salubrious of homes, but my two grand wasn't going to last for ever. Paying for somewhere to sleep would mean going without other things and I wanted to experience London to the full, make the money last as long as I could. The squat was a strange place. Not really my scene, but that was OK.

I took to drinking coffee up the road in Notting Hill Gate, sipping cappuccinos as slowly as I possibly could, whiling away the days as I mulled it all over and let it sink in, the big roll of notes in my leather pouch dwindling bit by bit. It was summer and everywhere was open late and the night-time air was balmy. I felt so cosmopolitan. I sat in trendy coffee shop after trendy coffee shop and I acclimatized myself to the city. To the heat of the summer and to the smell on the early morning air. I was fascinated by the women. They seemed so well put together, like something on TV. They all looked like they could be somebody and occasionally they were. I'd spot a singer or a model or an actress and my heart would pound and I knew that before long I'd look as if I might be somebody too.

11

I'll never forget those first weeks – the clear, cool summer mornings. The city smelled really good, full of the promise of warmth and, when I went out for breakfast, it floated with the aroma of freshly baked, yeasty bread and ground-up coffee beans. Sometimes I was so excited I used to break into a spontaneous run on my way down the street. I was a kid with a brand new toy – London.

Chapter Two

Lu: The Wanderer

I should probably tell you that when I got off the train the day I arrived, I wasn't a virgin. I'd done it with Mark Innes who lived down the road. And I'd done it more out of curiosity than anything else. We'd go over to his place after school when his mum and dad were still at work and we'd fool around for ages. Nobody knew about it, it's not like we ever went out on a date or anything, we just did it. Again and again and again, in different positions as if we were working our way through some kind of manual. I think I found it satisfying because I knew that I had some kind of power over him. He'd watch me in the common room at break times and wait for me coming out of the lunch hall. I knew Mark would have taken stupid risks to have me and I kind of liked that. I knew he'd have shinned up the drainpipe into my room at midnight if I'd asked him to. I knew he'd have done it bare-arsed behind the gym. But where I differed from a lot of kids was that I also knew that it wasn't love. Love was something else entirely.

How I got from an innocent shag with Mark Innes to taking money for sex I'm not very sure. I must have known what a hooker was, I was eighteen after all, but it was just not a career path that I'd ever considered for myself. Now though, well that's what I do. It's all I've done for the last God knows how long, four or five years I suppose. It's my job. And it turns out that I'm a natural. You see, you need poise, you need distance and you need to enjoy the power. Not the sex. The power.

I have to say that being a prostitute, the fact in itself, has never bothered me at all, but I suppose that's because I don't exactly look the part. Top end of the market, you see. I've always been a high-class girl ever since my very first day on the job a mere three weeks after I got off the sleeper – all five-star hotels and Chelsea apartment blocks. I picked up that film-star look quickly enough, that could-be-somebody veneer. Pretty and understated. The kind of girl who says 'where are you spending most of your time?' rather than 'where do you live?' I found out pretty quickly that there is a lot of money to be made if you can become the kind of woman who doesn't look like the kind of woman she is. And it all started with Eddie.

I'd seen him a few days in a row calling into the local juice bar for a 'Get Up And Go' – pineapple, mango, kiwi fruit and orange mix. He was kind of good-looking, with nice blue eyes and close-cropped, brownish hair. We'd nodded to each other, exchanged pleasantries and after two or three days we started to chat. Nothing too heavy, although he was pretty upfront about the fact that he was a pimp. When he talked about it I had been kind of shocked – firstly at what he did, shocked at the idea of me knowing some-one in the sex trade who was so nice and so upfront. Then, when he first suggested it, I was shocked at the prospect of having sex for money myself. It wasn't something I'd ever considered. But he carried on talking, my worries subsided and I gradually became shocked at how much money I could make. And by then, of course, I was sold.

And the moral issue? Well, its like this: everyone has so many preconceptions about taking money for sex, and so many preconceptions about sex itself, with or without payment, that unless you've actually done it I don't think people ought to comment.

'I say you look around yourself,' Eddie said to me. 'It's not always the cold girls who get the mink coats.' And he was right. All around me that summer in Notting Hill you could see them – women who picked up rich men and were kept in style. Passing out of Daddy's care and into the hands of some guy who could pick up the bills. To me, that's just socially acceptable prostitution and having to cook the dinner as well. The same thing only more dishonest. Maybe I was brought up around the work ethic for a bit too long, but I'd never have done what those women did. I wanted things to be cut and dried. I've always preferred to work for what I got, for things to be upfront, and it wasn't like I had lots of options either. So my young, excitable, thrill-seeking eighteen-year-old self saw what Eddie was suggesting as just another reckless adventure. A kind of gamble. And I love that kind of thing. Plus on top of that of course I realized how phenomenal the money was – you can get a couple of weeks' wages in one afternoon. Cash too. I mean, ladies of the night don't take credit cards. Not anywhere I've ever worked, anyway. I'm sure there are plenty of girls out there with the moral rectitude to turn it down and work in a burger bar for three fifty an hour, but, well, I wasn't one of them. No fucking way. Sex for me has never been like it is in films or books or magazines, some kind of great, romantic endeavour. I don't enjoy it and I don't not enjoy it. But I tell you something, I do like the money.

The evening I started Eddie came to pick me up in a taxi. I didn't have much stuff, just the small rucksack I'd brought from Scotland which I had been carrying around over my shoulder since I got there, because I was starting over, starting fresh. I climbed out of the kitchen window and Eddie and I headed across London towards the flat he'd sorted out for me, chatting in the back seat of the cab. Eddie was reeling off the names of good shops where I ought to buy my clothes and I was listening intently. I remember being madly impressed when he pulled a little box from his jacket pocket and carefully handed it to me. I squealed with excitement. It was Chanel. It was nail varnish. It was Rouge Noir. That summer Rouge Noir was big news. Uma Thurman had worn it in *Pulp Fiction*. It was the colour of the season and everywhere was sold out. Everywhere. But Eddie had got his hands on a pot just for me. At that moment, I know it sounds silly, but I believed he could pull anything off. Eddie was someone who could get me whatever I wanted.

As we pulled up at the flat, I sighed with satisfaction. Doughty Street. WC1. Sunny side of the road. First floor. We got inside and Eddie opened the heavy oak front door for me and I wandered into the bedroom and I just gasped because it was so full of light and it looked all golden, just like the place I'd been dreaming of living in, only when I lay down on the big double bed there was a mirror on the ceiling.

'You'll be all right here, darling,' Eddie told me as he languidly stroked my hair, and I looked at myself.

What I saw in the mirror that first evening in Doughty Street has stayed with me more than anything else from the time I spent in London. I don't think I'd ever really looked at myself before. Not like that. Not staring wide-eyed, knowing that I was beautiful. You don't know what the hell you look like when you're just some little schoolgirl, but that evening I stared at myself in the mirror and took it all in for the first time.

'I've done it,' I thought. 'I'm here.'

And like all the best ideas, things had just seemed so right. When Einstein first thought of the theory of relativity, you know, he didn't do it somewhere sensible, like in a lab. No, he'd been lying out on the grass on some hill somewhere, playing games, bouncing sunbeams back up at the orb of the sun. And it came to him. Einstein discovered his seminal theorem by instinct. I'd loved that story when I was a kid. I had a profound respect for physics and I'd spent a lot of time in Coatross bouncing things back to their source on account of relativity. Sounds in the night. My mother's unspoken resentment. The sarcastic comments of the geography teacher at school. Bounce, bounce, bounce. And Einstein's theory had worked for me. In the end, I remember thinking as I stared at myself in that mirror on the ceiling, I'd rather successfully bounced myself into a cushy little number in London, six hundred miles south of where I'd actually started out. I'd made it. Here I was. Strawberry blonde, long hair. Freckles. Blue eyes. 34–25–34. Meeting Eddie was fate. Kismet. And it changed my life. Cashmere jumpers in the wintertime and white linen all summer. A thousand pounds a night, seven fifty for the afternoon. Wouldn't you consider it too?

The only downside, of course, was the punters. Sometimes they came to the flat in Doughty Street, but mostly I went to them. Mostly they were from out of town. But the first time it was just a regular guy in a three-star hotel room in Hammersmith.

Eddie waited at the bar. I remember he drank Stella Artois and I thought that was cool. I headed upstairs and knocked at the door of the room number he'd given me. There wasn't any answer. I was really nervous and I flexed my fingers, taking courage from the immaculate Rouge Noir manicure I'd given myself that morning and the black trousers and loose, low-cut top I'd bought just after lunch. The girl in the shop had asked if I was a model and I had laughed. 'Too short,' I had smiled, 'I'm only five foot five.'

I knocked again and tried the door. It was open, so I walked right in. The room was full of smoke. The guy must have been puffing away for hours. He was sitting on the end of the bed, old and bald. It took me a second or two to hit reality. It wasn't very nice.

'You the girl?' he asked.

I smiled. 'Sure,' I said. It was like playing a part, I realized. I just had to get through it.

'You want it?' he asked and I managed not to laugh, which was quite a feat.

'I love it,' I said. 'I want it all the time,' and I walked over to him and bent over just slightly so he could see down my top.

'You sit here and watch TV with me,' he said.

So I did. And I waited for him. Slowly, he put one hand on my thigh and I faked a little moan. A sigh. He unbuttoned my blouse and he kissed me. It tasted horrible. All those cigarettes. Heavy tar. But I went with it. I stripped off for him and he caught me by the waist and pulled me towards him.

In the end it felt like five minutes, but I was up there for two hours. That old guy could go some. He pushed the money and an extra fifty into my hand and I smiled what I like to imagine was a dirty grin.

'Off you go,' he said, slapping me lightly on the arse.

Usually I'd stay all night. Mostly that's what they want. It's what they pay for. But that night I reckon the guy knew that Eddie was waiting downstairs. I reckon Eddie set it up just to be sure I could handle the job. I remember he checked his watch as he jumped down from his bar stool and he gave a kind of smug, knowing smile, then he took my arm and guided me outside and into the back of a taxicab without saying a thing. I didn't break the silence, I just pulled the money from my handbag and held it out to him like a kid who has something important to show their dad.

'We'll see to that later. We do that weekly,' he said, 'if you want to do it again.'

I thought for a moment. The old guy had tasted of cigarette ash and he smelled bad. He'd never normally have pulled a girl like me. Eddie waited for me to reply.

'I guess I'm not supposed to enjoy it,' I said and I put the money back into my handbag. If I'm honest, I like the look on a man's face when he can't help himself any more. Determined. Desperate. I get a kick out of that.

Chapter Three

T'ai: Peace

I worked out of that flat in London for nearly seven months and, to be honest, after that first day I can't really remember one of their faces or, for that matter, one of their names. I had regulars all right, but when it comes down to it they were all pretty well the same and my attention was taken up with other things – living in London, buying nice clothes, going out and seeing exhibitions, curling up for the afternoon in the movies. I must have seen *Trainspotting* half a dozen times when it first came out. And I went dancing sometimes and I liked reading, and I was quite happy. I was just being free. In fact, I spent quite a bit of time in my flat just reading and daydreaming. Relishing it. Being alone. They buy your body, you know, not your mind.

Once or twice a month Eddie'd turn up in a well-cut suit and take me out to this Italian place he liked at Charing Cross, so I got to know him a bit and I kind of took to him and, I guess, I trusted him as far as you can ever trust anyone in that situation. He groomed me, like some kind of guru. He'd tell me how to wear my hair and strangely enough, whenever I took his advice about stuff like that, people would stare. Walking into restaurants, people would stare.

'Just don't lose your accent,' he said. 'It's a winner. Gold dust. The guys love it.' Being Scottish, he reckoned, was cool. He arranged for all the style magazines to be delivered to my flat and when he came over he'd flick through them and point things out. It was very *Pretty Woman* I suppose, but it worked. I blossomed. And on top of that I was loaded.

We split things more or less fifty-fifty, Eddie and I. He had a big black guy on his staff called Elton James who used to laugh that his mum had married a guy with the name of the wrong apostle and that really he had been destined for stardom and missed out on account of his last name. Whatever. Anyhow, Elton used to turn up at Monday lunchtime and I'd give him the money from the week before. He had a key to my place, so he'd just let himself in and sit on the deep old leather sofa sipping a cappuccino from a takeaway styrofoam container.

'Everything OK, Kate?' he'd ask me, handing me a similar cup whenever I got it together to get out of bed properly and come over.

'Oh sure,' I'd smile. I was never really up before he arrived, so Elton always benefited from my rather great taste in nighties.

'Good week?' he'd ask me.

'Great week for shagging, Mr James,' I'd reply, looking defiantly into his dangerously still, toffee-coloured eyes.

Elton used to count it in front of me. Bill by bill on to the carved acacia-wood coffee table, his thick, nimble fingers making up little bundles of a hundred pounds at a time, and then stacking them into thousands. The coffee was good. He'd buy it on his way from a little kiosk just off Russell Square. He always used to put in sugar and although I don't like it sweet, I never really had the heart to tell him, which is kind of weird

21

because if I'd ever stepped out of line, like if I'd ever stiffed Eddie for some money or anything, it was Elton who would have come round to break my nose or worse, so I'm not quite sure exactly what I was saving his feelings for, but there you have it.

I know for most people being a hooker would be a strange sort of a job. I mean it's patently not normal, and some girls I've met, they have these awful stories and you know that being on the game is just part of some big, fucked-up problem, but it isn't like that for me. I come from a normal background. Coatross High School and a thin-walled, semi-detached house on the inappropriately named Hope Crescent. No cloying, groping uncles, no abusive, alcoholic mother, no early rape scene to scar me. Just the mediocrity which is exactly what people don't expect. Exactly what I hated. I was Ms Average until I went on the game, and I still think, even today, that it beats the pants off working in some office. No thanks. I've seen what that's like and I'd rather suck cocks for a living than kiss corporate arse. No matter what. And anyway, who is going to pay you upwards of £130,000 a year, tax free, for something that isn't a bit unpleasant?

I never did much kinky stuff, though I do know a few girls who specialize and the tales they tell would widen your eyes, if not your mind. I wasn't into any of that, although occasionally, once in a while, for a special client and always with the OK from Eddie I'd take on a special job. An individual commission if you like, but it always involved me doing things to them, rather than them doing things to me, so in fact it was even easier. Sometimes you don't even have to have sex at all, and for that kind of sicko, you charge double.

There was this one night in London that I did cry. Afterwards. It's the only time I've ever cried about it that I can recall. I'd been on the game a good few months then, and I'd come home a bit earlier than usual. I don't know who I'd been with. I can't remember. It hadn't been anyone special anyway, so maybe I was just tired. Who knows? Anyway, it was two in the morning when I got in and I just lay down on the carpet and stared at the lights from the cars which were playing along the ceiling, cutting through the shadows. It came over me quite suddenly, a gentle wave of unhappiness, and I got up and lit a cigarette, although I don't normally smoke at home, and I leaned up beside the window for a while and watched the dark, rainy street to distract myself but the feeling wouldn't go away. I stubbed the cigarette out and began to cry, hunch-shouldered, louder and louder until I was sobbing and wailing and holding my stomach and trying to catch my breath. For a while, I'm not sure how long, I was in despair but I didn't know why and I was feeling too much to really think about it and then, at last, as suddenly as it had started, it stopped. I'd let it all out and I fell, exhausted, on to the bed and into the open arms of a welcoming deep sleep. I didn't think about it much again. I didn't want to.

I suppose in the end you just sanitize it all inside your head. It's not that you switch off which would, I think, be a different thing entirely. I mean, you hear people say that about prostitution all the time and it pisses me right off, because to switch off you'd have to be switched on in the first place. And sex never had anything to do with love for me. Love is something really different and perhaps that was what I was missing that evening in London, the evening when I cried. Maybe I just didn't feel loved. Maybe I was lonely. Sometimes I hankered after a friend to talk to. Something normal.

To anyone else I must have looked like one of those Sloane Street girls with rich boyfriends – I certainly dressed more or less that way. Fenn, Wright and Manson trousers, a top from Whistles and a pair of Prada loafers with Armani sunglasses propped up on top of my head from April till October. It was a great cover, and most of the time I lived a good life in London. There was an endless stream of nice restaurants, and costly champagne. Of cars discreetly sent to fetch me and shopping trips in boutiques where you have to ring the bell. Of oh-so-subtle highlights in my hair and the best advice on make-up that money can buy. I just did whatever I wanted until my pager went off and told me where I had to be, or the phone went and Eddie left a message. London was great for months and months. I thought I was settled. I thought I'd made it. Every day I used to wake up and think 'here I am and isn't it fine?'

Every day, that is, right up to the time when Eddie lost more money than he could afford on the blackjack tables one Sunday night after Christmas and, in a fit of machismo and, I suppose, because it was just a business arrangement between us, he told his creditor that he had something better than money to hand over. To settle his debt he gave the guy a set of instructions and the key to my flat.

Chapter Four
Lin: Approach

Confucius had this really famous saying that if a man gets to forty and is generally disliked then there is no hope for him. That cold December day I took one look at Conrad Beckett and I knew that Confucius had him in mind. Conrad is a professional gambler among other things, so that gives you kind of an idea about him. Straight off it was clear that he was way, way too slick and, besides that, he didn't bring any coffee, which is kind of important to me first thing in the morning. Especially on Mondays because, after all, I was used to the Elton thing. Anyhow, he stood waiting while I got up out of bed.

'Who are you?' I asked.

'Conrad,' he answered. 'Eddie sent me.'

And obviously I thought he was a punter. A bit earlier in the day than usual, but, I figured, he must be special otherwise Eddie wouldn't have given him the key, so I just got on with the job of coming on to him and I started to do this thing with my eyes, which is really fucking hard before you've had any coffee in the morning. Beckett, though, had other things on his mind.

'It'd be really nice to go to bed with you right now,' he said. 'It'd be really nice to stay there all day. But we

25

have some other things to talk about first. I want to tell to you about a little business proposition I have.'

'I'm going to make some coffee,' I mumbled. I could have managed sex without it, but a conversation in which I was expected to participate was beyond me. I pulled a little pink chiffon slip round my body and headed for the kitchen.

Conrad sat down on the sofa, seemingly unperturbed by my nightclothes.

'You like it in London?' he asked.

'Sure. Where are you from?'

'The Far East. Macau. It's a Portuguese protectorate just off Hong Kong.'

'Wow.' I looked impressed because you gotta keep them going a bit and let them think that you think they are really glam.

'I want to take you there. Well, actually I want to take you to Hong Kong. I want you to come and work for me.'

I gulped. It was a bolt out of the blue, that was.

But there was no fucking way I was getting on a plane with the guy. No way. I had a real instinct about it. And besides, I could see when he moved that he was wearing a holster under his jacket. A fucking gun. And I wasn't going to get involved with that. Eddie could be dangerous, but hell, he never carried a gun. My danger-warning lights were on, so I said nothing.

'How much do you make here?' he asked and well, I knew by that stage that the guy was in the trade, dangerous or not, so I trotted off the rates at him. Hookers aren't coy about their earnings. There's none of that price-on-application stuff. There isn't any point. When I'd finished he just did this weird kind of grin.

'You get paid by the fuck? That's fucking outrageous.'

'Works for me. Self-employed and all that.' I smiled

as if it was none of his business and wondered how soon he might leave, how I might be able to get rid of him. But he just carried on.

'We'll pay you triple whatever you make a week, Kate,' he said. 'That'd make our offer around eight thousand sterling every seven days however much or however little you fuck. We need girls like you. In fact, to be specific, we need a pretty blonde girl at the moment. Not too tall. You'd be surprised. They're a bastard to find. And Eddie says you're really good. We need you.'

'I don't do kinky,' I replied, because usually to get paid that kind of money, well, I won't tell you what you've got to do, but it isn't pleasant.

Conrad laughed. 'You don't know Hong Kong,' he said. 'Kinky doesn't really come into it much. Local trade – the Chinks. Just poking a bit of blonde fanny is kinky enough for them. Not that we do a lot of local. My contacts cater for visiting dignitaries. Businessmen, pop stars, diplomats and bankers. Lonely bastards one and all. It's a pretty straight scene. We're in the hospitality business and we need a white girl just now. You get paid a lot to keep your mouth shut and leave in the morning. Those are the two things that our kind of customers really value in their pussy. They're too high-profile to dick around with anything less.'

I poured the coffee, thought about it for a moment or two and decided to come clean. I mean the guy had offered me a lot of money, I wanted to give him a chance to explain. As I saw it I was exploring the possibilities. Hong Kong began to sound kind of exotic.

'You're carrying a gun,' I said.

Conrad hesitated for a moment, taking it in. He looked like he was considering the best way to deal with me. How to talk me round. And he decided pretty quickly on pulling the gun from his jacket and laying it down on the coffee table.

'In England people aren't used to them,' he said with a shrug. 'Internationally, I'd say they're often mandatory.'

I sipped my coffee. He had an air of integrity about him when he said that, which seemed to come out of nowhere.

'You ever shot anyone?' I asked. 'Have you ever had to use it?'

'Once or twice,' he said, very gravely. 'Yes, I have.' And maybe it was his seriousness which made me feel that Conrad Beckett was a man you could trust with a gun. I'm not really sure.

Through the window to my left I caught a glimpse of our local bobby on the beat. He always walked past at the same time. They'd recruited a whole load of street cops and set them to work pounding pavements to make the public feel safer, and there he was, out doing his job, unaware of the stellar reading which would have registered on his crime-o-meter if he'd had one as he passed the door to my flat, unaware of just what he'd have to deal with if I ran screaming out of there chased by a gun toting, international pimp. I turned back into the room.

'How come Eddie's into this?' I asked him.

'Well,' Conrad said, 'Eddie didn't really have a lot of choice. I mean, he lost heavily last night at my table. But this isn't the white-slave trade, Kate. I'd write the money off if you didn't want to come. Really, it's up to you.'

'How much? How much would you write off?' I asked him.

Conrad shrugged. 'We played all night,' he said, his eyes meeting mine. 'I haven't slept. He owes me, let me

28

see, about fifty thousand in sterling.'

'And you'd write off all that if I just didn't fancy going?' I asked. I didn't believe him. It was too glamorous. Too showy.

'I don't think you realize quite how much money I make,' he said calmly. 'I just gamble for kicks these days. Let me take you out for lunch.'

Well, I had nothing better to do so I went with him. When someone offers you that much money, you have to give them the time of day, gun or no gun, and he was obviously a gambler. A dangerous liver just like me.

I can't honestly say that two hours later I liked the guy any better. I'd had a chance to study him though and he was very refined, perfectly turned out from his manicured nails to his handmade suit. He was, I figured, in his early forties and his hair was greying but hadn't yet started to recede and his eyes were a cold kind of uniform blue colour with no depth to them. Those were the first things I noticed. The superficial things. The secondary stuff, which I didn't pick up until later of course, was that he moved so smoothly, that he was perfectly at ease no matter what. It took a little while to realize exactly why he seemed so slick but then it came to me – Conrad Beckett had been taught perfect manners and he stuck to them. He ate beautifully, he rose as I left the table to go to the powder room, he walked to the kerb side of the pavement. I had the distinct feeling for some reason that though the guy had teeth he didn't necessarily bite. He asked a few too many questions though and by the time I had finished eating, I was beginning to feel as if I had been asset-stripped.

We had hit one of the upmarket restaurants off the back of Soho and we had a slow, leisurely meal. At three o'clock we were the only people still left in there, and Conrad's tales of Hong Kong had me hungry once again for a bigger city.

'Well,' he summed up when the bill came, 'it's a different class, Kate. I mean I know you're doing OK here, but with me you could really go to a different level. Of course my contacts are bigger-time than Eddie, there is that element of danger, but you're a white girl and to be frank, the Chinese in general won't find you that attractive. You and I both, I'm afraid and, well, they say that Caucasians just look like white pigs. Worse for women, that, I think. They say that white skin ages more quickly too, so your shelf life is pretty short. Let's say that it's a three-year contract or thereabouts. As soon as that thin skin of yours starts to look older than an eighteen-year-old's they won't want you around any more. But by that time you'll have made yourself quite a little nest egg, and, of course, you'll still be able to work the top end of the market in Europe for another six or seven years if you're careful. That's the deal.'

I finished my glass of champagne and sat back to peruse my options. There wasn't really much thinking to do. He'd offered me a lot of money, after all, and I couldn't really go back to Eddie after what he'd done. And the thing is, whatever city you live in, there's always somewhere brighter, isn't there? There's always somewhere bigger and more shiny on which to focus your dreams. Stuck in Coatross, London was my goal, my nirvana, but suddenly it seemed to me to be just a stopover, a training ground for the glittering lights of Hong Kong. So I figured, nothing ventured, nothing gained, right? I mean at least it would be exciting. The reckless gambler side of me loved it. Hong Kong. The chance to make big money.

'When do I have to go?' I asked Conrad.

'Hey,' he smiled. 'Whenever you want to, but I'm flying out myself early next week. I'll have done everything I have to by then. You can come with me if you like. First class.'

And I noticed when he pulled out his wallet to pay that he slowed down, almost imperceptibly, as if his battery had been removed.

We didn't have sex. That isn't so unusual for someone pimping you. It's a business deal after all. On the streets the pimps fuck the merchandise all the time of course, but that's because the girls are all messed up and they want love. Upmarket girls don't get strung out on smack, crack or devotion – not if they're successful. The best girls aren't junkies for love or any other drug. We're just like all the other professionals – doctors, lawyers, accountants. We do what we're good at and then we get paid. You could say that I'd been offered a good relocation deal with excellent benefits after a corporate takeover, and I did what anyone else would do. I packed my bags.

Three days before I went I bought five gold bars at sixteen thousand pounds a pop and I left them in one of the big safety deposit boxes at Barclays bank in Russell Square. You have to take precautions when you don't know how long you'll be. You have to have a stash which is fully realizable in times of trouble. It might seem weird, I suppose, to the nine-to-five crowd, but I think that would be the only difference between my profession and theirs. The level of personal paranoia you require to survive.

The day before we left I rang home. I got as far as dialling the number and hearing my father's voice at the other end, and then realized I didn't know how to explain, or what to tell him. A three-thousand-mile journey? An £8,000 a week contract? How I'd learnt to give brilliant blow jobs? What the hell was I going to say? It was a stupid idea.

'Is that you, Kate?' he asked after a long silence. 'Are you there?'

'I'm just calling to say that I'm fine, Dad. Don't worry about me,' I told him and then I hung up. I didn't really want to lie, so I figured it was best just to leave it at that. He suddenly seemed very far away, my father in Coatross, and I suppose he was. A million miles away at least and I didn't miss home one bit, though I shoved a thousand pounds into an envelope and sent it up to them by post. 'That'll pay off the hire purchase,' I thought. The ill-gotten gains of one night's work. And I realized how far I'd come.

The following Tuesday I flew out to Hong Kong via Amsterdam and my life totally changed again.

Chapter Five

Kou: Coming to Meet

The minute the plane swooped into the old Kai Tek airport I loved Hong Kong. From way up it just looked like a toy town and we came in so low that I could see people watching TV in their tiny one-room apartments. I sat deep into my seat and my heart was pounding as we plunged down and I had that feeling I'd had when I'd first arrived in London seven months before – the high of taking a risk, breaking free of everything. Things just felt so right. Conrad was watching me and I suppose my excitement must have shown, my eyes must have sparkled. He seemed mildly amused by it all.

'When we get off the plane,' he said, 'you'll smell it. There's an effluent plant nearby and the airport smells like shit. People say it's the stink of the dirty money.'

And I grinned at the thought, although I didn't take my eyes off the window.

It was quite something getting off that plane. I'd come from wintertime London with its low grey sky and oblique sunshine, the naked trees in Hyde Park standing bleak against the skyline, and Hong Kong was so warm and so intense. The sky was January blue and the air was thick and hot. I could hardly believe it. Conrad was right about the smell, though. I pulled the silk scarf I was wearing up over my face and we walked smartly into the air conditioning of the terminal building to pick up our bags. And that's how I arrived.

The city wasn't at all what I had expected, that much is for sure. None of it. For a start I thought that because it was a British colony, it would be kind of European. I'd read a couple of guide books before I left London and well, I just assumed that the place would be familiar and pretty westernized because Hong Kong viewed from the West seems that way. From the East though things are very different. Once you're actually there, you can forget all that and then some. Hong Kong is one big fuck-off Asian city. Outside the terminal Conrad and I slipped into the back seat of a large black car and the driver pulled out. 'We'll take a little tour if you like,' Conrad offered.

And off we set, me with my nose up against the window. Ten minutes later we were in the thick of it and I was staring at the crowds down Nathan Road and realizing that I was the only white person that I could see in the jostling, seething, tightly packed pavements. It was a weird experience. I mean, I'd always fitted in. Growing up in Fife, hanging out in London, I'd always looked like I belonged. But I realized straight away that there was no fucking way I was ever going to fit in in Hong Kong. Even with sunglasses. Even with a wig. I was an alien. When it came right down to it I moved differently from all these people and I suppose that was kind of exciting in itself.

The other thing I noticed on that first drive was the energy of the place. The life of it. The whole city seemed to vibrate like a bright blue strobe light at the very top of the spectrum. I'd found somewhere bigger and brighter than London and it was like moving to the big city all over again. It was a hit. A rush. The streets were crowded to capacity wall to kerb and every building was clad in neon and the skyscrapers reached upwards as if they were desperately grasping for some small space in among all the bustle. Conrad rolled down the windows and I smelled cooking everywhere and when we passed the open-air stalls the hot air wafted over, pungent with the dried fish and spices hanging there heavily in the humidity.

There was poverty too. Astounding poverty. I hadn't realized it when we came into the airport, but all round Kai Tek is really deprived. Whole families live in cages there, tiny cages with only one bed, and there are enough people living that way to populate a small town. You don't notice it because on the streets, people aren't begging like they are at home. It feels like there's money for everyone and there is just this tremendous sense of industry. It's glamorous and down-to-earth all at once. As we turned off on to Shanghai Road it was like floating in a dream and I knew even then that this was going to be somewhere that changed me for good. An experience I wouldn't regret. This was somewhere special.

Conrad dropped me off at a big house on Kadoorie Hill, which was where I was going to live. The car waited for him outside as he escorted me into the building and the driver dealt with my luggage. The house was beautiful. Space is at a premium in Hong Kong, so at first I didn't realize just how special it was. A study in luxury, really. God knows how much it was worth – you could pay hundreds and hundreds of thousands in Hong Kong just for a tiny apartment. That old place on Kadoorie Hill must have been worth millions. Downstairs there were three or four big public rooms, all decked out in sumptuous white carpets, carved hardwood furniture, ancient jade ornaments and blue-and-white porcelain. The air conditioning hummed in the background and when I looked up there were those old-fashioned fans hanging from the ceiling, like in *Casablanca*, for the particularly hot days. I felt strangely nervous. The place seemed very still, very quiet, and I was aware that even the noise of me putting my bag down on the table or my skirt rustling as I moved broke into that. Conrad was oblivious. He threw his briefcase on to a sofa and poured himself a drink.

'Now,' he said, 'I'd better show you round.'

And he began to guide me from room to room. First, into the kitchen where there were two maids cleaning out the fridge. Conrad introduced me and they both bowed. I wasn't quite sure what to do.

'Maids,' I thought. 'Wow.'

Conrad watched me as I said hello and then he led me outside to the garden where there was a verandah and a swimming pool. Upstairs there were four bedrooms, although as we went up there he explained that only I and one other girl would actually live in the house. The other bedrooms were for guests who might arrive now and again. I wasn't to ask about that. Nor was I to ask about, or to touch, the packages which might arrive from time to time and stand stacked in the hallway for a few days before being collected. Those were the house rules.

Conrad threw open the window of my bedroom, opened the wardrobe doors and spread his arms out like a magician who had completed a trick.

'Do you like it?' he asked.

'It's beautiful,' I replied, kicking my shoes off and running a hand along the silk sheet bound tightly around the bed.

Conrad sighed with satisfaction. Through the

window behind him I could see two Chinese men in dark suits walking up the garden. One was carrying a black briefcase and the other was holding an open-topped box. As I glazed out of the window, admiring the view from my new home, I saw that inside the box there were two or three guns. The shock must have shown on my face because Conrad turned around, instantly uneasy.

'Back gate,' he observed. 'Behind those trees,' as if this was adequate by way of explanation.

'Do you have an arsenal downstairs?' I asked him cautiously, half hoping he'd just laugh and produce a very logical, safe explanation but knowing deep down of course he wouldn't.

'They do,' Conrad replied, slightly too quickly and he began to shift towards the door.

'Don't they work for you then?' I asked, trying to get my head round things.

Conrad laughed. It made a snorting sound which seemed unlike him, but he didn't answer the question directly.

'You just do your job and everything will be OK,' he said and then he gave me a mobile phone and a pager and told me that I had the evening off, to get over my jet lag.

And the creeping feeling I'd had that things weren't quite right, started to become more concrete. I was out of my depth, that much was for sure. And those guys in the garden had sealed it for me. I had a bad feeling I wasn't working for Conrad Beckett at all. I had a bad feeling that the men walking up the lawn were mobsters. I'd heard of the triads. I'd seen them on TV – smooth-skinned men in suits with dragon tattoos snaking up their arms. But it seemed too bizarre. Too abstract. This was my life, after all, not some TV movie.

I followed Conrad back downstairs, not quite sure how to ask him about it. Not quite sure what to think.

'You can come and go as you please,' he said, 'but always carry your pager and phone so we can keep in touch with you.' He rounded on me in the hallway. 'You can make a lot of money here, Kate. You can do very well for yourself. Just don't question anything.'

And then before I could think of what to say, he left.

I sank down on to the thick white carpet and stared up at the fan on the ceiling cutting through the air right over my head.

'Oh fuck,' I said out loud.

I don't know why, but I had just assumed that Conrad's contacts were European. I mean, Hong Kong, I had thought to myself, is a British colony, although of course by the time I got there the Empire's time was running out. It hadn't ever occurred to me that I'd be working for a triad gang. I hadn't even asked. Stupid really, but I've met lots of pimps and they always rap on about their 'contacts' and usually that consists of their cousin and a couple of old schoolfriends. Conrad, I recalled, had asked me to come and work for him after all. It hadn't really been clear, but then, if it had been, I don't think I would have left London. I felt a bit sick. I may be on the reckless side, but even I have that much of an instinct of self-preservation. Organized crime, rather than Eddie's kind of crime, is very, very different. The triads' reputation is much more deadly than the mafia or any of the other crowds of inter-national gangsters which come from one ethnic group or another. I tried to convince myself that they had that reputation because they were so different, so alien. After all, I'd come from Eddie who was basically an East End heavy, and I'd done OK there. Pimps worldwide are dangerous people. But this was the big time, and as I stared down at the equipment Conrad had left me I realized that I was living in a house where there was no front-door key. A house where the door was always open because only a fool would come in if he wasn't supposed to be there. I didn't know what to do other than try to ignore how fast my heart was beating. With Conrad's departure the house had become unnaturally silent once more and I wondered where the two men with the box of guns had disappeared to.

At the thought of them my heart sank and my hands grew clammy. I was an idiot. I had followed my instincts thousands of miles round the globe, giving myself no escape route, no practical plan for if my instincts had gone awry. I had always thought of myself as a bit of a glamorous adventuress, unafraid of danger, but sitting on the floor in the hallway that very first day in Hong Kong I thought that this time I had gone too far. It was too dangerous and I was very unnerved by Conrad's rushed departure. I took a few minutes just breathing very deeply to try to calm myself down and I half considered just walking out of the place, going to the airport and going home. Not that there was anything much waiting back there.

But peculiarly in that greater danger, the thought which raced around my eighteen-year-old brain was something which Mr Pearson, the games master at school, had once written about me in a report: 'Kate operates well in any situation. She can defend or attack on the pitch. I have been very impressed with her ability to deal with whatever comes her way. She is extremely adaptable.' I don't expect that Mr Pearson knows how much he formed my young life, but I had been proud of that report. Mum had taped it up on the

39

fridge and I had believed it. I'm sure Mr Pearson's advice to me, had he been appraised of the situation in Hong Kong, would have been to 'Run Like Hell. Lather it back home, girl.' But I didn't. I sat on the carpet and I decided that I could handle it. I'd just have to handle it. And in the end, scared or not, I didn't really want to go. I like my heart pounding. I like it when my fingers quiver. It gives me a high.

'They're people,' I told myself, 'they're just people. I'll learn as I go along. I'll do OK,' and I got up and walked around the light, airy living room touching the furniture, familiarizing myself with the place, trying to see myself living there. It wasn't hard. Over at the window I caught sight of the lights of the city, spread out further down the hill. A place that shiny and bright just had to be fun, I consoled myself. Intriguing. Deadly even. And in the end it was just impossible not to try it, so I sloped upstairs to unpack my things.

That evening I decided to go out to see the city and as I walked all around the bustling streets of Mong Kok and Yau Ma Tei for the first time, I fell in love. The labyrinth of frantic passageways with their stalls and markets and brightly lit shops fascinated me. I don't think that I'd ever in my life seen so many people. I swam in the crowd. I moved with it until I made my way down to the water to stare at last at the bright lights of Hong Kong Island on the other side of the bay and relish the relative silence of the dockside, the black arm of the water slapping against the concrete of the mooring blocks, soothing me.

Later, back at the house, there was still no-one around but I wasn't tired. I had travelled eastwards so I felt as if it was still only the middle of the afternoon, when I suppose it must have really been two or three in the morning at least.

I stripped off at the poolside and cartwheeled around the lawn to stretch my flight-weary legs right out. I'd walked for miles and miles, the air thick and humid on my skin, and it felt good to have grass beneath my feet once more and the open space of the deserted back garden to cartwheel around in, noticing as my legs straightened out above me that it was as if they were slicing through the atmosphere like the sails of a windmill. Perhaps I was more tired than I thought but it seemed hard, out there in the open, to move independently. I'd only just arrived I suppose and I wasn't used to the humidity level, so I fooled around buck naked and then I toppled over into the water and splashed about for a bit. It was a balmy night, and from up there on the hill the street lights of Kowloon glowed amber and lit up the polluted clouds hanging in the bronze night-time sky. You couldn't see the huge stretch of water to the south where I'd been standing earlier. You couldn't see it at all. It was beautiful though and I felt OK. I felt that I'd made the right decision, and I was lying there, water against my skin, thinking, when a girl appeared silently up on the verandah like a glossy black oriental bird. She perched there watching me from one of the green linen loungers as I swirled around in the water like a long fish.

'You're new,' she commented, when I noticed her.

I pulled myself up.

'Kate,' I introduced myself, realizing this must be the other tenant of the beautiful house.

'I'm Rosie,' she said and she threw over a towel for me to dry myself. I walked up on to the clay tiles and settled down next to her.

'Busy night?' I asked casually.

'Always,' she assured me, nodding slightly so that the inky bob of her hair shone in the low lights which

41

rose up out of the grass and illuminated the whole garden. She had an astonishingly beautiful face. Perfect Chinese eyes, with long dark lashes and a wide mouth. Behind her, out of nowhere, one of the maids appeared with a silver tray which she set down silently on the table top before she evaporated back into the kitchen.

'You like tea or you like brandy?' Rosie offered me.

'Tea please.'

'Yes. English,' she commented with a smile. I didn't correct her. Hookers' force of habit that. Even Scottish hookers. Besides, I was curious about her. Rosie's reserve was fascinating, everyone thought so, and it got to me immediately. I wanted to ask her questions.

'Amazing house here,' I said. 'You been here for long?'

'Two years. My cousin came to visit me last month. She thought the house here was spooky. She told me that the ornaments inside still hold the spirits of all the dead people who once owned them. I like it though. Traditional. And if there are spirits, I think they are good ones. I think this is a lucky place.'

Then there was a soft knocking from the garden gate.

'My friends,' Rosie said vaguely and she got up to let them in. Two men appeared, young guys our age, both obviously drunk, and they kissed her on both cheeks. They didn't even notice me at first as they headed off down the lawn together towards the garden shed from where they emerged a few moments later wearing black short trousered wetsuits in which they tumbled joyfully into the pool, somersaulting off the edge with fierce abandon.

'Serge and Arthur,' Rosie tossed her head towards them and as she smiled her eyes sparkled. 'You'll meet them later. Serge is half Chinese. Arthur is from England. Just friends,' she said.

Serge pulled himself up out of the pool and waved over.

'Gonna light a joint,' he said. 'You want some?'

Rosie and I both shook our heads and we just sat there for a while on our cushioned recliners beside the house. Arthur was so blond, and Serge so dark. That night he looked really Chinese. But mostly I just remember them both being so beautiful as they took it in turns to topple elegantly over the edge and into the cool water, carefree and lean in the middle of the night.

'My God, they're the Empire, drunk and somersaulting,' I smiled. And after that, Rosie and I relaxed together and we were friends.

I fell asleep outside in the open that night and when I woke up they had all gone. Rosie had laid a soft tartan rug over me and as I opened my eyes the garden seemed too quiet and kind of empty without them. A dry leaf fell from a tree by the poolside and landed with a papery crack on the thick tiles and there was a moment of absolute silence before I pulled myself off the lounger and walked barefoot upstairs to my room.

Chapter Six

T'ung Jen: Fellowship with Men

I enrolled for lessons in Cantonese straight away. The second day of that first week, as I recall. Conrad just laughed at me. So did Rosie at first.

'You don't need to,' Conrad tried to explain. 'No-one else does.'

'You speak Cantonese. You speak Mandarin too. Rosie told me,' I accused him.

'Yeah, but in my business it's different. There are white guys in Hong Kong who only speak Cantonese when they get into a cab and they've been here for ten years. Look. *Um goy*, the Peak. Take me to the Peak please. It's all they ever need. You can just be like that. There's no point learning the language.'

'I want to,' I persisted. 'Please let me.'

What could he say? It wasn't as if I wanted to take a lover or something, was it? And I'm glad I made the effort. My Chinese isn't good by any means, but studying it has helped me to understand a few things. There's no tense in Chinese, you know. No past, no present and no future. When a Chinese diplomat tells a British diplomat that they will take back the colony, then it's as if it is going on at that very moment, it's as if it's already been done. It's the first cultural gap that you have to span to begin to understand things – the concept of time, the concept of perpetuity.

My teacher was a white guy called Max. He was a bit of a drunkard and he worked for some big news agency. He used to hang out all the time at the Foreign Correspondents' Club on Ice House Street and knock back neat whisky. He was in his forties and he had lived for ever in Hong Kong, since he was a kid, and he had really fluent Cantonese. I knew there was no point in trying to learn to write the language, I mean there are thousands and thousands of different characters, so I settled on the idea of conversational Cantonese to start with and once I had begun to get the hang of that I intended to move on to Mandarin. Of course, I've never actually moved on because Cantonese is so fucking difficult, but I can understand things now. I can speak a little bit. Max was really easy-going too. Sometimes I'd meet him at the club and other times he'd come over to the house, and then other times again we'd go for a walk to the Bird Garden, or wander round Victoria Park or wherever and we'd just talk and he'd teach me things.

'Your friend Rosie is really beautiful, but she's cold as ice,' Max smiled one day.

We were sitting in his flat on the Peak. It was one of the larger, older apartments and it was done out with shabby furniture which had obviously been shipped over from Europe years before. It was raining that afternoon and Max had left the windows open. I loved listening to the downpour and as I sat there Max taught me Chinese words for the weather. It must have been quite early on, I suppose. I was still picking up the basics.

'Cold as ice,' Max repeated, first in English, then in Cantonese.

'I like Rosie a lot,' I said. 'She's great to be around. I've always worked on my own before.'

'Practise your vocab on her?' Max enquired.

And I just nodded.

'Atta girl,' he said. 'We'll have you on the negotiating team yet.'

And when the rain stopped we walked down the hill a bit and hailed a cab. Max never let me out of his sight during our lessons. He'd pick me up and drop me off dutifully, like a gentleman. I remember finding it charming.

Those first months were idyllic. I mean the work was an absolute doddle and most of the time Rosie and I only worked at night, although usually it was all night that we had to work. The limo would crawl home with us at five or six in the morning and we'd sleep until after midday. It was just the two of us in the house on Kadoorie Hill. Two women in all that space, never touching the parcels in the hallway, never questioning the occasional visitor who would sleep in one of the guest bedrooms, lowering our eyes whenever we passed a man we didn't know on his way up the stairs. We became very close. We had, I suppose, an under-standing of the spaces between us, an ability to let each other be, which was as vital as the companionship and the intimacy we felt for each other too. I wasn't lonely any more.

In the afternoons Rosie and I would often go shopping in Tsim Sha Tsui. Rosie tried really hard to smarten me up. Jeans and cashmere jumpers might be just the ticket in London, but Hong Kong is a whole different headspace. She'd drag me away from the sale rails, muttering under her breath about how those were last year's colours, and then she'd march me around Gucci and Armani until I finally caved in and despite myself started to plump for understated elegance, which is what you need in Hong Kong for sartorial superiority. Clothes which are black, well cut and have a discreet label from one of the really big fashion houses are the only thing which cut the mustard in the Far East. Once a week the two of us would go for afternoon tea in the high-ceilinged hallway of the Peninsula Hotel, where we often had to return later on in the evening and take the private lift up to the restaurant on the rooftop. I had sex one time in the men's toilets there with an international investment analyst. He dragged me into one of the cubicles and he did it to me up against the wall, and as I left I noticed that the urinals were against the window and realized that if a guy was peeing it must look as if he was doing it over the whole of the city. Those corporate types must have loved that.

Other nights we'd be flown out by helicopter to Conrad Beckett's mansion house on Macau island. We saw Conrad quite a lot, a day or two every week normally, and then on top of that every couple of months he'd come into town and sit with me on the immaculate white sofas in the living room to tell me that I was doing very well, that everyone was pleased with me. Rosie had her own mentor – a Chinese guy called Bobby who would do the same, chat to her to make sure she was OK, tell her that it was all going to be fine. Bobby used to come more often than Beckett. He'd pick Rosie up every two or three weeks and take her out to Cat Street Market on Hong Kong Island, where they'd trail up and down the thin thread of passageways, picking stuff up out of the boxes on the ground. He bought Rosie a small carved perfume bottle one time. Another day it was a watch with an old black crocodile-skin strap. Sometimes he used to take her to the Man Mo Temple up on Hollywood Road, and watch her as she went in. It was old, the oldest holy place in the city it was said, all tatty and ramshackle and out of place, nestling in a cloud of joss just below a towering pink high rise. Bobby would sit over the road on a green bench beside the play park and he'd watch her make her devotions through the open shabby red doorway. I thought that Rosie got the best deal. Bobby really cared about her. Beckett was just doing what he had to for me. He was just doing his job.

He's a scary bastard, Conrad Beckett. Almost soulless. A white man who is heavily in with the triads, but I guess he hasn't had a lot of choice. He owns a whole load of casinos and hotels which his father left him and the gang run his security so he entertains for them a lot. Visiting dignitaries, diplomats, whoever the brotherhood are befriending at any particular time. Conrad is very rich and he does what he's told in order to stay that way, in a rapidly changing world where white men operating in the Far East need the Chinese on their side and boy, do the Chinese know it. White skin isn't quite so much of a privilege any more. Conrad told me that one time he'd been playing golf with a client, some big Taiwanese businessman, and they had been talking a lot so they let a couple of Chinese men play through on their hole, and as they had passed one of them had sneered at the Taiwanese guy, 'What do you want to play with him for anyway? Their time is past.'

As I got used to Hong Kong, as I settled in to the way things work there, it gave me a bit of an insight into Conrad Beckett. He had, after all, inherited everything he had, but then had to drag himself into present-day politics, where the word 'colonial' is something to be mildly ashamed of. And he'd landed himself a big job in a tough, violent world. So little by little I realized how dangerous Conrad really was. Very occasionally he'd get drunk and things would slip out. Tiny details. Too many people he knew seemed to have died. Behind his manners there was a blank, black nothingness held in place only by force of will. When he drank I could see his eyes, like endless tunnels, going nowhere. It made me shudder.

But if Conrad was cold, Rosie was a different kind of an experience. Rosie and I built bridges together in our daydreams. Rosie and I understood what it was like for each other. Rosie and I were friends, kindred spirits. Usually I think you choose friends because of that, because they're the same, because you have a lot in common, and perhaps the fact that Rosie and I both earned our money on our backs meant that whatever our other differences we would always have that bond. But it was more than that. I've known hookers before, and I've never felt so close to any one of them. Rosie was the first person I ever truly shared myself with and when I was around her I felt really positive about the future, about us. In fact, it wasn't dissimilar to the feeling I had in Coatross when I had known I was going to London and that my life was going to take off when I got there, although I didn't really know how. With Rosie I knew that whatever fell into my lap was going to be good and I felt that about her almost straight away.

I've never met anyone so focused or so together. One afternoon I walked into the living room to find Rosie curled up on the sofa poring over a Psion organizer. She was making entries like mad, in code. I peered over her shoulder and began to laugh as I realized that she was keeping a note of all her clients. You have to understand here that we'd probably see a few hundred men in a year but she'd keep records on all of them so that if they came back she'd know what they liked and little details of what they'd said. They must have thought they were so special. Maybe it's one of the reasons Rosie was so in demand. I watched as she typed in a date and some letters next to the name of a senior member of the judiciary.

'BJ' it said and a little heart.

'What's the heart for?' I asked.

'Likes you to say you love him,' Rosie replied.

'Before or after the blow job?'

'After, just where it is in the notes,' she shrugged as if I was a halfwit.

It was inspirational really, but whatever little details I give you about Rosie won't explain her. Not really. She's one of those people you can describe and describe and describe and still not get near to. It's strange. In my business you learn to sum people up pretty quickly. Men and women. Usually I can just look at people and I know what they want. I've watched wives at the Cricket Club and those keen but miserable young stockbrokers who'd rather inherit than work, and I know all about it straight away after a couple of glances and a casual conversation. I know all about their big, empty fun. I've watched other hookers at parties, bored but earning, or taxi drivers licking their lips, watching me in the mirror. I've seen that rare thing, a faithful married man, trying not to look me in the eye, avoiding temptation. In general you read people quickly.

Not Rosie though. She came from a million different places. She was difficult. For example, in all the time I knew her I never quite clicked into her sense of humour. One morning I came down and Rosie was sitting on the sofa chortling to herself and she just couldn't stop laughing. There were tears streaming down her cheeks.

'What is it?' I asked her. 'What's so funny?'

It took ages to get it out of her, but it turned out that a delivery man had dropped a parcel on his way into the hallway.

'That's it?' I asked her.

'Bang. Crash,' she nodded and it seriously took her hours to get over it.

She was childish like that, and then in other ways she was a long way ahead of anyone else I've ever met.

When we had a night off we would usually go out with Serge and Arthur. Rosie had known them for a while, and they were so cool. I took to them straight away. After that night when I had only just arrived, it felt like we were all meant to be together. We were friends instantly.

There was an edge to both Serge and Arthur which was apparent from the first. It was special. You often don't find it in people out there – lazy, fat-cat bankers playing the odds on their five-star lifestyles and never doing anything you wouldn't read about in some glossy magazine. Sad bastards. Souls for sale. But Serge and Arthur had a sense of adventure rather than just a sense of luxury. They had an edge. They did things for kicks. There was something off-the-wall about them which was kind of attractive. I suppose if there had been any question of Rosie and I having boyfriends, Serge and Arthur would have fitted the bill – Serge certainly had a soft spot for Rosie, sometimes I'd catch him just watching her reverently – but anything like that was out of the question. Being what we were, being in the trade, well it just didn't mix with that boyfriend thing, that regular-life stuff. It doesn't work and smart girls don't let it happen.

So neither Serge nor Arthur ever acted on any feelings they had, but neither of them ever seemed to see anyone else either. Girls, I mean. And the set-up worked. They were great. They were wild. Our closest friends, our confidantes.

The second time I met them, a couple of days after I arrived in Hong Kong, we all hired a sampan and took it out into the bay. Serge had brought a picnic – noodles from this great snack bar just up from the harbour and mango juice and the deep-fried, pungent, sweet bean-curd which made Rosie's eyes narrow with pleasure. Not that we ate much, as I remember it. Serge and Arthur got into an argument about something only they ever could. Something like the flexibility of the bamboo scaffolding used on building sites. Something stupid. I'm not sure how it got started but it escalated into the food fight to end all food fights, all four of us with our blood up and noodles flying all over the place. Rosie hated it at first and she tried to hide, but then she got angry.

'That's it!' she screamed, and I mean screamed.

The temper flashed up in her eyes and she got down to it good style and we all ended up exhausted and laughing, covered in soya sauce and beancurd, picking noodles out of our hair. I saw Serge holding Rosie down that afternoon. He had his arm curled around her back and she was struggling, slapping him with her palms which were sticky with mango juice, pushing his head back so that his fringe flopped up and down. The little tuft of hair at the top of his forehead fell over his eyes. Rosie went crazy that day and he just took it. Yeah, like I said, I think Serge had a thing for Rosie. But what could anyone do?

Come to think of it, the only time anyone said anything about all that was when Serge and Arthur took us up to Sai Kung. It was towards the end of March, and after a particularly hectic couple of weeks we had been given some days off.

'A good hooker is like a racehorse,' Conrad said when he told us. 'You have to be paced for peak performance. Three days.'

Rosie and I squealed with excitement, and that afternoon Serge had insisted that we all go away. We packed bags quickly and Rosie rang Beckett to let him know. By the time we got downstairs with the luggage Beckett had already rung around and Bobby was standing there in a black Armani suit, waiting for us. He didn't say anything, only held open the door of the study and followed us into the room, closing the door behind us. We hovered beside the desk, still clutching our cases nervously while he leant against the wall. His eyes were hooded with menace, his face almost like a mask.

'You understand how good we are to you?' he said.

Both Rosie and I nodded.

'You don't want any trouble?'

We shook our heads.

'You both work hard. Pleases everyone.' Bobby often talked of 'everyone' although Rosie and I never seemed to meet the mysterious hordes of people who were allegedly pleased with us.

'These friends. Men. You have to be careful,' he continued.

Rosie laid her bag down. 'You want us to stay here?' she said. 'We stay here.'

Bobby took out a gun from under his jacket. He laid it down on the desk.

'You don't have to stay. You have to understand,' he said.

Rosie was less shaken up than I was. I wondered at

the time if it was more a cultural thing – which is just really stupid. When Bobby left the house we had a couple of stiff whiskies.

'Don't tell the boys,' Rosie said.

And I agreed not to.

That night we all drove up to the New Territories along the jungle road to Sai Kung, way up north in the countryside. Serge had rented a house set back from Tsam Chuk Wan Road at Coconut Grove Lot and we spent our days zooming around the islands in the estuary on water motorbikes. Those jet skis can hit forty miles an hour over the water's surface and we made a racecourse for ourselves, agreeing a series of loops and turns between the islands as our circuit. Arthur scored us some grass in the village from a guy who did deals at the old pink building beside the bus station and for those few days we smoked every evening, lying out on the thick grass of the lawn behind the house, staring at the calm, silent blackness which led down to the water. It was a blissful place. Utterly heavenly.

One night Arthur just jumped in, fully clothed, and splashed around for ages, singing to himself and then Serge and he took out the jet skis and raced around some more, whooping in the dark.

'Once men get going it is difficult for them to stop,' Rosie remarked.

And we timed them. Over an hour.

On our last night we decided to go for dinner. Back towards Sai Kung there were fishmongers on the village front, interspersed between the restaurants all along the boardwalk. They had everything in their tanks from the alien-looking queen of the sea to sea bass and lobster. There were bundles of razorshells and buckets of cockles and murky, seaweed filled tanks piled high with oysters and squid. You could buy whatever you fancied and they would send it along to whichever restaurant you liked for it to be cooked.

We walked along the boardwalk, inspecting the fish in the big tanks at each of the shops. Rosie wandered over to the other side of the walkway and breathed in deeply. Even here, out of the city, the weather was heavy and the air was still dense with humidity, so full of water that occasionally you could feel the spit of a tiny raindrop on your face, as if the atmosphere just couldn't hold on to any more moisture without letting some drip to the ground.

Arthur was very taken up with the fish tanks. He pulled his golden hair right back off his beautiful face and crouched down in front of the glass of one tank after another, inspecting the eels and the king prawns and the red snapper, one by one while we waited, slightly stoned, listening to the water lapping against the rocks and the small boats moored up along the front banging together from time to time.

After long deliberation Arthur chose the fish – a pink-tentacled octopus to start with and some snapper for the main course, then Serge bargained with the guy over the price and the four of us walked in a clatter of leather soles on the wooden planks along to a shack right at the end of the pier.

It was a Thai restaurant with bamboo tables and heavy, hardwood carvings mounted up precariously on the thin board walls. Somewhere in the background, in the kitchen I think, a tinny radio was playing canto pop music and we could hear the clatter of mah-jong tiles as the kitchen staff played in between orders. Serge immediately spoke to the owner as we entered, telling him exactly what we wanted, and then we all sat around at a table to the back and drinks appeared as if from nowhere, borne in by pretty Thai girls who moved, like the maids in our house, without making a sound.

Serge proposed a toast. 'To a wonderful holiday,' he said, and at the moment at which we all clicked glasses in the middle of the table I knew, with a sudden clarity that nearly took my breath away, that my life was perfect. I had everything I wanted.

At the end of the meal we hired two little row boats to get us home. We were very drunk and it seemed like fun. Rosie and Serge got into the first one, Arthur and I into the second and Serge instructed the fishermen. Out in the black water Arthur and I gazed up at the stars, listening to the muffled murmur coming from the other boat.

'He adores her, you know,' Arthur said without looking at me. 'He'd do anything for Rosie.'

And then we heard the evidence of it. Serge splashing into the water and Rosie laughing.

That evening Rosie locked the door to our room.

'He begged,' she said by way of explanation. 'So I pushed him over the side.'

'He was just drunk,' I told her.

Perhaps if we had done something after that, if we'd sent Arthur and Serge away then, things might have been different. But the trouble was that we all got on so well. It felt natural to be together. We couldn't see how much things were set to change.

It was Serge and Arthur we were with the night before it happened. It was summer by then and we'd got into a routine of seeing them a couple of times a week, on our nights off. Hong Kong is just full of things to do, but we only went for the most thrilling. I suppose we were hitting out against our own jaded reactions, which is of course what you get to when you have half a brain and you're used to the high life, so we would go out just looking for kicks. And it was up to the boys to come up with the goods at which, it must be said, they excelled. They could procure comforting substances at any hour of the day or night, and they knew all the best nightclubs, illegal poker games, back-street restaurants and oddball parties.

Once we drove up, over the border, to go and see this magical underground cave, which was kind of cool. Other times, when weird people came to town, Serge and Arthur would somehow find out about it and sort us out with an audience. Not our usual clients, you understand, who had all made it in the mainstream, but people on the edge of things. People who couldn't afford to sleep with us. Fortune-tellers and poets, computer hackers and photojournalists. In the absence of films in English and live gigs, in the absence of anything cultural by which I'd normally remember what was going on, the boys provided milestones, challenging each other to come up with more and more offbeat experiences, thrills and spills until sometimes we were doing things that were just downright dangerous.

That night Arthur had outdone himself. I should have known when he arrived. He had a kind of triumphant dreaminess in his cornflower blue eyes as he downed his first gin and tonic in one while we were sitting in the silent white living room, waiting for Serge and Rosie to get it together so we could go out. Arthur tossed his light hair back from his face and grinned quietly to himself.

'You look like the big cat that got the cream,' I teased him.

'Aha,' he smiled, glowing with good health. 'Yes, definitely.'

'What?' I begged.

'You'll see,' he said as he leant forward to have his glass refilled, exposing his golden forearm in the process. He really is kind of like a lion, Arthur. A big lion, sitting in the shade of a tree, all playful because he's just eaten. King of the savannah.

'Tell me, please.'

'You don't mean that. Deferred pleasure. I know you. You'd really rather not know.'

'*Du le lo mah*,' I swore at him. Fuck you. See, I was getting the hang of it.

'I can't wait to see your face,' he ignored me. 'Tonight I'm going to find out what you're really made of.'

And with hindsight, that was the night that we all began to find out what we were really made of, so I suppose Arthur was quite right. But not in the way he expected.

A couple of minutes later the others came down and we headed out in a taxi. Arthur whispered to the driver, and he sat in the front with the rest of us in the back trying to guess where we were going. It wasn't far. He took us over to Kowloon City, to Nga Tsin Wa Road, so I have to say we weren't very impressed at first. Kowloon City is just full of restaurants. It was run-down because at that time it hadn't been redeveloped much. It was too near the airport so there were major height restrictions on the buildings and it was full of old low-rises which were kind of tatty, but there were a few good places to eat. Nothing much else, though.

'I'm not even hungry yet,' Rosie moaned. We always ate really late – like ten or eleven o'clock because, well, normally we needed the energy so that we could stay awake for most of the night. But she needn't have worried because we weren't going to eat. That wasn't Arthur's intention at all. He just laughed quietly to himself and then headed across the street towards this residential, pink, six-storey low-rise and we sheepishly followed him as he punched in the security code to open the front door. The hallway was really cramped and we had to go single file as we followed him in. Arthur forged ahead and began to climb the stairs. Up and up until we were on the top floor, and he still didn't stop and we followed him as he took great strides up a fire-exit ladder which led us out on to the roof.

'One of the guys at the Hong Kong and Shanghai told me about it,' he grinned as we climbed up one by one behind him. 'They bring all their new guys up here. To see who's really got the bottle.'

I looked over. Perched precariously on the edge of the building there were huge rows of air-traffic-control lights. They were pointed away from where we were standing, of course, because we would have been blinded otherwise.

'What is it?' Serge asked him.

'Sit down. You'll see.'

So we all sat down on the rooftop gravel and we didn't have to wait for long. I screamed as it came towards us. A huge 747. It came so close before it turned overhead that I swear I could have touched the fuselage. Everyone dived, lying flat on top of the roof. The noise from the engines was incredible. It really looked like we were going to be hit. As the plane receded and my ears recovered all I could hear was Arthur laughing, and then Rosie and Serge and I started to laugh too. We lay there for at least half an hour and there was a different plane every two or three minutes – 737s, jumbos, tiny six-seaters, even a helicopter roaring only a few feet away as we screamed our heads off with the excitement and the fear.

'There won't be anything like this when they move the airport out to Chep Lap Kok,' Serge said wistfully.

That night was fantastic, although I'm not sure that Rosie enjoyed it quite as much as I did. I think the first plane gave her a kick, but after that she wasn't really into it so much. She didn't like loud noises or physical danger the same way I do. Nightclubs, waterskiing, motorbikes and roller coasters. She just wasn't like that. I ignored her quiet frown, though. I was having a ball.

Afterwards we clattered back down the stairs in a daze, the roar of the planes still above us, but now of course we were close to street level and they just seemed so far away. We were elated, pushing through the heat and the crowds, following Serge who knew a restaurant nearby which we hadn't tried.

'Why are people staring at us?' Serge asked me, and I shrugged my shoulders before realizing that we couldn't hear properly because of the planes and we were shrieking when we thought we were talking low. We had to wait for half an hour for a table (which we considered to be a good sign) and when we finally got one we ate big bowls of spicy fish soup and drank coconut juice straight from the nut and clattered just as much as the other tables clattered around us. Afterwards Arthur was smug. It had been our best night out in weeks.

'I want to paddle in the sea in some peace and quiet,' he said.

'Let's go to Shek-O then,' Serge suggested and we all agreed. It's nice over there – just a sleepy village where there are loads of upmarket houses set back from the beach. It's really popular at the weekend. People go hang-gliding off the cliffs nearby. Midweek in the dark, though, it was deserted, which was just about what we were ready for.

Serge dismissed our taxi up at the cobblestone roundabout in the middle of the village and we all ran through the grove of cypress trees and down on to the sand, peeling off our clothes just in time before we got to the water. It was blissful. We swam up to the mouth of the bay, right out to the shark nets, and then we splashed our way back in again to the beach and lay out on the sand, our tired legs recovering slowly. It wasn't cold. I never find Hong Kong cold. Not even in the winter when most people complain about it. They're crazy. Even in December it's still in the high sixties. But it's all what you get used to I suppose, because some people sleeping rough down on the quays are said to die because of the low temperatures.

It was warm enough that evening though and the air was hot and heavy. We lay on the cooling sand making a million wishes, cordoning the cosmos into sections and sharing the stars equally between us, and then Serge gave everyone some downer or other which he had picked up from a drug dealer he knew who worked the underground station at Pacific Plaza. Serge always bought his drugs in the MTR station. It meant he could do his shopping on the way to work. He was kind of efficient like that. Anyhow, it was good stuff whatever it was and we just floated off to sleep quite happily. Rosie and I leaning together and Serge and Arthur on either side. The way it was meant to be.

The next thing I remember was my mobile phone going off. It cut into the silence, intruding on my dream and as usual in the morning, I took a few moments to figure out where I was and what I was doing there. You'd think that I'd have developed some kind of radar to give myself that information as I woke up, but no. I'm always a pretty slow starter first thing in the morning and I haven't really evolved a way of dealing with it. The phone had this awful screeching sound which I never noticed in the city, but out there, with the lush green behind me and the waves swooshing rhythmically on to the sand it sounded terrible. Then, before I could get it together to find the handset, which it turned out was right beside me, Rosie's phone started ringing too and there was a kind of weird hi-tech duet for a few seconds until we picked up.

It was Conrad Beckett for both of us, needless to say. He was having a party out at his place on Macau and he had been very perturbed to hear that neither of us had made it home the night before. I personally don't think Beckett ever sleeps. He just seems to work all hours of the day and all hours of the night and instead of sleeping he plays blackjack and poker for four or five hours a day. You never ring him and find that he is unavailable. He's always there, he's always on the ball. It was six thirty or so that morning. And he already knew what had happened the night before.

'What are you doing at Shek-O?' he asked.

'We slept here on the beach,' I said and wondered how he knew that we were there at all, because I hadn't told him.

'Right,' he said. 'Well, it's a lunchtime do, so I'll send you a chopper.'

'Aha,' I nodded as I pressed the button to hang up. Slowly, I began to get my bearings, hauling myself up on the sand and looking reproachfully one way up the beach at the shark-alert notices and then back down again to the sea. Rosie turned over on her stomach and kicked her legs. She reached out past me and fished inside Arthur's jacket pocket, pouring the last few drops of alcohol from his hip flask on to her fingers and licking them off greedily, sucking her perfect red nails one by one. She looked like a real vamp.

'Another lovely day,' she smirked, her Chinese eyes all dreamy. 'Just look at the sky.'

It was a gorgeous dawn all right, all orange and tropical, just above the waterline.

'How did he know we were here?' I asked her.

'Oh,' she lay back, 'there's a tracking device in our pagers. Didn't you know?'

Chapter Seven
Ta Kuo: Preponderance of the Great

When we landed on the perfectly manicured lawn at Beckett's place, he was sitting out on the verandah having his breakfast. It was his habit and, he told us many times, his father's habit before him to sit outside to eat if the weather was cool enough. It was still quite early in the morning and the sun hadn't quite kicked in when Beckett looked up from his paper and rose out of his brightly cushioned chair as we picked our way up the lawn towards him. I was still brushing the sand out of my hair when we got there, because when the chopper had landed on the beach at Shek-O huge dust clouds had billowed out from it and we had all got covered. Rosie had fixed herself up properly, but I hadn't quite got myself together.

As we swooped low over the bay on our way out of Hong Kong we headed westward and when the chopper began to climb I looked down on the lush green of the Peak, cradling the city in its ample lap, and then as we rose higher still I could just make out the huge mountains shrouded in mist beyond the Chinese border to the north behind the city. They rose even higher, seeming to engulf the whole tiny territory. Then we flew too far away and I couldn't see any more. Rosie had just finished sorting out her lipstick.

'Back to work,' she smiled at me and she put on a pair of navy sunglasses and sat back to take in the enhanced colour of the ocean below us. Rosie brushed up easily, of course. In fact, she's probably the most glamorous person I've ever met. She can stay out all night, and all she has to do is fix her lipstick, flick her hair around a bit and she looks perfect again.

Beckett offered us coffee and sugar rolls when we arrived. I was really hungry. I suppose it was all the fresh air and the excitement of the night before.

'There are clean clothes upstairs,' he commented, looking me up and down. Of course, he didn't say anything to Rosie. There wasn't any need.

The party was due to start at midday and we were to entertain some Chinese officials who had taken time out from their diplomatic schedule to cut some kind of a private deal with the triads. At home that would be scandalous, but in Hong Kong it barely merited comment. I stood up and stretched, stepping out on to the grass barefoot and flexing my toes. I was still kind of sleepy and I remember wanting to roll all around the lawn. To stretch out and jump in and lose myself completely.

'It's so lovely here,' I mused. 'It's such a lovely place.'

Beckett grinned, pleased. He always liked me to be appreciative, almost as if he was so jaded and cold himself that he needed other people to enjoy things for him. The house servants moved around the table, filling our cups with steaming, inky coffee and placing the warm rolls on to delicately folded monogrammed white linen napkins on top of the fine handpainted china plates. Rosie balanced her sunglasses on her head and began to nibble absent-mindedly, considering the day before us, and the kind of work it might bring.

'What are they here for?' she asked.

Beckett looked up. 'Drug dealers,' he said. 'Big-time. Two generals in the Chinese army. Brothers, I think.'

'Communists?' Rosie asked and Beckett nodded.

I came back to the table and sat down. Things were often a bit difficult when we had to entertain Communist officials. Most members of triad gangs had been on the other side when it came to the Revolution, or at least their fathers had been, so there was some tension from time to time. Injured pride. Not that it stopped anyone from cutting a deal of course, but sometimes you could just sense that things weren't, well, comfortable.

After breakfast Beckett went up to his office to work for a while and Rosie and I walked together around the garden. It was so lush there and as the golden light played on the greenery the garden just reeled us in. We had two or three hours before anyone was due to arrive, so I climbed one of the old trees beside the house and hung backwards from a sturdy branch by my knees, looking out upside down across the secure perimeter fence at the ocean. The bark felt satisfyingly rough against my skin. Below me Rosie let the wisps of the leaves brush against her face in the light breeze.

She really liked it out on Macau and she was one of Conrad's favourites so she got to visit him there a lot. He had recruited her himself, just like he'd recruited me, but I was already on the game when I'd signed up whereas he'd trained Rosie right from the very beginning. She had been just a kid – sixteen or seventeen – and she'd got a job working in one of Conrad's hotels helping to organize functions, wedding parties and stuff. He had spotted her almost straight away he said, and like Eddie with me, he knew immediately that she'd be good, that she'd do it well.

And she did. Rosie took to it like a duck to water, he told me one of those nights when he had drunk much too much vodka. He had started out just teaching her to gamble, and she had learnt fast. Within a week she could tell just from the sound of the cards when he was double-dealing himself a good hand from the bottom of the deck.

Beckett never laid a finger on me, you know. Never so much as patted my arse. Rosie though, well, they had a thing. Not that Conrad would have ever admitted it. Not that Bobby knew either. But to my knowledge Beckett didn't sleep with anyone else. Rosie was his girl and she kind of enjoyed that. It was a source of pride for her. And whenever she talked about it she'd bite her lip a little bit and her eyes would widen very slightly. But for Rosie, who was normally so elegant and so still, it was a big thing that her expression changed at all.

The blood was running into my cheeks and I shook my hair to get the last of the sand out as I hung there getting a bit of a rush from being upside down for so long.

'Fab place,' I smiled.

'His house,' Rosie said, 'is shaped like a birdcage. The luck here cannot escape.'

Conrad told me one time that they design casinos like that. The entrance is the mouth of a dragon, and the main body of the building – where the gaming tables are – is shaped like a cage. Feng shui, earth magic, to make sure that your money will not leave the building.

'I think I will wear my peacock-green dress,' Rosie said to herself. It was one of her favourites, that little satin cheong sam she used to wear. Conrad liked it too. I think Rosie must have fancied herself as a songbird in Beckett's house-cage. I mean, she tried to please him a lot. That was important to her.

I swung down out of the tree and we walked back into the mansion house chatting to each other about nothing in particular. We strolled through the marble hallway and upstairs to the bedroom we always used, where clothes suitable for every occasion were kept in a heavy mahogany wardrobe, just in case we should ever arrive unprepared. The walls in that room were dark, dark red and there were always fresh flowers. Even when we arrived unexpectedly. Rosie and I got ready together before we went down. It wasn't an unusual day. It didn't seem to be, anyway.

Old Chinese guys, well you get used to them. In our job we did a fair bit of entertaining for visiting dignitaries of all nationalities, but, of course, it was mostly the British and the Chinese. Rosie did her best to fill in the cultural gap for me when I arrived and the first thing I learnt was that Chinese men from the mainland are very different from Chinese men in Hong Kong. They had been through the Revolution, after all, and then the Cultural Revolution after that. It sounds really weird, but mostly they are kind of nostalgic for the old, forbidden Imperial ways. They're traditionalists at heart.

And when it comes to sex, it's like they don't have the words to ask for what they want. They don't know how to talk directly to you, so they play head games. Of course some come to Hong Kong to let rip and they want the full Western treatment of whores on tap along with all sorts of other capitalist accoutrements, but most old Chinese guys don't want hospitality like that at all. They have to be tempted to it, you have to be demure, lower your eyes and not look like you're enjoying yourself too much as they quaff their five-grain wine and order you around. So I spent some months polishing up my technique, learning to play the virgin, and I've had lots of practice. I'm good at it now. I give less eye contact. I'm a lot less vocal. I let them come on to me, really. It's what they seem to like. One night at Beckett's I heard two old Chinese diplomats bickering with each other over a couple of the girls. They called them 'cheap women', which is the colloquial term. I don't think they realized that they were in professional hands. They didn't understand just how much we were being paid to be nice to them.

That day it was a smallish party. There were perhaps twenty of us. Beckett had champagne served outside under a creamy canvas canopy and then there was a sumptuous lunch inside the cooler, air-conditioned house. After the meal the two generals and a couple of other men retreated into the crisp, fresh air of Conrad's shady, forest-green private study to make their deal, and the others – who were triads – sat out on the terrace and played cards while the deal was being struck. Bobby was among them. There was a guy I hadn't seen before too, Ron, who was a policeman they must have bought off. He didn't play cards with the others. He just came outside and sat around the steaming heat of the pool with us to enjoy himself while he waited. I suppose the triad guys were used to being around hookers, it was no big deal for them, but for Ron, a cop, all those beautiful women who were paid to be readily available were a bit of a thrill. He had slightly shifty eyes and it occurred to me that I didn't trust him. Not that you could have trusted anyone you ever met at Beckett's mansion house, but that policeman guy, well, I just had a bad feeling about him. Maybe it was an omen.

As well as me and Rosie, Beckett had arranged for a few other girls to be flown in and we knew them from other parties, though we didn't know any of them well.

They arrived by chopper, the same as we had. Beckett had a special arrangement with the Portuguese customs officers on Macau – helicopters which landed in his back garden were unregistered with them which meant that he could fly in whoever or whatever he liked. It must have cost him a fortune.

Out by the pool we all smoked pipes of Tibetan temple balls. There had been a silver platter of them at the lunch table with a little pile of white cast-clay pipes on the side, and it didn't take a genius to figure out that it was the stuff that the men were doing a deal over. It was good too. Opiated hash. You can't usually get it outside Tibet. The monks make it there – little one-ounce balls rolled by hand and when you smoke it your lungs just get very heavy and you laugh a lot. Now usually I would go for cocaine if I was going for anything, but I was relaxing and someone passed me a pipe and I smoked some. That cop guy, Ron, pulled one of the other girls away and they disappeared inside the house and I felt kind of glad that he was out of the way. The rest of us all sat around and we started to guess which one of us would end up with which of the men. I figured on Man, one of the triad guys, for myself. He liked me. He'd had me before. Rosie shrugged her shoulders and said that she thought she'd land up with one of the old generals. She was quite right too. Beckett never chose her for himself when he had guests. That would have been a commitment.

I suppose it was because we knew we were going to be there for a while, and because we were a bit high, that Rosie and I sat back on our loungers and luxuriated in the sunshine. We let go a bit. The other girls moved off and ended up sitting with their legs dangling in the pool and that looked kind of pleasant too, but to tell the truth I don't think I was quite up to moving.

'So you reckon that it'll be one on one this time,' I teased Rosie.

She smiled. It was a joke that week because on the Tuesday we had been sent over to entertain this black guy called Montel Sterling who was in town for a big conference. He was something important in the United Nations, and he was certainly very committed to interracial harmony because he took both Rosie and me to bed together and he seemed to get quite a kick from seeing our different-coloured legs tangled as we writhed around him. He was from Chicago, I understood. Sometimes, oh maybe only three or four times, Rosie and I worked together like that for a special request. It was always a bit of a joke. It was weird though, that time, because I think it had been a different experience for each of us. To me he was just another punter, but Rosie was somehow nervous of him. She was on guard. As we went back down in the lift the next morning Rosie checked her handbag to make sure nothing was missing.

'Lost something?' I yawned sleepily at her because I hadn't realized just how she'd been feeling.

'No,' she said. 'Just checking. Black man.'

Rosie cracked me up like that. She had no idea about political correctness or, for that matter, the difference between some big shot in the UN and some black cocaine dealer with whom she had had a bad experience a year or so earlier. That was kind of endearing after a while though. I mean, I hate bigots as much as the next girl, but I loved Rosie no matter what she thought. No matter how stupid it seemed. She was, in a strange way, extremely naive and you just had to love her for keeping that innocence when we were in the situation that we were in.

So anyway, we were in Conrad Beckett's garden by

the pool and we were out of it, and Rosie turned to me and took her sunglasses off.

'I've been thinking about making an investment,' she said. 'Buying a property. A flat. Somewhere in the Mid Levels.'

I nodded. It wasn't a bad idea. Property was at a premium in Hong Kong after all and the Mid Levels were really nice. I loved the open-air escalators which took you up and down the hill, going one direction first thing in the morning and the other later at night. It seemed like Rosie was on to a good plan.

'It's somewhere to live when I retire,' she said slowly, and turning her dark eyes on me she added, 'well, somewhere perhaps we could both live. If you'd like that. With a rooftop pool.'

I grinned this great big delighted grin and I reached out and touched her forearm. I felt I never wanted to leave Hong Kong. I didn't want to go back to Europe. You see, once you've got Hong Kong in your blood, it's a drug in itself. It was for me, anyway. The biggest of big cities. The fastest of them all. And Rosie was everything to me. I felt my face flush.

'I'd love it, Rosie. Maybe we could buy it together,' I suggested.

We stood grinning at each other like idiots, unsure of what else to say. That meant a lot. I mean, when you fake emotion for a living, when you make your money providing fantasies for other people, tuning into their worlds and then indulging them, you don't invite anyone into your world very easily. It's just not something that you do.

I suppose that's why Rosie really got me thinking that afternoon. I had never been sure about how long I was going to be on the game. In London with Eddie it had started as a kind of trial suggestion and then, without really deciding anything when the trial went fine, I simply hadn't stopped. Exactly how long I was going to work or what I was going to do afterwards hadn't ever been an issue for me, although, as Conrad Beckett had pointed out, I definitely had a shelf life. But in the meantime I figured I was getting to see a bit of the world and make a hell of a lot of money, although I wasn't sure exactly what I was going to do when the party was over. And then suddenly, Rosie and I had a plan.

That night we danced with the windows open all through the sumptuous public rooms on the ground floor at Beckett's house. And as it got late we began to pair off. Rosie got the old general and they sat together on a chaise longue and I saw him catch hold of her hand, and point to the jade ring she always wore, willed to her by her mother. Rosie's parents were both dead. She was the late child of a second marriage and she had grown up with that ring. Her mother had kept it in a green leather case at the back of her dressing-table drawer, the only thing she had left of her life in some old house in one of the northern provinces in China way back before the Revolution. Rosie's mother had walked to the border when her first husband had been shot. She had sold everything she had except that ring to secure safe passage to Taiwan. She must have been a Peking girl, I guess, with the pale skin and high cheekbones which right through history have always been the most prized, the most aristocratic good looks. That was where Rosie got her poise from. The ring meant a lot to her. It was carved from Imperial jade of the purest unblemished quality and quite apart from the sentimental value, it was worth a small fortune. She wore it all the time which I thought was kind of funny, seeing as jade is traditionally a symbol of the path of truth and duty.

I could see her beginning to tell the old guy the story, and I frowned. It was unlike Rosie. You don't tell punters the truth. It's an unwritten rule. You just don't do it. I mean, of all the fantasies you create for them, you tend to steer clear of anything real. But we had smoked quite a lot and I guess it put us all off our guard. I didn't have much time to think about it because Man pulled me into an ante-room and closed the high white doors behind him. He sat down on a low ottoman chair and I propped him up with shiny satin pillows and then I moved around on top of him with my black blouse open to the waist until he screamed '*Gweipah, gweipah*,' white devil, white ghost, as he stared up at my pale, pale skin and my yellow hair as if I was some kind of curious alien sex creature.

Chapter Eight
Shih: The Army

At ten o'clock the next morning I sat on the end of the bed in the red room with the lacquer furniture and drank cup after cup of cool, clear water, trying to get my head to settle down. Rosie was sitting at the black and gold dressing table combing her already perfect hair. Conrad had sent a message that he wanted her to stay on with him. Most of the men had left very early to get back into town. The generals had cut their deal and had been escorted down to the pier where they had disappeared over the horizon in a Red Army motorboat. It was only us who were left. The remnants. A few sleepy girls with killer headaches who would soon be sent off by helicopter back to their safe houses. Rosie perfected her lipstick and turned around.

'I will go up to him now,' she said. 'Are you OK?'

I tried to smile. 'Yes,' I mumbled.

'Bad drugs,' Rosie commented, sounding like a schoolmistress. Sounding like someone who hadn't done her fair share the day before. These things just didn't affect Rosie. I've never seen her with a hangover. I've never seen her ravenously hungry. I've never known her to really lose her temper. But I have seen her cry.

'Bad drugs,' she commented again.

'Tell me about it,' I said as she disappeared silently out of the bedroom and I collapsed back on to the heavily embroidered red satin bedspread.

Going back into town in the helicopter I sat staring at the waves flying by beneath us, trying not to be sick. There were a couple of the other girls there as well and they were talking about the men. One of them had had the other general.

'He tried to impress me,' she was laughing. 'He told me all about his golden palace. They have some place out in the countryside near Canton.'

We all laughed. Canton is a horrible, polluted hellhole of a province. If something glows golden it's probably radioactive.

'Didn't he realize he was on to a sure thing?' I asked cynically.

'Nah,' she joked, 'he thought he was doing great with me. He thought he talked me round.'

At the airport we walked across the heat haze of the tarmac and straight through the staff exit into our waiting cabs. I suppose all the ground staff knew who we were and, for that matter, what we were. I've never been stopped there in my life.

I was really glad to get home and I slept all day between the elegant vases of fresh white lilies placed at either side of the bed. In the afternoon, chicken and vegetable broth appeared as if by magic on my bedside table with a note which said 'nothing tonight'. I was grateful and by the evening I felt a lot better. The temple balls had been strong, right enough. I mean most drugs make you feel like shit the next day, but there isn't much which can consign me to my bed. The last time I'd tried them Rosie and I had been away for a lucrative few days in Tibet accompanying some Dutch businessmen on their trip. The businessmen were generous, even grateful, and there had been this one night up in the mountains where we sat up surveying the jungle, smoking, laughing, pretending to be friends. 'Maybe I'm getting old,' I thought to myself. I hadn't remembered feeling so bad the next day.

Rosie hadn't come back and I didn't really expect her. I woke up properly at about six in the evening and just lay there, unable to make any kind of decision. I wasn't sure what I was going to do until, at seven o'clock, there was a knock on my bedroom door and Arthur stuck his head around.

'They said you'd be in and I thought you might fancy going out for something to eat,' he grinned and I just nodded weakly.

We walked for miles. I had this idea that it would help to clear my head. Arthur and I often walked – it was one of those things which only he and I did together because Rosie and Serge just didn't get it.

'What did we come here for?' they'd say when we dragged them halfway up a hill, or down to the slums, or over to the docks to watch the sampans.

'We like a bit of filth,' Arthur always defended us. 'Too bloody sanitized down at your bit,' he'd tease Serge, who had been promoted at the bank and had moved up to a small flat worth a large fortune on the Peak. Serge and Rosie weren't interested – they were tame, rather than wild dragons – but to Arthur and me, probably because we had both been brought up in small towns in Europe, the endless streetlights of Hong Kong were more exciting than the stars.

It was a muggy night and I followed Arthur. We climbed a steep hill and looked down on the city, then followed a track of concrete and mud which rose up between the skyscrapers where the dense foliage of nameless tropical plants overgrew the pathway. In among the trees the track sometimes stopped at a makeshift shrine where golden bells and red rimmed pictures hung on the low branches of the trees. Other twists in the road turned this way and that for miles in the warm dark evening air. You could feel that there was a storm brewing. The blackness was heavy with it. We were right in the middle of the city, but I had the feeling that nature was breaking through. There were places where they had poured concrete down the steep slopes to stop landslides in the rainy months but the jungle in the Far East is very powerful, just like the hot, heavy weather, and there were small trees beginning to sprout through cracks in the barrier.

It was hard work climbing. Our cheeks were flushed and sweat was running down our foreheads. I was so hot that night that my hair was stuck to my skin and I had to push it back from my eyes to take in the view. It was amazing.

Arthur stopped and pointed proudly. 'See what I found,' he said. Down below us a whole skyscraper of spotless, yellow-lit windows rose up straight ahead, each room with its own air-conditioning fan pulsing in perfect time with all the others. This city grows, you know, all the time. It's alive. New places appear out of nowhere. You'll turn a corner and there'll be something totally different, totally new. Like there, in the dense jungle foliage, where I had suddenly found myself so close to a skyscraper that I felt I could touch it and, dreamlike, I could feel the rhythm of the beating fans in a whole column of homes I would never visit.

'That's Hong Kong,' Arthur announced. 'Come on. I've something else to show you.'

He took the lead again and headed further into the

suburbs, glancing at me now and then to make sure I was keeping up OK. The streets were damp. It had been raining the warm, heavy rain which falls in plump drops, soaking you in seconds. I'd slept right through all that and now the showers were over for a while, although the sky was brewing up rain for later. I could sense it.

I didn't feel much like speaking so I just let myself go and I walked with him along the dark pavements, sipping from time to time on the nameless liquor in his hip flask whenever he offered it to me, saying with a sparkle in his eye, 'Hair of the dog, Kate? Do you think that might help?'

I felt removed and dreamlike, the image of the skyscraper branded on to my imagination. After three-quarters of an hour or so we were out on Kowloonside in the middle of a whole load of cheap low-rise housing. We turned off the main road and stood under a banyan tree. Arthur shrugged his shoulders.

'That was the old Hong Kong,' he said, nodding back in the direction we had come. 'This is the new.'

Down below us there was an army barracks. I'd never been there before, never seen it, and I stretched out and leaned on the tree, my hand pushed in on the rough bark as if I needed to feel it to touch reality. We had tramped for miles.

'Red or dead? What do you think?' Arthur asked as we watched two red guardsmen checking for bombs under a military jeep returning from town. He kicked his heels against the red earth they call dragon's blood and the bright mud stuck to his boots. There were about nine months to go until the handover, and the Red Guard had moved into the barracks although the Scots Guards hadn't yet moved out. The British soldiers were taking it badly. Every night they got steaming drunk and ended up getting into fights in the crowded bars of Wan Chai. The papers had been full of it and I was surprised because there was, for some reason which I myself couldn't quite grasp, general relief that the Chinese weren't bringing any tanks with them. They'd brought their guns though. They still had ample firepower, of course. I wasn't worried. Not myself. Not with my contacts.

'They've sent their crack troops. All over six feet tall,' Arthur quipped.

'Just your type,' I quipped right back, and he poked me in the ribs.

We stood there for ages. Arthur and I were both fascinated by that kind of thing, although I'm not entirely sure why. Uniforms, guns, security checks. I don't know. But while I was confident about the future, Arthur's blue eyes betrayed him.

'It's the beginning, isn't it?' he whispered. 'Things are going to change.'

I just shrugged my shoulders at that. I felt more secure than ever before now that Rosie and I had made our plans together.

'Don't worry, Arthur,' I said, 'it's going to be fine.'

After we'd stayed for a while Arthur put his arm closely around my shoulder and we went for a drink in a bar up on the main road and got ourselves some noodles. I watched us sitting at the table together in an old cracked mirror propped up against one wall and noticed that our eyes were the same startling blue, though maybe it was only the light. It was very hot that night, more humid than usual, and my cheeks were rosy from the walking. The air was oppressively heavy. Arthur kept looking at me. It was like he was trying to see through my skin, his eyes drawn back again and again to the base of my neck.

'Feel any better?' he asked when the meal came and he scooped the noodles into his mouth with his chopsticks, just like a professional. And I realized I did feel better. My hangover had disappeared.

'You look good,' he said.

'Top of the world, Ma,' I told him, as he laid down his bowl and his chopsticks. I felt uncomfortable. Arthur was staring at me again and it was too, too hot.

'People are leaving, you know,' he said out of nowhere. 'A lot of people are thinking of moving to New York. They say that the market will crash after the handover. They say that things are going to change.'

I shook my head. When people say that about somewhere you consider home, it doesn't make any difference to you. When you want something badly enough it's amazing what you'll ignore.

Serge, Rosie, Arthur and I were drawn together like the four sides of a square. It was pure geometry. Rosie and I had a lot in common, all right. We understood each other so well, you see. And Arthur and Serge had complemented that without intruding on it in any way. So we loved them. The way Arthur was looking at me, though, it kind of threw me. I could see him in the cracked mirror, just staring, and I suddenly felt uncomfortable.

He was downing Seven Up from the can but he hadn't taken his eyes off me. I shrugged. Maybe it was only the weather.

'I love it in Hong Kong,' I told him simply, the vision of a penthouse apartment shared with Rosie ahead of me. 'I won't go,' I said, wanting to reassure him.

'Me neither,' he replied. 'Me neither.' Like it was a test of faith. And we shook hands on it.

Taxi drivers never try to talk to you when you ask them to take you to the house on Kadoorie Hill. There is a sudden air of respect when you give the address and they lower their eyes and thank you profusely when you tip them. After Arthur had paid the driver we both wandered in through the heavy side gate and I kicked off my shoes so I could feel the grass beneath my feet.

'Fancy a swim?' I asked him. The humidity was bearing down on me.

'Yeah, sure,' he replied, but when we looked up there were bats swooping out of the trees, low over the swimming pool and it had happened. Our own little storm had broken and whatever we'd shaken on, whatever we'd promised meant nothing, because Rosie was sitting up on the verandah, home far earlier than usual. She was home too early and it took me a few seconds to take it in because she was crying what looked like tears of blood.

Chapter Nine

Chen: The Arousing (Shock, Thunder)

I'm unsure whether Rosie didn't see us at first because she was so absorbed or whether she just didn't let on because she wanted to try to control herself. She wasn't wailing or howling or anything like that and it would have been just like her to calmly imagine that in the shadowy evening light it was impossible for us to see from a distance she was crying, because she was weeping without moving a single visible muscle in her beautiful face. The vermilion tears trickled down her high boned, moonstone cheeks in rivulets and ran straight off her jawline, falling noiselessly on to her pale chiffon dress in a roughly heart-shaped stain. Arthur and I ran towards her, and she pulled her palm across her face to try to wipe it dry.

'Rosie,' I gasped and she looked puzzled as she surveyed the palm of her hand which was streaked with red.

'Oh, velvette rouge,' she whispered, realizing what had happened, that it was only mascara. 'Very fashionable,' she gulped and then she heaved a sob from her guts and began to cry properly.

Arthur and I crowded close to her and I put my arms around her shoulders.

'What is it, Rosie?' Arthur asked gently. 'What's wrong?'

Rosie's fingers were quivering.

'I love it here,' she gasped inexplicably and then she began to wail again, howling her heart out to the crescent moon in desperation. I felt kind of bemused but Arthur flopped down on to the lounger and hung his head. He understood, you see. He knew straight away what was going on. Perhaps he had had an instinct all along.

'Where are they sending you?' he asked slowly and Rosie drew her eyes down to meet his rising gaze.

'China,' she whispered. 'I will be a rich man's concubine.'

Concubines, multiple wives, like so many other things in Revolutionary China, were outlawed as a corrupt and decadent practice hailing from the Imperial era. A man in China nowadays is only allowed one wife. Or rather, a poor man in China is only allowed one wife. What goes on in a rich man's house is his own business, until he moves out of step with the party line that is. Concubines are real third-class citizens. They have no legal status and as such they can't own any property themselves. They are housed and fed and clothed by their husband – entirely dependent upon him for everything. You'd want to not only really love your man, but also trust him blindly to go for that kind of deal, but Rosie didn't have much choice. She'd been as good as sold.

'That general?' I asked her, without really having to, because once she'd said it, it was clear. Some things you just know for sure.

Rosie nodded. 'Six weeks,' she said. 'When he delivers the drugs.'

She should never have told that guy about her

mother's ring. Hookers and the truth are a heady, powerful combination. She shouldn't have told him. But it was too late then. It was way too late.

'Why can't you just go as his mistress?' I asked.

At least that would have been better for her. Mistresses usually have apartments of their own. It's a slightly different deal from being a concubine, for God's sake. The mistress of a rich man in China can live a very good life. I've heard men at parties laugh that they like to keep their mistresses out of Hong Kong, somewhere like Shanghai, because there are fewer designer shops there so it works out cheaper. But Rosie shook her head sadly and I remembered Bobby's face the day we went to Sai Kung. The mask he hid behind as he laid his revolver on the leather desktop in the study. I felt goosebumps rising all up my arms and I shivered involuntarily as it dawned on me. The old Chinese general had gone for the whole traditional deal and that was that. There was no room for negotiation. There was, it seemed, nothing to be done.

Eventually Arthur and I got her up to her room and soon she was sitting up in her vast white bed, scanning the pages of clients in her Psion organizer, the blue neon light from the tiny electronic notebook lighting up her pale, desperate face. She wouldn't talk. There wasn't much she could say. I knew she was looking for a man with some influence who could help her, and I knew it was hopeless. All those hundreds of names, all those intimate secrets, and not one person you could call on.

I felt as if the carpet had been pulled out from under me. The first concrete plans I'd ever made, my very first commitment to another person and it wasn't going to happen. It couldn't. I'd probably never see Rosie again.

When we had turned the lights off and Arthur had

gone downstairs Rosie let out a long sigh.

'I feel so stupid,' she whispered, her eyes closed and her forehead wrinkled.

I picked up a pillow and I kicked it across the room.

'Fuck,' I said, 'fuck, fuck, fuck.'

She was right. We had been stupid. We'd been morons. We'd thought we were invincible, instead of just pawns on a chessboard. Close to the important pieces but expendable nonetheless.

'Canton,' Rosie murmured miserably.

'Tell me,' I said.

But she shook her head, shrugging her shoulders and bursting into tears. Eventually Arthur came back upstairs with three crystal beakers of whisky. We stayed in Rosie's room all night, falling asleep at last some time after three o'clock in the morning as we lay dog devoted on the thick cream carpet at the foot of her bed. When it was light again Arthur gently nudged my shoulder.

'Kate, I have to go to work now,' he whispered and I pulled myself up and saw him down to the front door. The house felt uneasy and as we came downstairs the maids in the kitchen, who had been chattering, fell suddenly silent.

'Take care of her and don't worry,' Arthur said quietly and he squeezed my arm. 'We'll think of something.'

As I waved him off I noticed that there was a black BMW parked across the street two spaces up from the front door. Its glossy paintwork was covered in a light dusting of blossoms and leaves and tendrils from the overhanging trees and I realized that it must have been there all night. Inside, the black-suited Chinese man didn't even glance as Arthur headed off down towards the main road. In Hong Kong, where only a fraction of the population are white, let alone blond, Arthur's honey-coloured hair and skin always attracted attention. Just like mine. People stared in the street. It wasn't a good sign that the guy pretended to ignore him. It meant that we were being watched.

I closed the door and slipped back up the stairs into Rosie's bedroom, followed by one of the maids who was carrying a lacquer tray of green tea and sugared toast. It was far earlier than we'd usually be up of course, and as Rosie gradually came to, little worry lines creased up around her eyes.

'I don't want to go,' she said simply, as she sat up and I handed her a small cup of the infusion. She grabbed my hand and squeezed it hard. 'Oh, Kate,' she cried. I laid my other hand on top of hers.

'Tell me what happened,' I replied. 'They're watching the house.'

Chapter Ten

Chien: Development (Gradual Progress)

Rosie hadn't been supposed to find out, of course. When General Ho had included her as part of the deal for the Tibetan temple balls it had been agreed quickly between all the men there that she should only be told at the very last minute. But Beckett, astonishingly, had slipped up. The next morning in bed, either before or after I had left the building, he had said that he would miss her when she was gone and then, of course, he'd had to tell her what had happened. Every detail. Rosie said she'd pleaded, begged him to help her, but Beckett had stood firm, his hard blue eyes merciless as he coldly got dressed. He wasn't sticking his neck out for anybody. The rules with Beckett were the rules.

The very first day that Rosie had agreed to come and live on Kadoorie Hill Beckett had taken her over to Kennedy Town in a black-windowed limousine. He had wanted to scare her. To show her how powerful he was. Rosie had sat placidly in the back seat next to him until the car had stopped at a run-down, seedy shooting gallery. Beckett had walked like a general inspecting his troops up and down the bare boards of the room where derelicts huddled in corners, their skin smeared with grimy sweat and their clothes filthy. They were people who'd given up on any semblance of a normal life. He'd made her sit and watch the down-and-outs as they injected the drugs, the dirty needles shaking in the hamfisted grasp of their trembling hands. He had called her over to inspect the steaming brown liquid the poor bastards were shooting into their arms and legs. He'd made her look closely. It had scared her half to death. That had been the idea.

'You don't ever inject drugs. You don't take anything we don't give you. Understand?' he had told her and Rosie had nodded, wide-eyed. On the way home they had cruised the red-light district in Mong Kok and Beckett had kept the windows down so that the pungent whiff of the streets had pervaded the car.

'Women like these,' he had said airily, pointing at the crowds of short-skirted street girls huddled in the doorways, 'earn next to nothing. This is where you'll end up if you don't abide by the rules. I won't come to get you.'

The general had, apparently, chosen her. He wanted to save her, Beckett had said, from the ignominy of prostitution and bring her back to her rightful place in the enclosure of his private estate where the traditions of Imperial China still flourished. It was the kind of household her mother had come from, before the Revolution had sent the Kuomintang into retreat and everyone who could get away had fled. Rosie was horrified at the thought. She twisted the little jade ring round and round her finger as she tried to think of something.

'I have six weeks to get away,' she said in a half-hearted whisper, but all I could do was hang my head. You don't get away from the triads. You can't. In cases like that, individual gangs pull together. There are so many stories of girls falling in love and their boyfriends trying to buy them out and in every one of those stories, whether they get out of Hong Kong or whether they stay, the couple mysteriously disappear and then some months later their bodies, or should we say their remains, are found. The brotherhood doesn't stand for desertion. It doesn't matter where you go, they'll do anything to find you. It's a point of honour. From Moscow to Panama, from Reykjavik to Sydney, there's a worldwide network from which you can't escape.

'Where do you think you could go?' I asked her.

But Rosie just pulled her knees up to her chest. 'He said it was a good deal for a girl like me,' she sobbed. 'He said I should be happy because the general is a very rich man.'

I knew Conrad Beckett was a hard-hearted bastard. I'd seen that in his eyes pretty well the first time that we'd ever met and since then, over the months, there'd been plenty of evidence to back up the theory. His coldness and his detachment gave him power. He was tough. There was this one time when we had been out in his garden together, just relaxing, and he had decided to sunbathe but when he had taken his top off I'd seen that the whole of his chest was covered in tiny white scars. I remember being really shocked. He always looked so self-sufficient, so groomed and so complete and in control that somehow you just didn't expect him to have that kind of imperfection. I remember that I'd been so taken aback that I gasped and he had grudgingly turned to me and told me, although he hadn't been able to look me in the eye as he'd done so, how he'd got his 'designer skin', as he called it. He'd been punished when he was younger, for some disagreement he'd had with the brotherhood. It was a trivial thing. A difference of opinion over the timing of the sale of some shares. He'd almost bled to death.

Maybe that broke whatever humanity he'd had to start out with. Maybe he'd been hard all along. I don't know. But, knowing the way she felt about him, saying what he did to Rosie was unnecessarily cruel.

We couldn't eat anything. The little plate of toast lay untouched beside the bed. Then just after ten o'clock we heard the bell sound and the maid came upstairs to say that Max had arrived. I was supposed to have a Cantonese lesson that day.

'You go,' Rosie said. 'I want to have a shower. I want to take some time to myself.'

I left her there, pulled on some clothes and walked downstairs. Max was waiting in the living room. The maid had brought him a beer.

'Before lunch?' I teased him.

'No spirits,' Max defended himself with a grin. 'Don't go getting puritanical on me.'

He kissed me on the cheek and we sat down together on the sofas. But it felt like I wasn't really there. When he talked to me I couldn't quite tune in to what he was actually saying, kind of like one of those long-distance calls when there's a time delay on the line.

'What do you fancy doing then?' he asked. 'I have some great new recipes for you.'

Max had this thing for disgusting Chinese dishes. I mean, really disgusting Chinese dishes. Boiled chicken's feet and live monkeys' brains and all that. Max had a running collection of the most revolting-sounding ones. He always said that one day he'd bring out a recipe book for Westerners. *The Little Yellow Cook Book*, he called it. A guaranteed bestseller.

'Rat in red ant sauce,' he said with theatrical vigour. 'It's real. Look,' and he pulled a grubby newspaper clipping out of his pocket and showed it to me proudly.

'Let's go to the Pen,' I said abruptly. I wanted to get

out of the house. I wanted to go somewhere with high ceilings and cool air. Somewhere I could sit comfortably and think. So Max knocked back his beer and we left Kadoorie Hill, walking down to the main road where we hailed one of the red and white cabs which were speeding towards the centre of the city. I must have looked as disconnected as I felt.

'Something up then?' Max enquired gently.

I suppose he couldn't have just ignored my behaviour. Perhaps he thought it was something minor.

I knew of course that I had to be careful who I told, but I had known Max for some months and I liked him. He wasn't really friendly with Conrad or anyone else we knew, he was from a different world. He worked in a news agency and I always reckoned he was kind of smart. His advice might have helped us a lot so I wanted to tell him what had happened but something held me back. I didn't feel I could really trust him because I was worried about the concept of journalistic instinct. Way back in London, Eddie hadn't given me much advice about clients but one thing he had told me was to steer clear of the press. We didn't take them on as punters at all, which probably cost us a small fortune in lost earnings but journalists were a risk which Eddie calculated just hadn't been worth taking. He'd always said that there was only one thing which turned a newspaperman on more than a nice bit of totty, and that was a story about a nice bit of totty.

Eddie's advice had stayed with me and while I figured I could trust Max not to take a backhander, I wasn't so sure that he wouldn't want to break the story to the tabloids. Shock Horror Shame of Nubile Prostitute. I mean, I'd known him all that time and I still wasn't exactly sure about his job, what it was that he actually did, and I felt that I had to know that before

I could tell him. After all, there aren't that many rules to the game, so the few you do have you tend to try to keep. I needed to think on my feet. My mind was racing. Rosie was leaving.

'Max,' I asked as the taxi turned down Nathan Road, 'what is it exactly that you do?'

'This and that. Import, export,' he joked with a wink. 'Nah, I'm a heavy-duty political editor. It's boring as fuck but you get to meet some great girls.'

I laughed. Max had a really charming way about him. A veneer.

'Do you fancy telling me what *you* do? I mean, in sick, graphic detail? I don't mind listening,' he carried on.

'Your heart wouldn't hold out,' I said. 'You're too old.'

And he just grinned, but I still didn't tell him.

When we got to the Peninsula Hotel we walked through the marble-floored shopping arcade. Only the very best at the Pen, you know. It's a five-star joint. Handmade chocolates, Gucci handbags, Hermès scarves. In the arcade there is plate glass from floor to ceiling and never a fingerprint anywhere. Someone told me that they employ a lady just to keep it clean. She checks the windows every thirty minutes and polishes the prints right off. It's her full-time occupation. Max and I wandered in and looked around. I was in a bit of a daze and I felt myself drawn into the menswear shop at the end of the row. I was pretty spaced and there was something reassuring about the smell of it, expensive aftershave and cured leather. Max followed me dutifully as I stroked the brightly coloured silk ties which were laid out in a fan shape on the polished rosewood table.

'Can I help?' the assistant asked.

And for some inexplicable reason I said, 'No, I'm just looking for a present for my husband,' and then I blushed as the guy's eyes fell to the nakedness of my marriage finger and he eyed Max suspiciously as he loitered beside a display of Italian leather belts. I wasn't quite myself. I was scared.

Triad gangs have an array of trained killers with different skills, their steady, smooth hands always at the ready. They can cut you up within an inch of your life, inflicting painful wounds which stay safely clear of all your vital organs so that as long as you make it to a hospital you'll probably live. That's if they want to keep you alive. That's what happened to Conrad Beckett, I guess. He'd driven himself to the hospital with blood pouring all over his smart new Mercedes. He'd driven himself there and booked himself in. What a fucking control freak. And wandering around the luxurious Pen, I realized that it wasn't the right place to be that day. People knew me there. People knew who I worked for. It wasn't safe. It hadn't occurred to me before but as soon as it did I knew we had to get out of there so I took Max's arm and we walked through the main hallway of the hotel and out into the heat. I was aware that I must have seemed very irrational. I was aware that I must have seemed a bit nuts.

'Right, you want to walk now?' Max asked, but he didn't push me for an explanation and I just nodded without saying anything and turned left on to Nathan Road, thinking the whole time that it couldn't really be true. Rosie couldn't really be leaving. It had to be a mistake.

We headed up a couple of blocks through the crowds into Tsim Tsa Shui East and into a cafe. Max ordered a beer straight away and I looked at the menu. I hadn't eaten anything yet that day.

Max had clearly decided just to carry on as normal. He sat back in his seat and tilted his head so I would turn around. Maybe he thought that it would take my mind off whatever it was that was obviously freaking me out.

Behind me there was something worth seeing. A little vignette of Hong Kong life to distract me. Over at the service counter two young tourists were trying to order noodles and a frantic conversation of two languages and gesticulation had broken out.

'There are no noodles. None left,' the waitress was saying in Cantonese with increasing impatience. The kids didn't understand, though. They just kept pointing to the menu and shouting more loudly. One of them was getting angry.

'How can you run out of noodles? We're in Hong Kong for Chrissakes,' he shouted in an American accent. 'That's like running out of Coca-Cola. It's impossible.'

Then this Chinese guy got up and went over to the counter to help. Max was listening intently. This was right up his street. A lot of the time that was what we'd do together. Hang out and watch other people. Listen to what other people said, how they dealt with things, and then analyse it to learn the lessons. It's not a bad learning method, eavesdropping.

The guy who'd got up to help put himself between the waitress and the tourists like he was some kind of an inscrutable barrier and Max didn't seem concerned about me at all. He was just watching that guy, hanging on his every word.

'The lady says there are no noodles,' he told the two young tourists calmly, in English.

'Have they got any won ton then?' the kid asked rudely, assuming the guy would just translate for him. It was exactly the way to get a Chinese person's back up.

'You want them to leave?' the guy asked the waitress, this time in Cantonese.

The waitress nodded. 'So rude,' she said, 'just like babies.'

'Busy morning. Nothing left,' the guy started to explain to the boys, the more intelligent of whom had already picked up his rucksack. 'They're making more won ton but it will take an hour or so. She says she can make you chicken feet or pigeon head. If you want noodles you should try next door,' he translated for them and the kids grudgingly left.

As the door closed the waitress smiled eagerly. 'Thank you officer,' she said to the guy, who must have been a policeman I suppose, and a regular customer. I mean, he wasn't wearing a uniform or anything, so she must have known him.

'Stupid kids,' he sneered. 'They can't even order right.'

And after all that the waitress smiled at him and innocently asked the question, 'So do you want noodles like usual, then?'

The guy didn't bat an eyelid. 'Yeah, that would be nice,' he replied as beside me Max began to snigger into his beer and I grinned openly. The guy was a policeman so she'd serve him whatever the hell he wanted. If you're rude you get nothing. It was so like Hong Kong, that. Max ran his hand over his forehead and smoothed his fringe backwards and I noticed that his hair was receding a little bit.

'That's your lesson over for today, then,' he laughed. 'You'd want to remember that one don't you think, Kate?'

And at that moment, with him sitting there smiling, I decided to tell him. I decided to ask him for help.

'Max,' I whispered, lowering my head over the

Formica table top and pulling him towards me, 'they've sold Rosie off. She has to go and marry this old guy from the mainland. He's a general or something. He's selling them drugs. I don't know what to do.'

I'll never forget that moment. It was like night and day. Another little Hong Kong vignette for me to learn from. As soon as I'd said the words Max's eyes narrowed. He got so angry that he almost spat his answer at me. It was instantaneous. He was suddenly a completely different guy from the roly-poly, thick-skinned, heavy drinker I'd come to get along with so well.

'Fuck you! Are you crazy?' he said. 'Don't you go telling me any of that shit, Kate. You might be a whore but you don't have to be stupid. Keep it to yourself for Christ's sake. People get caught up in that shit and they get hurt. Don't you know anything? Don't you know what they do to people? Keep it to yourself.'

And it was like an automatic barrier came crashing down and Max was on the other side of it, his eyes all bloodshot at the corners, staring through the shield, and him safe and sound over there completely unfeeling, completely unaffected, just watching me. Just like Conrad. I felt sick. I wanted to shout at him. I wanted to hit out, but the waitress came over to take our order before I could say anything. I was so shocked I was speechless. I mean, Max had always been so nice to me. I'd never, ever seen him like that. I'd never seen any sign of it. We'd spent a lot of time together and I'd never known he could be so aggressive. He pulled right back in his seat and stared at me without smiling and I realized suddenly why he'd lasted so long in Hong Kong and how stupid I had been to even ask him for help. He knew that helping Rosie would impose its own death sentence. He knew just how dangerous it was going to be. Whatever defence system Conrad Beckett had, Max patently had it as well, in spades. I saw quite clearly that both of them would stick to the rules no matter what. I took a sharp breath in and I could feel my cheeks burning, like a small child who has been fiercely reprimanded for something they haven't done. I felt like a fool. A self-important idiot. A pawn close to the king.

The waitress had her pen poised over her order pad and there was an uneasy stand-off between us as I pointed on the menu to a bowl of chicken broth and also ordered some weak tea. Max was knocking back his beer and as the waitress moved away, before I could say anything, before I could even try to make it right and tell him what a cold, unfeeling bastard he was, about how you should stick by your friends, he pulled a roll of red notes from his pocket and left one on the table. It was an insult, a clear indication that he wasn't involved with me at all, that he was the powerful one. It was just like one of those customers who want to stick the money down the front of your knickers. Cold and emotionless. Distant and smug.

'Here,' he said, 'this lunch is on me. You enjoy it. I'm going back to work now.'

And he walked out.

I knew I'd never see him again. I didn't want to. But I'd learnt a valuable lesson: you can't trust anyone. You can't ask for help. And my hands were shaking and there were tears of humiliation welling up in my eyes. We were alone. No-one was going to help us.

Later, after I'd eaten as much as I could, I wandered, light-headed, up Nathan Road towards home. I had cried a bit in the noodle bar, just quietly to myself and I'd had a little time to think and to calm myself down and face facts. Rosie was going, any fleeting hope I had

had was gone and I knew that the whole thing was completely out of our control. I couldn't think of one single thing that Rosie or I could possibly do to stop the spiral the triads had set in motion. My fighting spirit had dissipated and I just felt confused and frustrated and insignificant. She was going and that was that. 'Thank God I have a British passport,' I thought to myself rather hazily, although it was scant consolation really. I mean, if it had happened to me I scarcely think the British authorities would have been able to protect me. And I realized haltingly that it *could* have happened to me. It could still happen at any time. Another day, another drugs baron and nobody willing to even listen, to sympathize, let alone help.

Suddenly Hong Kong didn't seem quite so glamorous any more. The sour-sweet aroma of the Mong Kok streets was bringing me to my senses. It was midday. The sun was blaring down through the clouds and my skin was sticky. It was like wandering around in a bowl of soup. Hot and heavy. Dreamlike and in despair. As I made my way northwards, I hit the red-light district. The street girls were out already, touting for business. A couple of kids postured in a doorway just off the main street. Hong Kong carried on around me.

'They can't be more than sixteen,' I thought to myself. 'Too young.'

Street girls. I'd never be a hooker like them. Desperate. Badly dressed, parading themselves, transparent. I wouldn't sink that low. It stopped me in my tracks for a second and I stood there staring, and one of the girls caught my eye. She was pretty. Looked like a Thai. And she was wearing a black sheer nylon blouse tied in a knot at the waist and a pair of black plastic hotpants. She must have been half suffocated with the heat, but she didn't let on. It was so hot and my limbs felt very heavy. I was frozen there for a moment or two and I'm not sure why, but I just gazed quite openly at her. I suppose I felt so powerless, so lacking in confidence that I wasn't absolutely sure any more of the difference between someone like me and someone like her. The difference between a designer original and a rip-off copy. I couldn't move and she held my gaze fixedly before she flicked her long straight hair over her shoulder and then casually lit up a cigarette and sauntered across towards me.

'Looking for someone?' she asked me in Cantonese.

I stared blankly at her. 'How much do you make?' I replied.

It was more a matter of professional interest than anything else. It had been quite a morning already. It felt like a strange dream, unpredictable, disjointed, verging on a nightmare. Heavy. But I wanted to prove to myself that she was different from me. I figured that if I couldn't do that I wouldn't be able to do anything. The girl cast her eyes over my discreet Hermès handbag and the perfect linen of my Shanghai Tang trousers. 'Two hundred dollars,' she replied. Two hundred dollars in Hong Kong currency is about twenty quid at home. Still, it was over the odds for a girl like that.

'Show me where you work,' I said and the girl flicked her cigarette into the road and fell into step. We walked past the street stalls, further up the hill, and then she turned off up a seedy stairwell where the walls were plastered with the telephone numbers of escort services and strip shows. I wasn't sure what the hell I was doing. I didn't really have a plan. I just wanted to see what it would be like. To prove to myself that even under the plush interior design, the tranquillity that big money buys, where I worked was different. That she and I weren't the same.

'It's up here,' she said and I trotted obediently behind her.

We walked along a narrow corridor into a grubby white box of a room with a low bed in one corner and a pile of tissues on the floor beside that. There was no air conditioning and the room was already unbearably clammy. She would be working in there all day, I supposed. It made me shudder.

'You could die here,' I thought.

The girl sat on the edge of the mattress and held out her palm for the money. I reached into my bag and pulled out two red notes and then watched the kid's hands, her thumb and first finger rubbing together, the slight clamminess of her fist as it lay on the shiny plastic of her hotpants, the obviousness of her cheap high-heeled shoes and bare legs. The room was full of the smell of sex and men and cigarette smoke. She spoke first.

'I could give you oral pleasure,' she said in English, learnt by rote. 'Would you like that? Or maybe you like a massage?'

I shook my head slowly. It felt like a sauna in there. 'What's your name?' I asked her in her own language.

She lifted her eyes. 'Pamela.'

'I want to know what it feels like,' I started. 'Tell me about the men.'

Pamela looked bored. She really didn't know what to say. She sat on the edge of the bed for a while. 'Well,' she said eventually, 'they just want sex really. That's all. They want you to want them. Dirty bastards.' She laughed a laugh between girls.

'Do you ever want them? Even a little?' I asked her, turning my back and casting my eyes over the sticky white walls. 'What the hell am I doing here?' I thought.

Behind me there was the tiniest hesitation; only the

smallest pause; then the cogs in Pamela's mind whirred into motion. She thought she had clicked. She began in graphic detail, talking dirty and assuming this was a turn-on for me, her new, two-hundred-dollar client. My mind wandered half in memory, half in imagination. It was fucking surreal. In a daze, I reached into my bag and handed over some more money, crouching down in front of the kid as I did so. Pamela's hair fell forward softly as she looked down to shove the notes under the mattress. I reached out to touch it and the coarse locks felt sticky with dried hair gel and cheap shampoo. I pulled her face up towards me and kissed her on the lips. It was all she was fit for but it still felt like an experiment. Weird. I slipped my hand under her blouse and felt the nipple raised over the strange, plump flesh. Pamela pretended to get excited. It was really funny. She started breathing fast with a practised conviction. She hadn't even noticed that I wasn't into it. It was a floorshow. Useless. I took my hand away.

'You should get out of here as soon as you can,' I told her. 'You shouldn't be doing this.'

And then I clasped my handbag to my stomach and backed out of the room and along the corridor leaving her still and silent on the grubby sheet of her bed.

It had been a bit of a revelation, and I winced at the memory of her sitting inept and helpless on the single mattress. I'd never been on the receiving end before and as I came back out into the street I caught sight of myself in a mirrored shopfront on the other side of the road. Well dressed, well heeled, clear skin and bright eyes. Clean-looking in comparison with every other working girl in range. I looked so competent and I knew that I was competent too. There is such a subtle sensitivity in being a good hooker, but it makes all the difference and I knew that I had it. A fifteen-year-old came up to me, a little girl, and she pulled at my sleeve.

'Is everything all right, lady?' she asked.

'Leave me alone,' I snapped. Perhaps it was a bit harsh of me, but I just wanted to get away from there. It was like getting a hit straight into my bloodstream. Knowing how good I was. What a different scene I had fallen into. All my confidence came flooding back and I felt I could take on the world again. Max didn't matter any more. After all, there are bastards all over the place, it's just that I had thought I could spot them. My momentary lapse of confidence was over.

'God, we're good at what we do,' I said out loud, feeling myself again. Feeling professional, back in control. 'We've got to be able to do something about Rosie,' I thought. 'Whatever happens, we'll deal with it. We'll definitely cope.'

Chapter Eleven

Ming I: The Darkening of the Light

When I got back to Kadoorie Hill I left my handbag on the hall table and flopped down on to one of the big sofas in the living room. The doors out to the garden were open and the sheer white curtains were wafting this way and that in a hot, heavy breeze. I felt like I'd achieved something and I kicked off my shoes, stretched my toes out and stared up at the ceiling, listening to the faint sounds of movement upstairs in Rosie's room. She wasn't up there alone. I wondered of course who was with her, but in a brothel you don't go barging into bedrooms so I stayed put. A minute or two later I heard her bedroom door open and shut and then Bobby came down the stairs with another man.

'You're too soft,' the man was saying to Bobby. 'People gonna take advantage of you.'

I saw Bobby move his shoulders like he was shrugging the guy off, then they went straight out of the front door. I don't think they even noticed me sprawled out on the cushions. I was too low for them to see. A nervousness twitched in my belly. When a triad tells another triad that he's too soft, something bad has to be up.

'What the fuck have they done?' I thought frantically

and I jumped to my feet and ran up the stairs to see.

Rosie was lying on her bed. They'd broken her right wrist for no reason other than that she was unwilling to go to China. She was holding her hand in place, pale and shocked and crying quietly when I burst into her room. It was a seminal moment. A turning point in my understanding.

'What have you got,' I thought, 'if you haven't got friends and freedom?' And there was the answer in front of me. I sat silently down on the edge of the mattress and stroked her hair. If I'm honest, I was relieved that they hadn't hurt her any more. The stories you hear of people fed through mincing machines, people having their stomachs turned inside out while they're still alive, people with their limbs hacked off. Death by a thousand cuts. It makes you terrified when you know they've been up to something. Anything at all. Though I expect they break wrists more than they indulge in insane torture.

'It's like a watch,' she whispered without emotion, repeating what he'd said to her as he'd done it. 'An alarm clock. It takes six weeks to heal. When it's healed I have to go.'

'Hush,' I said. 'Dr Harry will be on his way.'

I hid my anger, telling her to breathe deeply and concentrate on the breaths. I'd read somewhere that's the best way to cope with pain. I began to breathe deeply myself, trying to keep calm. It was horrible seeing her like that and I told her that stupid story about the way my grandfather decided to die. I was relieved when I heard the front door open and the familiar steps of the doctor coming up the stairs.

Dr Harry's kind of a regular feature round the place. We're used to seeing him. He's our in-house doctor if you like, our personal physician, and he's just how you'd imagine a Chinese boffin – thick black rimmed glasses and thin hair surrounding his balding pate. His skin is a pale tan colour and he has a few sun freckles dotted over his face and deep wrinkles around his eyes. Dr Harry always wears a pale brown suit and a cream shirt. His shoes are slightly scuffed. Rosie and I knew him quite well because he was the only doctor who was allowed to tend us. Once every month or so he'd come and take tests to make sure that we were clean because they have to keep the merchandise up to scratch. They can't, after all, have their VIPs contracting anything nasty, so Dr Harry had us permanently on antibiotics so that we didn't get thrush and always took blood tests to make sure that we were HIV negative and urine tests to make sure that we didn't have herpes and that we weren't taking any drugs or at least no drugs apart from the ones that they gave us. He supplied our contraceptive pills too – the strong kind which stop you bleeding every month – he weighed us to check that we weren't piling on the pounds.

He's a funny little guy really. His English wasn't up to much, in fact it really only consisted of the technical stuff he needed to do his business, so when he first came to examine me, before I could speak to him in Cantonese, we always had these bizarre conversations.

'You had anal intercourse this week?' he'd bark in pidgin English. Or 'You got plenty oral contraceptive? You got condoms?'

One day he had been about to examine me and someone must have been joking with him, teaching him stuff in English.

'Rie back and fink of Engrand,' he said.

And I had been convulsed.

Dr Harry was permanently on call. Not just for the girls of course, but also to patch up triad heavies who got into fights. Hookers and heavies, we were Dr Harry's job. He cleaned up bullet holes, set broken bones and sewed up open knife wounds whenever someone couldn't or wouldn't be taken to the hospital for one reason or another. The brotherhood look after their own and I knew that Bobby probably rang him before he'd even laid a finger on Rosie's arm. The doctor didn't ask any questions about how it had happened – he never did – he just set out his things quietly and competently put a support around Rosie's wrist, avoided all eye contact, and then he left some painkillers on the bedside table in a small brown bottle before disappearing as unobtrusively as he had arrived with a slight slow bow of his head and a solemn and formal 'Goodbye'.

After he had gone we must have lain there for ages, the two of us. Two slim bodies in a wide bed, side by side. One of us dark and one of us fair against the crisp white sheets. Neither of us said anything. We were both too preoccupied and the silence of the house engulfed us. It was as if despair was seeping out of Rosie. It was like she was lying in a pool of it, whimpering. She had given up. And I just lay there beside her like a sponge, soaking it in. As much as I could take.

I didn't tell her about Max, I didn't say anything about that girl in Mong Kok, I just lay there in sympathy, letting her go as low as she could, being able to take it. Sometimes that's just what a person needs. For over four hours we hardly moved, then at six o'clock my pager sounded and a message appeared telling me to go to a suite in one of the new five-star hotels over on Hong Kong Island. Every evening was a different five-star hotel it seemed but suddenly, for the first time, it all felt so empty. I didn't want to leave

Rosie behind. Once you've found someone to share things with it's difficult to go back to the way it was before.

'They won't let me work any more,' Rosie mumbled quietly in self-pity.

I pulled myself up a bit on the bed and spoke very calmly after the long silence of the afternoon. I had made my decisions.

'I can't promise that we can get you out of this,' I said very definitely, gently pressing her uninjured hand. 'I can't promise that. But I do promise that I will do anything I can. I promise to think of something, Rosie. I promise to try.'

She turned towards me. I think she had seriously expected me to give up on her, to take the Conrad Beckett line, the Max point of view. I think at that point she'd given up on herself.

'We'll never get me out of Hong Kong. They'd kill us both,' she said.

I nodded. 'There must be something we can do, though. There has to be. We'll set our minds to it. We'll come up with something smart. I'm not going to let you go without a fight.'

The corners of Rosie's mouth turned upwards and a little of the light came back into her eyes. 'I always liked Bobby before,' she said, and she glanced down at her arm. 'He's an orphan too, you know. He says it is an advantage with our occupations.'

I reached out and I held her close to me.

'Rosie,' I whispered, 'you and I, we're like family. I'm not going to give up. We'll think of something. Together.'

Rosie smiled again. It was an open smile this time. A grin. She pulled back against the wide pillow behind her and nodded.

'Tomorrow,' she said, 'we should go out for lunch. I know a place we can talk.' And one solitary tear squeezed itself out of the corner of her eye and trickled down her cheek.

As I left the room I wondered if I ought to leave her alone there with all those painkillers. She had been so silent all afternoon. But I glanced at her through the open bathroom door, splashing cold water on to her face with her left hand, and she looked up towards me and smiled not with her mouth, but with her eyes. It was a brave smile and I realized that I'd always had Rosie down as a survivor. Just like me. And I knew she wasn't going to do anything stupid. Not that night, anyway.

When I came back it was very, very late and I noticed that the triad in the car outside had gone, which immediately made me wonder if they'd had bugs installed inside the house instead. Crazy, isn't it, how paranoid you have to get? I went inside and crept up the stairs into Rosie's room, utterly exhausted. I had sat up late downstairs in the hotel lounge on high stools at the padded leather bar with an old fat white man who worked in shipping. We had drunk gin Martinis one after another and there had been a cabaret. Three Filipinas in electric blue cheongsams had done Frank Sinatra numbers with all the appropriate hand movements to the accompaniment of a keyboard synthesizer. 'We're Maria, Leonie and Janey,' they had sung at the end of their set, with wide, open-eyed smiles, and then they'd worked a couple of the tables and had drinks with the punters before they left. The shipping merchant had loved it. He had sung 'I've got you under my skin' afterwards, upstairs in his plush suite of rooms as he'd laid his plump, loose-skinned hands on my thigh. And he'd been mercifully quick when he finally lay on top of me and pushed himself inside, grunting like an old pig.

When I crept back into the house Rosie was fast asleep. It was well after four in the morning. She'd been out on the balcony, I realized. The chairs out there had been moved around. She'd been watching the trees over on the other side of the main road, I thought. At night you could see little neon threads like spiders' webs in the rain, strung between the branches around the old courtyard over there. They glowed in the dark, like Christmas decorations all year round. She must have sat out there for a while. Now, though, she was breathing deeply, even peacefully. Beside her two books lay on the sheets. An atlas from the bookcase in the living room and a volume of Chinese poems which lay open at 'The Song of Sadness'. I picked up the poetry and began to read the English translation at the bottom of the page.

> *I have married a man*
> *Far from where I belong*
> *In a foreign land*
> *Where he is king*
> *I live in a palace*
> *But I am alone*
> *No-one speaks my language*
> *No-one knows my dreams*
> *Always thinking of home*
> *Sadness around me*
> *I wish to be a cloud in the sky*
> *To float back again.*

The text was over two thousand years old. I closed the book and put it to one side, then crept into my own bedroom. Arthur had left me a message. I would, I decided, ring him when I woke up. My eyelids were heavy and my eyes felt dry. I dropped my clothes at the bedside and slipped between the sheets. It had been a long, hard day.

Chapter Twelve

Ts'ui: Gathering Together (Massing)

Serge and Arthur turned up uninvited very early the next morning and woke me from a fretful sleep. They had both taken the day off work and when I opened my eyes Serge's face was right up against mine wearing a very intense look.

'Kate,' he whispered into my ear, and I almost jumped out of my skin.

Sometimes I watch Serge. On some of our slower evenings, that is, when I have the chance. He's so beautiful. Half Chinese, half English, you see. Some days he looks just like the photographs I've seen of his mother who lives in Taipei. Then other days he could be some fresh-faced, good-looking kid from London, which is, I suppose, what his long dead father was many years ago. And Serge, well, I always thought that he just floated along with all the ease of a deep and dream-filled sleep. White in one light, yellow in another. Always fitting in. Things have always seemed to come so easily to him. But he looked worried then. Just at that moment. And I realized, looking at the two of them, that they had probably been up for most of the night. It felt good to have friends. To be together.

'Kate,' Serge whispered again. 'Wake up.'

I sat up in bed and tousled my hair, groping on the bedside table for my little black crocodile-skin clock. It was only just nine thirty. Behind Serge, Arthur was lurking in the doorway.

'We came to do something. We came to help,' Serge said in a stage whisper and he sat down on the edge of my bed. 'We can't talk here.'

I knew the moment I got up and dressed I was heading down a difficult path. Hong Kong is a place where many roads converge. That year it was the crossroads between Communism and Capitalism. The fading-out of one Empire, the stoking-up of another. That year Arthur, Serge, Rosie and I decided to travel together. And I knew that once the boys were involved it would become more serious, more dangerous. But I'd bought my tickets and I'd travelled first class and this was where I had ended up, so I got out of bed and splashed my face with water and I pulled on my clothes and then the three of us crept across the hallway to Rosie's bedroom and got her up too. The cavalry had arrived. Then we left the house, hailed a cab and Arthur told the driver to go to the Old China Hand where we could get a good old-fashioned English breakfast.

Rosie ate carefully, her right hand in her lap, swaddled in bandages. She ordered scrambled eggs so that she wouldn't have to cut anything up and she used her fork painfully slowly, grasped ineptly in her left hand. Afterwards I helped her to take two tablets from Dr Harry's little vial of painkillers and she washed them down with hot sweet tea. Bobby had really hurt her, more than just her wrist I mean. She had trusted him in a way, she'd really liked him. She considered him, I suppose, a kind of professional friend. Bobby had never had sex with her. No minder was allowed to. But I'd seen him looking and so had she and it's always hard to believe that someone who'd look at you that way, in awestruck admiration, and buy you little gifts and spend more time than they strictly needed to with you, would actually hold you down and snap one of your bones.

'He said it would stop me eating with my *gweiloh* friends. He said it would stop me getting fat before I go,' Rosie announced proudly, her moonstone cheeks glowing over her empty plate.

Arthur lit a cigarette and ordered us another pot of tea as the waitress cleared away the remains of the meal. When she had gone we all leant low over the table and huddled together so that we could talk without being heard. We had taken one of the dark red velvet booth seats up at the back of the restaurant so we knew that there was no-one hovering around us, no-one who could hear. It reminded me of being in the playground as a very small child. It reminded me of having those passionate childhood secrets, whispered from ear to ear. Of sharing confidences with people you trust absolutely, blood brothers and blood sisters. It had been a long time.

We had a few ideas between us. It turned out the boys had spent the previous evening up at the Cricket Club drinking beer and knocking balls into the practice nets as they came up with one thing after another. Police tip-offs and Interpol information. Amnesty International and the Court of Human Rights. Newspaper exposés and everything. The boys had been thinking big. They had, I suppose, been thinking about Justice.

We had been more pragmatic, aware that a high-class prostitute might not find much in the way of sympathy in her progress through the legal system or the tabloid press, and also, more importantly, that the triads don't mess around. That grassing them up to anyone at all was a sure-fire shortcut to being found dead in some black place in the middle of the night. So Rosie and I had been considering less direct courses of action. She had been fruitlessly scanning the atlas for sight of some tiny corner of the world where she might be safe. I had been imagining deals we might make to buy Rosie back. All hopeless stuff of course, but when you're desperate you'll claw on to anything. One by one we voiced ur plans. One by one we shot them down.

After that first round of everyone's terrible ideas, Arthur walked off to go to the bathroom, his arms stretched out in frustration, his fists all clenched up and tight. He looked, I thought, like some kind of Christ figure walking around searching for a cross. It was agonizing for all of us. When he got back to the table, Serge took control and things seemed to get a bit better.

'Look,' he said, never letting his eyes meet Rosie's although they were sitting opposite each other, 'no-one else is going to help us here. The police aren't going to come in and make it OK and there isn't some kind of magical agency for lost girls who will take up Rosie's case. There isn't anywhere to hide from the brotherhood. We're not going anywhere. If any kind of authority, customs, police or press get hold of this then we are all most probably dead. We have to keep it a secret. It's down to us. We have to hit right at the source. We have to do something to fuck up their deal.'

There was absolute silence round the table. After a moment or two I laughed nervously. This was thinking big. Wanting to get Rosie off the hook was one thing. Fucking up a drug deal in the process was quite another.

'Fuck up their deal?' I said carefully. 'Serge, you're out of your mind.'

'No, I'm not,' he said seriously. 'It's the only way.'

'They'll kill us. Slowly.'

Serge shrugged. 'If they catch us,' he agreed, and he turned towards Rosie. 'As I see it, there are three or four elements to this – which means that we've got three or four chances. There are the drugs. I mean, if anything happens to the drugs the deal doesn't go through. So we could approach it from that direction. There is the transport, the point at which the stuff is in transit. If we can find out how they're bringing it in then we could possibly sabotage that although that may only be a short-term solution because they'd try again. Thirdly, there is the money. That is replaceable, but we ought to look at it, just in case. And then of course, there is you, Rosie. I mean, it's a last resort, but if anything happens to you, your part of the deal won't go through,' Serge finished apologetically.

We all glanced at her then of course, and her eyes were dark and hard. She looked like she would rather have died than go through with it without putting up some kind of fight. I clung to the feeling I'd picked up from her the evening before, when I'd seen the steady, low light of survival in her eyes, and I told myself that when it came right down to it, Rosie wouldn't do anything stupid.

My heart missed a beat though. It was so unfair, so completely unjust. When we had passed under the estuary in the taxi that morning I had seen her lean her head against the window and stare out as we came up into the light with sad, still eyes. Rosie loved Hong Kong. She belonged there. There was no doubt about that in my mind. It had taken her mother years to get to the big city, to escape from the Communists, get over to

Taiwan, make enough money to move, to find herself a free life, the life she wanted. And I told myself that there was no way that Rosie was going to go backwards willingly. There was no way that she was going to leave Hong Kong, no matter what it took. She belonged there among the neon-clad skyscrapers and the swarming pavements. It was her home and there was, I hoped, a natural justice which would make sure that she stayed there – although that natural justice might need a little bit of help from Rosie's friends. This plan of Serge's though. It was insane.

'Not my face, OK?' she said. And I shuddered.

'Don't even say that,' I snapped.

'You got a better idea?' Serge countered.

I shrugged my shoulders. I didn't have any ideas at all.

'Do you really think we can pull this off?' I asked.

Serge considered this and then nodded slowly. 'We've got to try,' he said and Arthur put his hand out over the table and one by one we each laid our palms on top.

'So let's try,' he said.

Looking back on it, that morning was the phoney war – all goodwill and positive thinking and gung-ho bravery – which had to come before I really began to understand properly the kind of tactics we were going to need in order to win. We were used to living in a glamorous, privileged, movie paradise, and in movies people decide to do crazy things and actually get away with it. Our whole friendship was based on reckless adventure, aeroplanes and nightclubs and playing chicken. Gambling against the odds. We were so used to playing games that it just didn't seem real.

We walked out into the sweltering heat of Wan Chai, crossed the main road and cut through the back streets towards Central. The locals say that Wan Chai is like a char sui roll, a roasted pork sandwich, because there are all these shabby pink low-rises in the centre of it and then around the outside there are tall, white, pristine new skyscrapers. We decided to go to the temple to pray, and Rosie wanted to shake the sticks and have a priest tell her fortune. It might seem weird and I suppose that strictly speaking all four of us were atheists, but you make your own luck and we all knew it would make us feel a bit better. A bit of ceremony can sometimes be quite important, especially when you've just pledged yourself to do something absolutely crazy. Something so crazy you can't quite believe it.

We took the overpass across the main street. It was packed as usual. Serge and Rosie walked ahead, two ebony heads bobbing in front of us. It was only seconds before we lost sight of them in the teeming crowd. I took Arthur's arm. The temple was a ten-minute walk away and we knew we'd see them there. I suddenly felt safe.

'We seem to have our fingers on the pulse,' I smiled at Arthur.

'Don't be silly, Kate. They're going to kill us all,' he said sadly with an air of great resignation. 'There's no way we can get away with this. We just have to do our best.'

And after that, I just shut up.

Chapter Thirteen

Ta Ch'u: The Taming Power of the Great

In the first wave of the blitzkrieg Rosie and I agreed to gather information and we split up to do it. I met Conrad Beckett the following day at a rooftop restaurant on Hennessy Road. There was no point in hanging around, both Rosie and I wanted to get on with something, so I had rung Beckett the evening before and arranged to meet him for lunch. It was a Japanese place and although we hadn't booked we had, of course, the best seats in the house, right up at the grill with a panoramic vista of the city beneath the clouds and this amazing view over to the racecourse at Happy Valley. It looked kind of ragged, because there had been a rainstorm the night before, but it still felt like thunder was coming. The clouds were dark and the air outside was even heavier than usual.

I had just about managed to drag myself along the pavement in order to get there, but it had been like walking in moon boots. The heavy weather of high summer was long gone and the uncertain, shifting humidity of autumn was coming on. The air was dense, you could tell that the storm was about to break. From the bird's-eye view of our black marble lunch table on the twenty-eighth floor we could see little men scurrying down from their towering cranes on building sites all over the city, almost falling in their haste to be out of the sky before the lightning came. Beckett smiled and watched them as they reached the ground and disappeared into the huddle of tiny men in hard hats who had gathered at the bottom of each crane. When they were all safe and the only thing left to see was ordinary pedestrians scratching around the streets like mice he turned his attention to the lunch before him.

It always somehow shocks me when I find myself in a suit sharing a meal with a man who is also in a suit. It always feels strange. Kind of grown-up, as if it's a game, although that day I wasn't working of course, I was playing grown-up games on my own time. I remember that nothing that lunchtime actually seemed real and I was anxious, but I had said I'd do it and at least it was something I could be getting on with. When I arrived I scooped the complimentary box of matches on the table into my handbag. Rosie collected matchboxes from cool places and I'd taken to picking them up for her. From time to time she would draw one from her bag with a flourish and offer to light someone else's cigarette. Great style, very impressive our Rosie.

Beckett was in a bad mood. Not that an untrained eye would have been able to tell. There wasn't so much as a crease on his forehead. But I could see it. Beckett was wearing his poker face and his hands lay gentle-fingered on the table top, absolutely static, posed to make him look relaxed even though he wasn't. He had ordered grilled tuna. I had the salmon.

'So,' he started smoothly, once the food had arrived and he had his chopsticks in his hand, 'why did you want to see me?'

Conrad Beckett would have done well in politics but

then there probably wouldn't have been enough money in that to satisfy him. He knew damn well why I wanted to see him. He was just curious about what kind of lie I would make up about it, how inventive I could be.

'It's Rosie,' I said, apparently coming clean, and he smiled, thinking to himself that I wasn't even clever enough to think of a cover. 'I'm worried because I don't want what's happened to her to happen to me, Conrad,' I continued. 'I want your guarantee.'

Beckett dipped a little parcel of tuna into a dark pool of soya sauce and then placed it carefully into his mouth. It occurred to me then that I had never noticed Conrad Beckett chewing before. We'd had endless meals together of course. But I'd never actually noticed him engaged in the act of eating. Food just seemed to slip down so smoothly.

'I can't guarantee anything,' he said, 'but Rosie, well, she's Chinese and you're not. There is a difference. No offence, but I really doubt anyone's going to want to marry you, Kate. You'll be living the life of luxury back in London yet. Don't worry.'

It seemed to me that he'd bought it, and I knew that Conrad understood selfishness. Selfishness came naturally to him and that was why I'd started by asking about my own interests. I figured he'd understand that, I thought it would put him at his ease. He knocked back a small black cupful of sake and seemed satisfied that the only reason I had wanted to talk to him was for my own welfare.

Having established that, I decided that I could try for some small talk. See if he might let something slip in casual conversation about it all.

'I wish she didn't have to go,' I said.

'It's not a bad marriage for a girl like Rosie, really,' Beckett started. 'She'll do all right. I've heard his house is a palace. Those guys line their own pockets pretty well.'

'Yes, he said something about that,' I lied. 'His place sounds amazing.'

'He's a smart guy really. Good businessman and all that. I think he'll treat her well. And Rosie won't be far from Canton at all. A couple of hundred miles or so. She'll just have to get used to it. Canton isn't so bad.'

'They're opening that club there,' I smiled, keeping the conversation going. It had been in the news. The China Club, the hottest ticket in Hong Kong, had taken premises over the border. Despite the astronomical membership fees, there was a waiting list to get in. I began to toy with my food, pushing the fish up and down the plate, leaving little streaks of soya sauce on the pristine white china. 'I suppose your common or garden drugs baron has got to spend his money somewhere,' I said.

Beckett laughed. 'Did you try that stuff?' he asked.

I nodded. 'Heavy,' I pronounced. 'I felt really bad the next day.'

'That's the opium, you see,' Beckett replied. 'That's what it does to you. High content.'

'No wonder the Chinese went to war over it,' I said. 'Though how they ever got it together after a night on that stuff, I don't know.'

'That's the funny thing,' Beckett said. 'I mean, it isn't for the home market if you know what I mean. It's going abroad,' he lowered his voice, 'and the old guy thinks he's some kind of ethical investor. He thinks he's waging his own little opium war on the West in historical retribution. Crazy bastard. He's got it in for Europe all right. Wasn't even happy about me being there at the meeting at all. Wouldn't surprise me though if the Chinese government had given him the nod.

Some of the stuff they go for is pretty wild and far-fetched. The advance guard on China's assault on the Western world. Opium balls. Who knows? Anyway, you liked it?' he asked and I just nodded and smiled.

Outside the sky suddenly darkened and the storm broke. Sheets of rain flooded out of the heavens and the cracks between the grey clouds became dazzlingly electric. One time there had been a storm like that and Rosie and I had danced around the garden of the house on Kadoorie Hill. We had been drenched in seconds but it didn't matter. The rain was beautifully warm and afterwards the air was light and fresh for a while before the humidity set in again. When it's raining like that you just feel so alive.

Beckett had finished his main course. He sat back in his black leather chair and smiled an ominous kind of smile.

'Look at it,' he said, staring out of the window at what he considered to be his city. 'Hong Kong. The ultimate Chinese takeaway,' he drawled.

I'd never known Conrad to discuss politics. He'd never really mentioned the handover before in front of me but I suppose it must have been on his mind. It was only a few months away, after all, the biggest sea change in Far Eastern politics since the Communist Revolution. Markets all over the world were due to be rocked and it must have concerned him. But the people who lived in the territory just *had* to believe everything was going to work out, whoever was in charge. There was too much money at stake for it not to. Hong Kong is just a tiny spit of land really, like a fart bubbling into the sea out of China's arse, but it's worth a fortune. Surely, people were saying, China would want to take advantage of that prosperity. Surely nothing would change. I suppose it was easier to think of China as a benevolent, corruptible power rather than some demon dragon, biding its time ready to terrorize Hong Kong whenever it wished with one great flick of its mighty tail. The whole place was in denial.

It had been like that with Rosie, and I suppose it had been like that with me too. We had known the triads were dangerous. We weren't stupid or anything. We had just thought that as long as we kept our noses out of trouble and we were good at our jobs, we'd come through the whole thing. We hadn't reckoned on trouble coming to find us. It just hadn't crossed our minds.

I laid my chopsticks down and pushed the plate away from me. I was interested in what Conrad had to say.

'Do you think things will change much after the handover?' I asked.

But by the time I'd got the question out Beckett's poker face was back in play and his fingers were once more laid gently on the tabletop.

'Not for you, Kate,' he said, 'you just have to spread your legs as required and you'll be fine.'

And that was the most I could get out of him. I mean, if I'd pushed him, he'd have wanted to know why. So I settled back in my seat and we ordered some coffee and then we just sat there watching the storm blowing itself out from our vantage point. Safe and sound. 'This is what it's like to be Conrad Beckett,' I thought, as plump raindrops slid down the window panes in thick streams and, lunchtime drunk from a few cupfuls of sake, I couldn't feel a thing.

Chapter Fourteen
Meng: Youthful Folly

That night was the night of Rosie's last trick. A kind of a swansong which she shouldn't have turned because if they'd ever found out, she'd have ended up with more than a broken wrist. You work when you're told to, and only then. But God, she wanted to. I guess she was a bit emotional because she'd had a hectic afternoon. I guess when it came down to it Rosie clung to what she knew in a time of crisis, just like anyone would. And what she knew was the Game. She missed it.

After lunch Beckett had left the restaurant and disappeared into the back of a leather-seated air-conditioned Mercedes which had taken off into the crawling mid-afternoon downtown traffic. I had declined his offer of a lift and decided to walk instead. I made it all the way over to Admiralty, just turning things over in my mind endlessly. I wandered in and out of a few shops without buying anything and I found myself fascinated by the name tags on the salespeople's uniforms. Chinese people pick rather astonishing English names for themselves. There is a guy over in Tsim Sha Tsui who works in a hi-fi store and his English name is Electric Fan. No shit. It's not an urban myth or anything. This guy really exists. Arthur took me to see him and we bought a couple of speakers more or less just because it was so over the top.

'Can I call you Electric?' Arthur asked the guy.

'Sure, mister,' Electric smiled.

That shop must do a roaring trade on account of Mr Fan, but he's not alone in the crazy-name stakes. I heard somewhere that the most popular English names for guys are Jesus Christ and Michael Jackson. That day, after my lunch with Beckett, I saw a couple of shop assistants called Elvis, but that wasn't unusual enough to make me want to buy anything.

I didn't realize how angry I was. I kept catching my hand in doorways or banging my elbow as I turned corners, like I was trying to let it out somehow. By the time I made it down to the concrete garden at Admiralty I was so pissed off I kicked one of the big statues really hard. Only the base of it. People stared though. 'Fuck,' I said out loud, 'fuck him.' And then when I saw a policeman looking at me, I knew I had to calm down.

I decided to take the ferry over the estuary. The lunchtime rush was over, it was about three o'clock or so, and I sat up in First Class on the shiny wooden bench seats at the front of the ship, restoring the fluid level in my body with sips from a bottle of mineral water I had bought from one of the booths at the ferry terminal. It had been a while since I'd taken the Star Ferry. When I had first arrived the old green boat had been my favourite way to cross the Pearl River from Kowloon to Hong Kong Island. It had been a bit of a change from crossing the Thames by bridge, a bit of a thrill because it seemed so traditional, so old-fashioned, like riding in a horse-drawn carriage or something.

That afternoon when I'd had my ride and I finally walked out of the terminal building at the other side of the water, the sun was beaming down again and a group of crazy old ladies were practising their t'ai chi on the wet concrete of the pavement beside a temporary display of tropical plants. I kicked one of the palm trees half-heartedly and then I hailed a cab and went home, still processing the little information I had managed to get from Beckett, still pretty pissed off, even if I hadn't done too badly. Rosie was moving to somewhere near Canton. The drugs were for the foreign market. It wasn't much but at least it was something, and I hoped that Rosie had done a better job in finding out what was going on from Bobby that afternoon than I had done with Beckett over lunch.

When I got into the house she wasn't back yet, which seemed quite promising. On the verandah I pulled off my clothes, dived into the pool and just swam. I'm not sure how long I was in there, but my skin creased up and when I got out of the water there was a towelling robe and a pot of tea laid out for me in the shade and a note which, it seemed, had been delivered by hand. I glanced this way and that, but the maid had gone. I wondered who had sent me a message. Maybe something had happened. Maybe it was good news. I tore open the envelope which was damp at the edges where my fingers had touched it and then I let out a little shriek. I was really pissed off. It was from Max.

Dear Kate,
I'm sorry that I can't teach you for a while. I have a lot of work on just now and it looks like I will be away for most of the time over the coming months. I will get in touch with you when I get back, but I

know how keen you are to learn so please feel free to engage a new tutor. You've made so much progress already it would be a great shame not to continue. All the best.
Max

The bastard was covering his back. I crumpled the paper up and let it fall to the ground. 'They can read it if they want,' I thought, and my breath became shallow and I bit my lip and shrugged it off even though it was so insulting. All of it. Max's cowardice. Beckett's detachment. Rats from the sinking ship. Both of them were really low and, I told myself, they weren't worth the worry.

I sat there by the pool, my eyes stinging, trying to be brave and fuming inside. But fuck them, fuck them all. Rosie, Serge, Arthur and I were together and that was all that mattered. My mind went over and over the possibilities and the betrayal as I stretched myself out and then slowly I drifted into an afternoon of sleep. I must have needed it, I guess. A three-hour siesta from four till seven in the haven of the leafy green garden from which you couldn't even hear the traffic up on the main road.

I had to scrabble around on the paving stones in the pockets of my skirt to find the pager when it went off. I was disorientated, realizing over a few seconds that it was early in the evening and the sun had set very suddenly while I had slept. Darkness comes like a blanket in the Far East. There isn't much dawn or much dusk, only light and dark. That's all. The garden lights had been switched on already and I looked at my watch in one glance and then over to the pager in another. Cradled in my hand it flashed with a suite number and an address over on the main island and the words – *meet client in rooftop bar.*

I got up slowly and wandered barefoot through the living room, stretching my toes out on the thick, soft carpet, relishing the cool air conditioning on my skin. Rosie hadn't come back. Her room was untouched. I shrugged my shoulders and wandered into my own bedroom where I sat down in front of the mirror to apply my lipstick and then pulled a strappy, sheer black dress from out of the cupboard and wriggled into it. I still smelt faintly of the swimming pool. As I leant over to pull on my shoes my hair fell in a cascade over my face and I heard the front door slam and Rosie come up the stairs. She burst into my bedroom and stood triumphantly beside the dressing table with a little-girl grin on her face.

'Bobby?' I asked and she nodded. If you hadn't known you'd have thought she'd just come in from the most amazing date.

'Eight hundred and fifty kilos,' she burst out. 'And he showed me on the map just where I am supposed to be going. The generals have this house together, but they also have land there. They grow their own.'

'Drugs?' I asked her incredulously, keeping my own voice low to try and encourage her to do the same.

'Home-made,' she replied. 'Cultivated. There is a factory there, to make the temple balls. They even use their own people. They own the whole village. Makes for very cheap price. Kate, this could work. It could work,' she said and then, bright-eyed and enthusiastic, she ran out of the door and returned seconds later with an atlas open in her arms.

'Look – there's jungle all around him. He's protected by the Red Guard,' she said, her finger pointing elegantly to the right place on the map.

I peered at the open page but the scale was too large

to tell anything much from it. Eight hundred and fifty kilos of the stuff though, that had to have a value of a couple of million quid. Off the street. It was a big deal all right. No wonder they'd treated both the generals so well and were prepared to throw in one of their best girls to seal it. 'No wonder,' I thought as I glanced at my watch and nodded my head sagely while Rosie peered at the map, holding it up closely to her face to take in every small detail. She was on a high. For a second or two it was infectious. Then I realized what the information could do for us. I remembered Arthur's air of resignation outside the Old China Hand. It was crazy. I think Rosie saw it in my eyes. She put the map down on the dressing table and smiled weakly.

'I have to go out,' I said. 'To the Heavenly.'

And Rosie said she'd come too.

Personally, as hotels go, I like the Heavenly. Up in the rooftop bar you can get cocktails and most evenings there is a fat black jazz singer and a thin white band who are kind of good, which makes a change from Filipinas singing really crass cover versions. I'm Western so I'm a bit snotty about my music. If there's one thing I miss about the UK it's indie. There was no chance of any of that going on though. Not even at the Heavenly. It has this plush but eccentric feel about it which is different from most of the five-star establishments where I usually work. For one thing, there's the lift. It's probably the least discreet lift on the island because it's not only glass-sided, but it also has an amazing fifteen-storey mural of Chinese hills behind it, which flies past you as the lift moves and draws attention to the fact you're in there as you go up and down. Staying at the Heavenly, one thing was for sure that evening. The punter wasn't going to be a diplomat.

Rosie and I elected to get the MTR over to the other side of the water. We walked down the main road to the station together and we weren't really in any kind of a big hurry because response time is usually around an hour from when your pager goes off and we figured, in the evenings, the trains aren't too crowded although they come almost as promptly, every three or four minutes. I like the rocking of high-speed trains. It's soporific. I think it's a nice way to travel. Taxis are taxis the whole world over but underground systems are kind of individual. The Hong Kong underground, the MTR, is devoid of graffiti. It's spotless in fact and the announcements come quickly in a kind of clipped Cantonese, and then slowly in a heavily mannered, badly pronounced English. Some of the stations are subject to terrible draughts, which can send an empty bottle spinning along the clean shiny black platform at speed. Kids sometimes race them. Rosie and I picked up some fresh kiwi juice from the stall beside the station and sipped it as we took the stairs down and waited for the train, Rosie clicking her high heels impatiently against the tiled floor. The place was deserted.

'New money tonight then,' I laughed at the thought of the Heavenly.

Rosie finished the last slurp of her juice and threw the carton into the discreet rubbish bin by the stairs. We stood and waited, and paced, and after a minute or two Rosie's heels became suddenly still and she looked at me quizzically.

'I don't want to go and I miss work already,' she said sadly and then asked, absolutely straight-faced, playing with a strand of her glossy black hair, 'is that funny? I miss it even now.'

I shrugged my shoulders. I mean, I suppose I understood. I'd have missed the parties and the nightlife too. I'd have missed dinner out five times a week and the odd stint of riding in a black limousine all over town. I've never not worked and working the way that I do, well, it's an occupation. You live at a certain pace, a certain speed and slowing back down to normal life must feel frustrating. It's like taking exercise every day for months and months and then just sitting watching TV for a week. Your body doesn't like it. It doesn't feel nice because you're hooked. Once you're on the pleasure express, it's hard to get off and switch to another, slower service.

And I missed her already. There was part of her that already wasn't there. I laid my hand on Rosie's shoulder.

'It's going to be OK,' I said and then the train came.

We stood in silence, side by side, holding on to the chrome pole near one of the automatic doors and even in the harsh light of the train I thought to myself that Rosie looked very beautiful and also very distant. There was something compact about her, something separate. It's hard to explain really. But even then, at a time of great need and a time of crisis, Rosie still had the air of someone very independent, someone who, despite all evidence to the contrary, could look after herself. And now, I realized, she might have to. Things were going to change. We weren't going to be together like this much more, no matter what happened. Not for a while. We might not work together ever again.

At the Heavenly the doorman recognized us and pulled the glass back with a flourish. Rosie nodded elegantly as his eyes came to rest on her broken wrist and we ignored him and glided on together through the pale marble hallway and took the lift upstairs to the bar where I was due to meet the punter. The band weren't playing that night, and there was piped music, although the stage was set up with a mike and a couple of spotlights were focused on to it.

'What's that all about, d'you think?' I asked Rosie as we scanned the lounge area.

She shrugged her shoulders. 'Soloist, I guess,' she said.

When the waiter came up to seat us he must just have assumed that we were both there on business, which of course would have been usual, so we ended up sitting at a table together beside the window, waiting for the guy to come down from his suite. I don't know why I didn't say something, why I didn't point out earlier that she would have to go soon, that we shouldn't have been sitting there the way that we were. I was thinking, I suppose, about other things. I had evaded responsibility all my life. I'd never cared about anything. I'd prided myself on it. And now there was Rosie.

We ordered some drinks and then Rosie checked her watch against the neon colour clock on top of the new Bank of China building. You get quite a good view of it from the Heavenly although I've never quite got a handle on how it works. I mean, there are a whole load of colour codes to memorize. Green for quarter past the hour. Blue for half past. It was, Rosie announced, quarter to eight by her reckoning. I got my head together.

'He'll be down soon. You better sit somewhere else,' I told her.

'I'll move when my Martini comes,' Rosie replied. 'And then when I've drunk it I'll ring Serge and Arthur and tell them what we've found out. Maybe I'll go and meet them after they've finished work.' The boys, well everyone working in Hong Kong really, put in pretty mad hours. It would be normal for them not to finish until nine or so at least and quite often we'd hear of them working clear through the night on something. There were showers in the offices and little crib beds where all-night employees could catch a couple of hours' sleep before turning up at eight in the morning, shaved and ready to start again.

I felt suddenly jealous at the thought of Rosie leaving the hotel and going to meet them. I had a flash forward to the conversation between the three of them while I, I thought to myself, would be drinking away, listening to some boring businessman who was too far from home. I could almost hear the infectious lilt of Arthur's laugh, and I was surprised at how much I'd rather be with him, Serge and Rosie. There I was. Professional to the last. An ice maiden if ever there was one, usually dedicated entirely to money and to all that it could bring and I'd have paid anything to get out of working that night.

I'm not sure how long Rosie and I sat there. We didn't say anything much, only sipped little by little on our drinks and I kind of lost track of time for a few minutes. Rosie should have left ages before but then before we knew it the waiter had brought a middle-aged American to the table – my punter.

'Hello ladies,' he smiled, and well, force of habit, we just introduced ourselves.

'I hadn't expected two of you,' he grinned once he'd shaken our hands, settled down in his chair and ordered himself a Scotch. He must have been fifty and, I noted, like most wealthy Americans his teeth looked a good twenty years younger than the rest of him.

'You hurt yourself?' he asked Rosie.

'Yes,' she said.

'You'll still manage, though?' he asked.

I was about to explain to him that Rosie had to go, and that I was his date for the evening, when Rosie piped up herself and got in before me.

'Oh I'll manage just fine,' she said, cool as anything. 'My friend has to leave soon if that's all right by you.'

And suddenly, out of nowhere, I had the night off.

Chapter Fifteen
K'un: The Receptive

We swapped our pagers and our mobile phones. It meant we'd still be able to get in touch with each other, of course, but that no-one would know that Rosie was the one upstairs in the suite at the Heavenly instead of me. As I left the cocktail bar the stage was all lit up and a skinny, scruffy, small kind of guy came out and started telling jokes to the audience in a thick Irish accent. A sea of nervous laughter wafted me towards the lift and I smiled to myself, knowing Rosie wouldn't get any of the jokes. Downstairs in the hallway I borrowed the phone at reception and rang Arthur at his desk, telling him excitedly, like some eager child, that Rosie and I had discovered stuff, whispering some details down the handset to him in a kind of impromptu secret code which he seemed to instinctively understand. I didn't want to use Rosie's mobile just in case. I suppose I was getting cagey and careful.

Arthur told me he was nearly finished for the day and that I should pick him up from work. He said that he'd get in touch with Serge himself and arrange somewhere for the three of us to meet and talk so, fully instructed, I drifted out of the hotel building and straight into the back seat of a cab which I directed down towards

Central and Arthur's office. I felt almost hysterical. I was supposed to be upstairs in the lap of luxury and I'd done a bunk. And it seemed I was getting away with it. I loved the thought of getting one over on Conrad, of me and Rosie tricking him. She was a daredevil, though. There never was any stopping Rosie.

Half an hour later Arthur and I were walking around Lan Kwai Fong, standing in the middle of D'Aguilar Street, trying to figure out Serge's directions which had been supposed to take us straight to this little restaurant where we were all going to have dinner. It was a balmy kind of night and the streets were buzzing. Lan Kwai Fong is about the only place at night in Hong Kong where Europeans pretty well outnumber the Chinese. In the swish bars just off the main road blue-eyed models and brown-haired stockbrokers chat with back-packers and drug dealers. It's a place of short skirts, bottled beer and suntanned faces – a succession of pickup joints really. Meet and greet city, where the punters spill out on to the pavements and some nights even crowd over, blocking the road itself. We didn't usually hang out there as a rule, Arthur, Serge, Rosie and I. Working on the principle that on a non-professional basis, you should never sleep with anyone whose troubles are very much worse than your own, well, the place speaks for itself.

I caught glimpses of our reflections in the gold-plated panels of the office entrances as we walked along. The night air was pleasant and we kept going right up the steep hill, which made my bones ache a bit. The humidity sometimes makes it difficult to move, so I was glad when, referring to Serge's instructions which he had jotted down on a grubby Post-it note, Arthur suddenly turned left and we picked our way down a tiny dark alley which surprisingly opened out on to a small terrace at the end. It was a bright, busy pocket of light away from the main road and Chinese faces once more predominated. From D'Aguilar Street it hadn't looked like there was anything down there at all, but once you made it through the alleyway, the place was teeming. There was a black fronted comic shop which was still open, and it was busy too. Through the window I could see kids shuffling between the racks, leafing through the collection of fanzines and fantasy mags from around the world. By the door, perched on a high-backed chair, a girl with skin as white as Lux flakes and hair the colour of ginger biscuits sat haughtily in a miniskirt and a man's shirt reading a volume of *The World Compendium of Tattoos* entirely, it would seem, for effect. Arthur moved left across the terrace and I followed him.

'It's here I think,' he said, as he stopped outside an open-fronted noodle bar. The place looked like it belonged in some kind of stylish sci-fi movie, *Blade Runner* or something. A classic. It managed to look dusty and hi-tech all at once. We sat down at one of the Formica-topped tables out on the street. The free-standing fans from deep inside the restaurant blew a pleasant breeze out towards us and Arthur ordered us some Coca-Cola, which arrived immediately, served without ceremony in the can. No glass provided. We opened the drinks up and toasted each other, laughing manically. Serge, if nothing else, obviously had a sense of the dramatic.

As I stared up the terrace, watching for his arrival, a short, squat, Vietnamese man passed by. He stopped a couple of yards away and spat loudly on to the rough, muddy street.

'Asian men,' Serge's voice said, with humility, 'are so

unattractive.' And there he was right behind us, as beautiful as ever.

We ordered some greens, ribs, noodles and Chinese tea and settled conspiratorially around the table.

'There's a bar around the corner where they have meetings all the time,' Serge said, and it occurred to me that it was beginning to seem as if he was running on some kind of inside track. 'Chinese dissidents, gay rights campaigners, artists and stuff,' he continued. 'I figured it was the right end of town for us just now,' he said seriously.

I looked sideways into the restaurant at the other customers who were wielding chopsticks with great dexterity all around me and I wondered what they were plotting, who they all were and what they were doing in what had now grabbed my imagination as a Den of Thieves.

The waiter came with bowls of food for us and Serge waited for him to leave and for us to start eating before he spoke.

'I've brought maps of the area from the office,' he said. 'We have detailed layouts of the whole of Southern China because we underwrite development loans there. For roads and stuff. I also ran both of our generals through the computer and came up with their biographical details and political profiles, though I haven't read them yet.'

I pushed some of the noodles from my bowl into my mouth and coughed as a strong piece of ginger hit my throat. That whole night was a bit surreal. It felt like we were in a James Bond movie and I half expected something vital and dramatic to happen very quickly and lots of people around me to die. I hurriedly swallowed the food in my mouth and gulped down some Coke and then I spoke.

'What exactly do you think we're going to be able to do, Serge? Do you have a plan?' I asked him.

Serge toyed with some greens and then picked up a rib and sucked on it thoughtfully. 'Don't really know yet,' he said. 'But I do know that the more information we have, the more chance we have of figuring something out.'

'Yeah, and we don't yet know how they're planning on bringing the stuff over here, or where they are going to land it,' Arthur said. 'It's got to be most vulnerable in transit, hasn't it?'

Serge nodded sagely. 'Yeah,' he said. 'That's something we need to know. That would be really handy.'

I don't think it had actually occurred to me before that Serge intended that we were about to become some kind of commando unit. That as far as he was concerned we were going to have to have a pretty hands-on approach. It's one thing thinking that you want to help save your friend, but it's quite another parachuting into enemy territory and booby-trapping crate loads of cargo yourself. Personally.

I shoved some greens into my mouth and gulped down some more Coke, noticing my neatly painted nails and thin fingers and thinking how inappropriate they seemed in the face of the conversation. I suppose that everyone has actually done things that are naughty or dangerous, at which they might get caught. The time you kissed someone you shouldn't. The time you shinned down a drainpipe and away from the house without your parents knowing about it. But then your friends and family would be unlikely to actually torture you physically for any of that. You'd be unlikely to die for what you'd done, whereas the triads employ people specifically for that job. Give a triad a couple of hours

140

and a mobile phone and there's no-one they won't be able to get to. They say that the top triad hitmen know over three hundred different ways to kill a man, although as far as I can see, they generally prefer to use a gun.

I stared at Arthur, looked deep into his blue eyes and realized why he'd said that time we'd been on the overpass in Wan Chai that we were all going to die. Serge looked very serious too. It struck me that they were pretty brave when it came right down to it and there was a sneaking suspicion inside me that I wasn't really up to it, that I wasn't as brave – or maybe as foolish – as they were expecting me to be. I wanted to save Rosie. I wanted to try whatever we had to try. But there had to be something better than this kind of plan. Foolish, noble, desperate and doomed. There had to be something which would really work.

'Whatcha thinking, Kate?' Arthur asked gently and leant over towards me. I guess my face must have been a picture.

'I dunno,' I said. 'I just kind of thought we were planning to do something more subtle. Something less, well, physical.'

Serge pushed his empty bowl away and sat back in his chair, and I suddenly understood why he was paid so much. He had this air of complete competence about him, as if the way he saw the world was necessarily the way it really was. As if he was totally in the know. He got quite cocky about it.

'A bloodless revolution, eh?' he replied.

'Look, no offence,' I said, 'but I'm a hooker, not a commando, and you two are bankers, for Christ's sake. We aren't cut out for this. No way.'

Serge looked me straight in the eye. I think I'd offended him. He had been ready to put his life on the line, after all. But someone had to say it sooner or later.

'Do you want her to go?' he sneered. 'Do you?'

'You know I don't.'

'Then what else are we going to do? Means to an end, Kate. What the hell else do you want? Someone to just deal with it for you, like everything else in your life?'

'Fuck you,' I said, angry now.

Arthur leant forward. 'Hey calm down,' he murmured, his blue eyes unblinking, 'we need to stick together. And for the record, I'd lie down in traffic for Rosie, but I'd rather not have to. Maybe Kate has a point.'

Serge kicked the ground. The waiter came over and cleared our dishes and there was an uneasy stand-off, Serge avoiding my eyes, Arthur's fingers twitching as he fiddled with a paper napkin. When the waiter had gone, Serge looked up.

'Mercenaries are expensive,' he said. 'We don't have enough money for that. It would cost a small fortune.'

I think I felt relieved. It wasn't that I'd wanted to get in mercenaries, it was just that at least Serge was giving a little. Perhaps, I thought, mercenaries would do it. Maybe that was the solution. It sounded a lot less dangerous than parachuting in there ourselves. I dived down into my handbag, pulled out my change purse and threw it over the table towards Serge, my blood up. But he only grinned.

'Small change,' he laughed at me. 'A good unit would cost a lot more than you can carry in a little thing like that.'

'Open it,' I said seriously.

So Serge tipped the coins out on to the table.

'There must be a whole $10 here,' he said and looked at me questioningly.

I grabbed my purse back and pulled out the key

which was attached inside to a chain. It felt good to make him look foolish. Like he wasn't clued in.

'Safety-deposit box,' I explained. 'In London. There are five gold bars in there. Worth eighty grand when I left.'

Arthur smiled.

'We've got lots of money,' I said. 'Money isn't our problem. Between us Rosie and I must have three or four times that again in the bank. What we need is a plan which will work and for that we need professional help.'

'I'll look into it,' Serge promised and after that he seemed to take me more seriously.

Arthur didn't say a thing though. I don't think he had realized quite how much Rosie and I were getting paid or maybe, the deeper in we got, he was realizing the dangers too. And it wasn't what I wanted either. You can't trust mercenaries. You can't trust anyone you have to pay and really, they can't trust you. When it came down to it we were middle class and safe at heart. We were soft. We'd squeal if we'd been pressed. A mercenary would have to be crazy to take us on as clients. The only one of us with a backbone of iron was Rosie.

Chapter Sixteen

Hsu: Waiting (Nourishment)

When I got back to Kadoorie Hill that night it was late. After we had left the open-fronted noodle bar, we caught a cab and drove up to Serge's flat on the Peak. The new plan was beginning to sound just as far-fetched as the old one and I could hardly believe that I had got carried away and offered to underwrite it. As Serge talked on I felt more and more uneasy and when he insisted that we pore over the small-scale, detailed maps he'd brought until we found the site of General Ho and General Tang's house I was relieved at least to be dealing with something real. There it was, the Palace of their Desires. It was in a poor, rural area, the kind of place where people feed their cattle more than their starving children – if they're lucky enough, that is, to have any cows at all. China is so huge and the infrastructure is so ropey that in backwaters like that, people might not have heard yet of Mao Tse Tung's death, let alone of the impending death of Deng Xiao Ping. It's quite possible that people in communities like that wouldn't know who Deng Xiao Ping was at all. It's a different world, that place where General Ho and General Tang had their households. Remote and backward. And that's where my lovely, sophisticated, glamorous friend was headed.

Serge stood in front of the huge, floor-length windows of his minimalist white living room which faced out towards the city, and drank neat brandies while he detailed his plans for further searches, to get as much information as possible about the generals and their intentions. He'd even commissioned a photo search to try and get us some actual images of what the place was like. It was a fairy tale. La la land. As I listened to him I found my mind wandering away, out over the rocks and bushes which made up the sheer landscape of the side of the the Peak to the brightly lit streets of skyscrapers down in the big bay of Central Hong Kong Island and then the inky thick blackness of the Pearl River Estuary which lay beyond. And north of that was Canton.

General Ho and General Tang were cousins, Serge informed us. They had denounced Ho's father as a traitor during the Cultural Revolution after the old man's death. It was said that they had done so with the old man's permission to gain political advancement for themselves. He had been some kind of high official in the province where they had lived at the time, some kind of political accountant, and in the days of the Cultural Revolution denouncing others was how you secured advancement for yourself. Ho and Tang had entered the army and had quickly gained promotion. They had always been hard men and now they were hard old men, in a position of power. The Red Army is corrupt. It always has been. And in its ranks, to advance, or even to survive, a soldier has to be corrupt too. It would seem, from what Serge had found out, that General Ho and General Tang had done well for themselves out of their positions. Serge estimated their annual income at some half a million pounds sterling, mostly from bribes and scams, smuggling and extortion. This would be, as far as he could make out, their first foray into the production of drugs. This was, he pointed out, them really hitting the big time.

'Up until now they've made a lot of money, but they will have had to spend it too. At least half of their income must go on having to bribe others. Maybe more than that. It's just like paying insurance premiums, in their situation. There's no question of *not* paying.' Serge shook his head. 'This will be their first real, big money. They have enough land here to produce a lot more than eight hundred and fifty kilos. That's less than a tonne. You'd need very little space for that, comparatively. You can get a tonne of dope from just one acre. I'm not so sure about the yield for opium, but I'll find out. It can't be too substantial in any case. They have a lot of land there, a lot more than they need, so what they're making now is the trial run on a sustainable deal. Once they've done it the first time they will be able to produce more of the stuff and do the same kind of deal again and again. Probably on an even larger scale. Bobby's bosses are selling Rosie to him as a goodwill gesture, I reckon. So he'll deal with them again. If it all comes off they each stand to make millions.'

There was something fascinating about Serge that night. Something crazy and wild and free. Something purposeful which almost made him shine as I looked up towards him. His face looked really Chinese in the warm, shadowy, evening light which filtered up from the city and he looked like a young guerilla general, his eyes bright as he directed operations over his small-scale maps. Noble and doomed.

'How did you find all this out?' I asked.

And he just stared at me, as if I was crazy. 'I work in a bank,' he said by way of explanation. And before I knew it Serge was walking up and down with his hands behind his back. He was talking about 'buying in hardware' and how Arab mercenaries would be best for the job. He was talking about 'budget restrictions' for Christ's sake and suitcases of cash in sterling. He sounded crazy. I couldn't quite believe that Arthur was just sitting there letting him rant on, but this time, addled with brandy, Arthur was nodding. He was up for it.

If I'd had a moral map there, if one had existed for the road upon which we found ourselves, I'm sure it would have been bordered by red-rimmed signs saying STOP NOW BEFORE IT IS TOO LATE. We were definitely on the wrong road, I could feel it, and by and large my sense of direction is good. But what the hell was I going to say, there in the half light of Serge's smart apartment when I'd just offered to finance the whole crazy thing? *We shouldn't do this. It's too dangerous.* I couldn't say any of that because it seemed to me that it was tantamount to just letting Rosie go which was, for all of us, completely out of the question. And I felt a coward because when Serge had sneered at me, when he'd said that I just wanted someone else to deal with it, well that was the truth.

I had a very bad feeling though. This was too big a deal for us by far. The more Serge talked the more it dawned on me just how dangerous this was going to be, and how conspicuous, and I tried to calm myself by rubbing my thumb and forefinger together and concentrating hard on how the soft skin on the ball of my finger felt. It's something I've done from time to time with punters, when I've wanted to take my mind away from what I'm actually doing. This time though, it wasn't just all going to be over in an hour or two and I felt lost, because I didn't know what to say or what to do to bring the whole thing back into control.

'You guys are amazing,' I smiled but I don't think I've ever felt so distant from Serge and Arthur as I did that night. As it turned out the house of our friendship was built on two supporting walls – Rosie and I. And Rosie was leaving.

Out in the night air, in the relative darkness of the Peak, away from all the neon, Serge waved Arthur and me off and we slipped into a taxi silently and headed for Kowloon.

'You still think we're gonna die?' I asked him.

Arthur just shrugged his shoulders. 'Swings. Round-abouts,' he observed, almost as if he didn't really mind. When he finally dropped me off at home around midnight I kissed his cheek, drawing his face close to mine with my fingertips and smiling at the light in his amazing blue eyes before I hopped out on to the pavement and he disappeared away down the hill back towards his flat on the fringes of Mong Kok.

I wonder now if I could have said something then to make it all turn out differently.

I fell asleep waiting for Rosie to come home. I wanted to talk to her about it honestly. I was looking for an ally and I wanted to hear her opinion. She and I existed in the same world, you see, and it's a world where you just don't take risks like Arthur and Serge were planning. Not normally. It's a world where you play by the rules, where you plan every move like a chess player and I knew, almost without realizing it, that the only way to win this battle was strategically, just like a grandmaster would win it, rather than storming in like some kind of World War One general. There was a big difference between being a bit spirited like Rosie or a bit reckless like me, and what the boys were talking about. I wanted to hedge my bets. To stay small and smart and on top of things, and avoid the carnage which seemed to be the only logical outcome of Serge's plans.

I lay downstairs on one of the wide white sofas in the living room, my shoes cast carelessly into the middle of the floor and a cream shawl wrapped around my shoulders. And lying there in the darkness, I dreamt, for the first time since I'd left, of Coatross. Of my mother's cheap yellow Formica kitchen which always smelled of soup and my father's favourite brand of cigarettes. Regals in a white box with red stripes across the corner. The smoke used to stink out the little toilet under the thin plywood stairs fitted with cheap blue corded carpet. It was the only place in the house that my mother would allow him to light up though. Dangerous, really, if you think about it, but there you are. It's not, you understand, that I wanted to go back – I've never been homesick, not once since the day that I got on the overnight London train – it's more that I was afraid, that I was returning in my imagination to a place and a time where I knew what I wanted, where I was going and when.

I woke up in a panic at two in the morning, took a deep breath and went into the kitchen to find a glass of iced tea in the huge double-doored fridge. I kept gulping in air. In fact, I think it was only my deep inhalation which was keeping me upright. I felt like some kind of blow-up figure, as if my body would have collapsed in on me if I hadn't kept breathing in as deeply as I did. My limbs felt weak. I had a flash all at once of how much I didn't want to die.

'I mustn't panic,' I thought to try and reassure myself. 'It will be fine.'

And I tried to sip the icy tea and ignore my rising fears.

Rosie didn't come in until after four that morning, by

which time I had returned to the sofa and fallen deeply asleep once more, lying out low on the thick squashy cushions. I don't think I was visible from the hallway of the house but I suppose, in the pale light filtering into the room through the French windows from the direction of the garden, she must have seen my dark shoes on the white carpet, and she crept into the living room, crouching down next to me. I woke up immediately, and turned around on the sofa so that I was facing her. 'OK?' she whispered, and I just nodded, trying to catch my thoughts and cram them into a few coherent sentences in my mind before I said anything out loud.

The American punter had obviously done the trick. Rosie wasn't tight and frustrated any more. She wasn't confused at all. In fact, while I was scrabbling about in my mind, trying to find the words I needed, Rosie was busy doing things, busy organizing herself. She was clearly more at ease with her body than she had been earlier on and she moved smoothly like a traditional dancer, her thin white arms stretched out elegantly. I was glad. She drew my pager and phone from her pocket and popped them into my handbag which was open on the ground, delving in and retrieving her own devices with her long pale fingers.

'Thanks,' she said.

I sat up slowly and then stood up and we both walked out of the room and silently up the stairs together, side by side but not touching. Just Rosie's presence was very calming and I felt extremely near to her, very drawn in and quite emotional in the face of that calmness. A wave of admiration or love or what-ever else you might call it washed over me and I realized, that is I recognized, exactly what the big deal was about. Exactly what had hit me. Why I'd been gulping in air in the kitchen like some kind of deep-sea diver surfacing to replenish oxygen supplies. Why it mattered so much that she was going away and why I was so anxious to make the right plan. Rosie and I were really close. Genuinely. Close with the depth of real feeling. Love. If there is one person in the whole world I've ever felt real love for it's Rosie, and the prospect of her being taken away just made me feel desperate and helpless.

I was on the point of finding the words I wanted to say, of asking her opinion, of really beginning to talk to her when Rosie laid her hand on my forearm.

'It will be all right,' she said calmly, as if she knew where I had been that evening and exactly what I had been thinking. 'We'll let them plan whatever they want, but in the end we know what is possible and what is not.' Rosie is so amazing like that. It was as if she knew just what Serge had said, exactly what we were all taking on to try to save her and how afraid I was. And she hadn't been there for dinner that evening, she hadn't seen Serge's maps or heard his crazy ideas, but still she knew and that calmed me down. She and I were taking the diplomatic route, playing a political game. Letting things go on until we were ready to take control. And I had confidence then that between us we'd do something which would turn out to be right, and I felt a tightness leave my chest.

I've never been so scared before that the only time I could admit to it was in the middle of the night. I think I smiled and just nodded without saying a thing, and then Rosie turned towards the door of her room and disappeared inside with that incredible poise of hers and I went into my own room and flopped down on the bed. 'She's something else,' I thought. 'She's amazing. A true friend.' And I liked the way that when she was

151

weak I'd been strong for her, but when I'd needed her she'd been there for me too. It had a kind of pleasant balance to it, I thought, as I listened to the silence.

Chapter Seventeen

Hsiao Chu: The Taming Power of the Small

The next morning the sun was shining through the clouds and I woke up quite late. I rolled over and checked the clock on the bedside table. It was after eleven and I could hear the shower in Rosie's bathroom on the other side of the hallway, the maid sweeping up dead leaves on the verandah below my window and the sound of someone moving downstairs. I wondered for a second who it might be and flushed at the thought that perhaps Max had come to give me my Cantonese lesson after all. That maybe he'd had a crisis of conscience or something. Fat chance. I guess I was just confused. I pulled one of the thick goosedown pillows over my head and decided it was probably someone just cleaning, or a man with a package for the hallway. It was probably nothing to do with me. The house was awake though. Everyone else was up and about and it was another day.

I smiled to myself as the night before fell into perspective. All it takes, you see, is a bit of time, and you can come to terms with anything. Everyone in Hong Kong seems to be so disconnected sometimes. Everyone seems to be getting away from something or someone else. There are so many guys I've met, white guys, who came to the colony in the first place to get away from their families, as if putting all those thousands of miles between them, kept their mothers and fathers at an emotional as well as a physical distance. As if running to the other side of the world put them in control.

I thought about Serge and his mother, who was holed up in Taipei. She came to visit him two or three times a year, although I never met her myself. And while she was staying Serge would make this pageant, this array of arrangements, all designed to show her how competent he was. I don't think the old lady really even noticed his spectacular show. She seemed to spend a lot of time during her visits buying plants to improve the feng shui of Serge's apartment and flinging out the dry, dead, twisted foliage which she had installed on her previous visits and which Serge never tended properly.

Arthur's mother and father never visited. He hadn't been back home since he arrived. But whenever he talked about his family he always made the same point, over and over. How incompetent they were, and how he had taken responsibility for his life. How he had got the hell out and made some money. And it struck me then that the four of us really had that in common. Families that we claimed didn't matter to us but which, nonetheless, provided a spur, if you like. A reason to succeed. So many good things seemed to drop into our laps and we were all the kind of people who really made the best of that.

'That's why the boys are so keen to do something hands-on,' I realized, 'they think if they do, they'll be in control. Whereas Rosie and I know that the less you do the better.' And like most things, once I knew the reason for it, I felt that I could cope. With Rosie on my side, it wasn't something to worry about. I stretched out under the sheets, arched my back and yawned as I recovered my equilibrium. The mattress felt quite cool at its edges and I turned over and decided it was time to get up.

I trailed lazily across the bedroom and into my shower and then dried myself and put on some clothes. Downstairs on the verandah the sweeping had stopped and I could hear men's voices, but I couldn't make out exactly what they were saying so I switched the air conditioning off and then opened the window so that I would have a better chance of catching the words. It was like an oven outside, a low, baking oven, and the heat came through the window in a block and pushed its way across the room. The men were speaking in Cantonese. It was Bobby and Man and they were discussing two containers which were going to come through customs.

'*Ho sarng yee,*' Bobby was saying. Business is good.

And so it should be. Hong Kong is the second biggest container port in the world after Rotterdam. Up in the New Territories to the north of Kowloon, there are whole container cities which sprang up in the Eighties and early Nineties.

'Two big containers,' Bobby was saying, 'forty feet size. We can check it all up there and then ship it out. Hong Kong customs will be no problem, but in Rotterdam we will have a more difficult time. We need to buy them off with a dummy shipment.'

You don't live in the circles I live in without knowing about that kind of stuff. A dummy shipment is basically a gift to the customs men. The smugglers pass it through the port only a few hours before the real shipment is due to go through, and it can work in two ways. Either it keeps the system so busy that the real shipment is unlikely to be detected, or it's agreed with the customs men that the dummy shipment will be sent through, so they can look good and meet their targets for drug detection as well as benefit from a backhander, probably planted in among the goods. Drug dealers often stockpile stuff which is suitable for dummies, low-grade stem marijuana, batches of chemical hallucinogens which go wrong, that kind of thing.

'And Rosie will be delivered to him by plane once it is checked?' Man asked.

'Yes,' Bobby replied, 'I will take her myself. With the money.'

And I think that I detected a tightness in Bobby's voice when he talked about Rosie going away, although that may only have been wishful thinking. There's little enough expression in spoken Cantonese in any case. Little enough to the Western ear. But nonetheless I thought that I heard something in his voice as I strained to listen.

'This stuff,' Man started to ask, 'this stuff is like cocaine?'

'No,' Bobby told him. 'Designer drugs. Fashion.'

And I could hear Man grunting his approval. Fashion was, after all, a very important thing. And then, as I moved sideways, I caught a glimpse of another face – that policeman I'd seen at Conrad Beckett's house. He was sitting on one of the chairs on the verandah just listening and nodding from time to time, but obviously involved in the whole plan in some way or he wouldn't have been there.

I sat on the thick carpet below the window and I listened. The men were drinking something, and I could hear them as they clicked their glasses in a toast. I have yet to figure out exactly what they were doing up in the house on Kadoorie Hill that day – they didn't really seem to have much of a purpose there, although triads often dropped in, particularly if they were on their way to the airport, which was only fifteen minutes away if that. It struck me that perhaps Bobby had called in to see if he could catch a glimpse of Rosie. Just to bump into her, as if casually, and then I thought to myself that maybe the guy had been right the other day – perhaps Bobby wasn't really tough enough to do his job. Anyhow, maybe they'd turned up at the house because they wanted to show the place off to that policeman. It was a pretty lush house. Who knows?

I got on to my knees and peeked gingerly over the window sill to see whatever I could. Bobby had started to walk across the lawn and around the swimming pool, so I ducked down again in case he might turn around and see me peering out of the window over his head.

The conversation seemed to be over and there wasn't much else to hear, but I still sat there, just in case. 'The stuff's coming into Hong Kong in containers,' I thought. 'Canton, Hong Kong, Rotterdam.' And I tried to see it in my mind's eye, but whenever I did there were always dark-faced soldiers parachuting down from the sky with missile launchers blazing. I'd stopped paying any attention to the men in the garden by then and I almost screamed as the door of my bedroom swung open and then I breathed a sigh of relief because it was only Rosie. I brought my finger up to my lips so that she wouldn't speak, and she glanced questioningly at the open window as I crept across the room and took her by the arm, whispering that Bobby had been talking about the deal with the Chinese generals and realizing in that moment that there wasn't really any question of not making every effort to do something to stop the deal. We had to explore every possible escape route, however crazy. Even if it meant Arab mercenaries.

I was desperate because of Rosie of course, because somehow we had to stop what was happening. I know it sounds insane, but when you were with Rosie she had such a quality of glamour entangled with her vulnerability, her naivety, that you would have done anything you could to stop them taking her away.

Chapter Eighteen

Ting: The Cauldron

We got ready and headed downtown. Rosie had received a brief message from Serge. He wanted us to come to his office for lunch. As we slipped out of the house, we could hear Bobby and the men leaving by the garden gate. We hovered in the doorway out of their sight as they piled into a car and pulled away, then Rosie sauntered to the edge of the pavement and stuck out her hand to hail a taxi.

Serge worked for a very swish company. We arrived slightly too early and sat on a white bench in the entrance atrium of the huge office block. The cupola was fifty feet above our heads and the sky glowed like a blue light through the glass. In front of us there was a marble oasis with palm trees and a bronze Renaissance statue. There had been a huge scandal about that statue. It would have been pretty run-of-the-mill in Europe – just a nude male figure by some unnamed Italian sculptor living three hundred years ago. In Europe it would have just been art. But when it was unveiled the censorship committee in Hong Kong had demanded that the investment company who had built the office block apologize to the public for the affront caused by the statue's nudity. And they had insisted that the statue should have a plastic fig leaf attached to its groin. The papers had kicked up a stink about it, art critics from all over the world were flown in to give their professional opinions and even the Governor's office had got involved. In the end they had let the statue be. A fine figure of a man too.

Rosie perched on the edge of the bench and checked her watch.

'You know,' she said, 'this all seems like such a fuss. I can hardly believe it.'

'Two forty-foot containers,' I said as I tapped my forefinger on the back of the bench. 'That's a party. That's something to fuss over.'

'How many of the balls could you fit in one of those things, do you think?' Rosie mused.

'Twenty-eight grammes a ball, rolled by hand,' I said by rote and I held up my thumb and forefinger in a little circle to show the approximate size.

It was a hell of a lot of drugs, even considering that there would be packaging inside the containers as well. It was two enormous rooms full of the stuff in each big box, when you thought about it.

Rosie pursed her lips and pulled a packet of cigarettes out of her handbag. She drew the soft felt of a filter up to her mouth and struck a match to light it up.

'Well,' she said, 'all this crazy stuff Serge and Arthur are into, there has to be something cleverer we can do. Once men get started it's difficult for them to stop.'

I nodded, and we sat there in silence for a few more minutes.

'At least,' Rosie suddenly shrugged her shoulders with uncharacteristically dry humour, 'I suppose it will stop them clutching at straws.'

I laughed out loud. Rosie really was something.

'Look,' she said, 'I think I have an idea, Kate. But you aren't going to like it.'

'What?' I asked.

Rosie paused for a second. She looked around us at the teeming marble concourse, and took a deep draw on her cigarette. She seemed reluctant.

'What?' I repeated. 'Rosie, it can't be worse than hiring fucking mercenaries to burn out two million quid's worth of opium.'

'It's much more difficult than that,' Rosie said, her brown eyes still and defiant.

I took a deep breath, but just as she was going to tell me we saw Arthur come into the atrium through the swing doors and it was time for us all to go up in the lift together and whatever Rosie had on her mind, she definitely didn't want to tell the boys.

Serge of course had carried on planning his James Bond adventure. In his fifteenth-floor office the three of us sat around his desk picking at a platter of sushi, while he closed venetian blinds on each of the four glass walls around us. Then he came back to the desk and pulled a dossier out of his bottom drawer. Those guys at the bank worked fast. 'There,' he said. 'It came through this morning.'

Rosie opened the folder and we crowded round her. It was full of photographs Serge had bought from some American information agency working out of Singapore. I guess if you're prepared to pay enough you can get photographs of anything these days. Serge had done his job well and the dossier was pretty comprehensive. There were aerial shots of the house where Rosie would be sent to live as well as photographs of the surrounding area, which seemed to be jungle right up to the perimeter of the old men's estate where the carefully manicured gardens were guarded by soldiers, safe in aerial lookout towers. From a thousand feet up, the lush, dark jungle lapped up against the harsh, clear, manmade lines of the confines of their property, and inside the lines, the greens were far lighter and the areas of different shades of colour were set out in clear shapes. There was no definite evidence of drug production apart from a few outbuildings set in the farmland which bordered the south side of the estate and, of course, huge fields of poppy flowers, which by themselves proved nothing, and fields of what looked like marijuana plants covered in thick green netting which meant, of course, that we couldn't really tell. Serge had also looked into the methods of production – exactly what was necessary to combine opium and hashish – and it turned out that all you need is a big cantilever boiling pot, some simple tools and the manpower. All of which, of course, were easy enough to obtain and easy enough to hide. There was nothing really obvious from the air. Nothing that we could identify in any case. The only thing which stood out was the house itself – and that was huge. We couldn't see inside, but it was patently a large traditional enclosed household with a peony garden and a fish pond. There were two storeys of accommodation topped by a red clay roof below which, we figured out, there must be at least twenty good-sized rooms. It was pretty plush.

On top of that there were also file photographs. A shot of General Ho and General Tang together at some kind of military ceremony earlier on in the year and a picture of General Ho's wife whose name was Jung and who, in a life long before she met her husband, had been a nurse in Ho Chi Min City. She was an elegant, slim lady with long, grey hair and dark, almost black

eyes. The photograph of her was dated on the back –
1992 it said – so we figured the woman must be almost
as elderly as her husband. Certainly well into her
sixties. Rosie turned the print around and around in her
hand, examining it carefully. Ho's wife was old enough
to be her mother, and that wasn't all. There were
photographs of four children – a son who had followed
his father's steps into the military, a younger boy about
whom there were no clues, and two pretty girls in plain
nondescript black clothing.

'Stepchildren,' Rosie murmured with her fingers
stretched out and the prints balanced on top of them
as if she was begging, 'they will hate their father's concubine,' she said and she began to cry because
suddenly, I think, it seemed very real. Serge and
Arthur kept their eyes on the contents of the dossier.
They didn't seem interested in Rosie's tears. Girls
only cry in James Bond movies so that James Bond can
save their lives.

As Rosie began to sob, I pulled the photographs from
her hands.

'Don't give up,' I said, reaching out and stroking her
arm. 'Here, don't worry,' and I passed her a tissue.
However brave and sussed Rosie seemed, she was
obviously shaken and upset too. Her nose was red and
slightly swollen. She blew on the handkerchief and
smiled at me.

'OK,' she pronounced.

'I'll have them fetch us some iced tea,' I offered and I
went out into the main office to find Serge's assistant.
When I got back Rosie had completely stopped crying
and had dried her cheeks but there was an
unaccustomed frailty in her eyes.

Serge was sitting in the old leather seat behind his
desk. Arthur was leaning against a bookcase to one side

of the room. He was holding a bottle of beer in his hand, which Serge had evidently given him while I was gone, and he looked thoughtful as he flicked the bottle open with his thumb and took a long swig. Serge used a metal opener on his and poured it into a glass. There was silence. We were all thinking. About different things. Eventually Serge started.

'I've made some enquiries,' he said, but I cut him short right there. I didn't want to hear it.

'Oh shut up,' I snapped angrily. 'You're like a kid with a fucking Christmas list, Serge. You're so caught up in what you want that you don't even notice anyone else. All that stuff might be good for your ego, but it isn't good for Rosie.'

Serge's eyes narrowed. 'You think this is about my ego?' he said. 'Is that what you think? Maybe it's about your ego, Kate.'

'Oh for God's sake,' Arthur joined in. 'Listen to you both. You're quarrelling over nothing. All that's important here is Rosie. Keeping Rosie here and not getting killed.'

'What do you think I'm trying to do?' Serge shouted. 'I'm the only one who's done anything about it. Don't you even care?'

'When they cut into us,' Arthur said, 'we will seep real blood together. You and I both, Serge.'

I felt sick. Rosie stood up with her hands out in front of her, like she was trying to calm an eager crowd of kids.

'I'm all right,' she said. 'It was good to see the photographs. It's important to know. Now Serge, if we are going to go on with this you have to be careful. You understand, don't you? You know we could all be shot?'

Serge nodded as if she was some kind of schoolmistress who'd asked him a stupid question.

'Right then,' she said, 'you can carry on, but we each have power of veto. This is just an idea we're checking out.'

Serge nodded, but I could see that he thought this was the only possible option. There was something ominously obsessive about him, something crazy in the slow, half-lidded blink of his eyes. No-one felt like sushi any more. Serge folded the dossier together and put it back in his desk. Then he walked us all as far as the lift, patting Arthur on the back to make up, I suppose, for screaming at him.

Downstairs Arthur saw us into a taxi and we decided to go home.

'We should have called him off,' I said as soon as the door closed on us. 'Serge is crazy. We're walking a very thin line.'

Rosie held up her bandaged wrist. 'I know,' she said simply, 'I know.'

Chapter Nineteen

Sun: The Gentle (The Penetrating, Wind)

We decided to walk part of the way back and the taxi dropped us off at the green police station on the main road about fifteen minutes away from the house. We bought some more cigarettes from a kiosk and smoked them together as we strolled along through the humidity. There was building work going on and yellow dust covered the pavement, falling from scaffolding up above us. I felt shiftless, groundless, like I was in a nightmare and I couldn't get a grip. Rosie stopped in front of a shop window. It was an estate agency. She stood for a second or two looking at the display cards for apartments in town, the kind of place we'd wanted to get together.

'You said you had a plan,' I murmured.

Rosie stubbed out her cigarette with a kitten heel.

'Let's go and get stoned,' she said, and walked on.

An hour later, in our own garden, we lay giggling on the sun loungers, animation flickering across Rosie's face. I was pretending that nothing had happened and I was comfortable with that. I've always backed off from anything too real, and it was a relief just to forget it. To make believe that this moment could go on for ever. To lie there laughing at the clouds.

'How old is he, do you think?' Rosie asked, at length.

The picture of Ho had been a grainy black and white. It wasn't flattering.

'Seventy, I suppose,' I replied.

'Exactly it,' she leaned over. 'That's my idea. The one you won't like. That's it.'

'What are you on about?'

Rosie sat up. 'The real plan,' she said. 'The one which will work. He'll die. He'll die before I do. And when he's dead I will come home again.'

I began to cough. I couldn't believe it.

Chinese generals, in fact all the higher echelons of the Chinese junta, are renowned worldwide for their longevity. Those wrinkly old bastards just live on for ever. Someone like Ho might well still have a good twenty years in him. Maybe more. It certainly wouldn't be unheard of. I stared at Rosie, hardly able to believe that this was what had kept her so calm. She was twenty years old and just sitting it out seemed to be her best plan. Now that's long-term strategy and I suppose in one way she was quite right because it was certainly the surest thing we had yet come up with. Rosie has always been a bit of a survivor, she comes from the right stock for that, but still, serene as it was, her plan lacked a certain spirit and indeed, urgency. Rosie ignored the look of shock on my face. I knew I had gone deathly pale.

'You have to look after my money, Kate,' she said, racing ahead as if it was decided. 'Power of attorney.'

Rosie had been working in Hong Kong for three years, and during that time she had saved most of her money. Like I said, apart from clothes and the odd meal out there wasn't a lot we needed to shell out for. Certainly not rent, and rent in the city is extortionate. You've no idea. Rosie and I got paid in line with quite senior management jobs, but we didn't have the expenses. Between us, if Serge didn't blow the loot, we had saved a packet. The money just kept going into the bank account in my name which Conrad Beckett had set up for me at a downtown branch of some European bank with whom, it seemed, he had a special arrangement. I'd never had a bank account before. I'd never seen money earn money all by itself just sitting there. The first time I'd seen an interest payment go into the account I had just been stupefied.

Rosie, as it turned out, had saved a lot of money over the time she had been working. Even I was surprised.

'High-interest savings,' Rosie continued as I sat there absolutely stunned, listening to her. 'Safe investments.'

Her life was at stake. Her freedom. And she was talking about junk bonds. I couldn't believe it. She was as cold as ice, just like Max had said. I sobered up pretty quickly.

I got up and walked to the shaded part of the verandah. The sunlight on the garden made the grass look a strange, very bright green. The pool looked as if it was glowing a pale, seaside, Brighton kind of blue and the little gold mosaic tiles at the edges glinted up at me. As I turned around I could feel the heat on the back of my head although my face was still in the shade. Rosie was hanging on to the edge of her lounger, waiting to see what I thought. She was going to be disappointed.

'You can't, Rosie,' I said very definitely. 'You can't just give up like that.'

Rosie's face became hard. She looked about ten years older all at once.

'I need your help. We need to plan,' she said. 'There are so many practicalities. I need to change my pill. I'm not having any children there. I'll never get out of that place if I do. We've got to get years of supplies and find some way of hiding them so I can take them in with me. The kind where you still bleed every month. It has to look normal. They'll check. In a place like that, they know everything. We have to plan this properly,' she explained.

I thought about it for a moment and then tears welled up in my eyes and I looked away pulling my hands up over my face. She had already decided and was being so brave about it all. So practical. So committed. And my heart felt like it was breaking. I was horrified at her cold determination and I have to admit that there was part of me which actually preferred the suicidal insanity of Serge's crazy rescue plan. What Rosie had come up with on her own might be sensible but it was too cold. I wanted to at least try something even if it failed. I had to do something because I'd be so desperate without her.

'If it's this difficult for me it will be close to impossible for the boys,' I thought. And I realized that she'd sent them off on a wild goose chase just to keep them occupied. I realized that I was the one she really trusted. She needed me.

'I don't want you to go,' I whispered. 'Rosie.'

And then my voice broke completely and my shoulders began to shudder. It was the thought of being alone again. The thought of her going away for such a long time, for good. My eyes stung with the tears. I couldn't stop. I cursed myself for smoking the dope. It made me too emotional.

'You're my friend,' I said. 'You're my only friend.'

And I sobbed for what felt like a very long time with Rosie begging me to help her, to be practical, to see sense. In the end I finally agreed with her and fell in with the long-term view. I didn't feel very brave, though. I felt trapped and hopeless as if it was my future which had been taken away, which, in a way, I suppose it had.

'Don't cry, Kate,' she whispered. 'You're so pretty. I hate it when you cry.'

But I couldn't help it. I howled so much that strands of my hair stuck yellow to my wet cheeks as Rosie and I crouched in the corner together in some kind of childish pact, and held hands.

Chapter Twenty

Chin: Progress

I didn't do my best work later that day. I had to drag
myself away from the house to supply personal
services at a conference which was on in town. They
were world-renowned ceramics experts, it turned out,
who had come to Hong Kong for a symposium on early
Chinese porcelain. There was a large exhibition of
pieces from the Shan and Quin dynasties which had
been staged especially, and an auction too. Early
examples of Chinese ceramics are very rare because it
was Imperial policy to smash up and bury the pieces
of anything which wasn't being used or had been
damaged. I should have been rolling out all my best
conversational pieces for intellectuals – observations
about China's strong links with the past, about how
it's the only country whose writings of up to 1,000 BC
are still readable in the language of today, how time is
far more perpetual, and history so much more
immediate. I had a line of patter for Western visitors of
a more academic frame of mind. My concentration,
however, wasn't on all that. My mind was with Rosie
back at Kadoorie Hill.

I had never really had anybody before. Not like
Rosie. Not anyone who I could feel that close to. In

Coatross I had known I was leaving all along so I kept myself distant. In London I hadn't met anyone I felt I could trust. It's a big gulf between me and anyone else, the sex-for-money thing. You can't tell many people outside the game, and even if you can tell them, like with Arthur and with Serge, they can never really understand about what you do. I don't think so anyway. The only way in which what I do for a living is a big deal is the way other people see it. From time to time, Arthur asked me questions about what it was really like to be on the game. He had a bit of a fascination about it, I think. Well, that's blokes for you. Once or twice, when we were out on our own, watching late-night art movies in a cinema just off Pacific Plaza, he'd whisper questions to me in the dark, but he never seemed to understand what I said in reply. No, it was only Rosie who got it. She was the only one who really understood. And she was leaving. It could have been any city in the world flying by the taxi windows that afternoon. I didn't focus once.

'What's all the money for anyway?' I wondered, and well, that tells you how spaced out I was. But for the first time the money just didn't seem to matter so much any more because they were taking away the person I wanted to share it with. I hauled myself out of that taxi though, I got myself downtown. There was no sense in me getting beaten up over Rosie leaving and I knew Bobby could arrive at any time. I had to follow orders. I was miserable enough as it was.

It was around five o'clock that afternoon when I arrived down at Tsim Sha Tsui East and booked into the hotel. I immediately went up to a room on the tenth floor which had been allotted for my use. I'd brought an overnight case with me – just a few clean clothes and a toilet bag. We'd work like that a couple of times a year when some big event brought a host of clients into town all at once and our more normal, leisurely pace speeded up considerably. Usually working like that gave me a buzz. Men. Boom, boom, boom, one after the other. Working at speed, freshening up quickly between each punter and back into the fray. It happened seldom enough to be exciting. Something different. There would often be three or four girls working an hotel when something special was on and we'd all share the same changing room, swapping tales as we passed each other going in and out on our way to freshen up. The last time it had been Rosie and I, passing each other in the corridor, slapping palms as we went. Racing. Comparing how many guys we could fit in in the limited time that we had. Then it had been a diplomatic weekend, some kind of conference.

That day at the ceramics do there was only one other girl. A sullen Chinese eighteen-year-old I'd met a few times before and never liked much. I think her name was Amy. I nodded peremptorily at her and exchanged a few pleasantries as I unpacked my clothes into the redwood wardrobe and laid out my toiletries in the glass and chrome bathroom. Then, following the instructions posted on my pager, I took the lift up a couple of floors to my first client.

Professor Robin Stimson probably advised someone important somewhere on their collection of ancient porcelain. I don't think that the professor, though, was quite used to or prepared for the kind of attention he was about to get from me. He was in his sixties and unremarkable in a bookish kind of way and he wore a short-sleeved thin cotton shirt and a pair of pale lightweight trousers in some cheap fabric. His long fingers were agile and he spun a pen between them as he took down notes whenever the telephone went, which happened a few times while I was up there.

'This is quite unnecessary,' he said as I arrived, and I feared for a moment that he, like the Mancunian shipping expert I'd had a couple of weeks previously, would start into a long and protracted conversation about his wife. He didn't though. It seemed he wasn't married, or if he was he never mentioned it.

I took in the saggy, freckled, olive skin of his arms and the lines of flesh around his neck as I lit a cigarette. Old men are easier. They seem to feel that they have less to prove.

'It's quite normal to have an escort in Hong Kong,' I told him.

He clicked his false teeth and spun his pen between his nimble fingers while he considered this.

'Where are you from?' I asked politely.

'London,' he said. 'I work there.'

I noted that he had a nice smile. In fact, his eyes danced and his face kind of lit up whenever he grinned. He seemed a sympathetic kind of person. It didn't really matter, but it was nice.

'I lived in London for a while. Near Russell Square,' I said. 'Why don't we have a drink?' And when he agreed, I opened the minibar and poured him a whisky and added a little splash of soda. Then I prepared a drink for myself.

'Vodka and just about anything going,' I told him, 'tart's cocktail.'

And he laughed. It must have been a bit of a change for him, I thought, from afternoons in some musty office somewhere in a museum or university. He was willing, though, and we chatted with each other for a while and it wasn't quite seven o'clock when he'd done with me and I moved on to another suite further

174

down the corridor and a jetlagged American investment analyst. There were no complaints, of course, but I knew I wasn't on top form. My mind wasn't, you might say, really on the job.

Later, over dinner with a British-born Taiwanese business tycoon who had come to bid at the auction, I was kind of reaching the end of my tether. For the first time in my life, I really didn't want to be there. It wasn't just that I wasn't particularly interested. I actively wanted to leave. I got up and went into the bathroom, listening to my heels clicking on the marble floor, sweeping dreamlike past the grey-haired toilet attendant and into an empty cubicle where I took a seat and lit up another cigarette. I guess I must have been in there for a while because the toilet attendant rapped on the door and asked if I was OK and I realized that the cigarette in my hand had turned all to ash and that I was crying again. I opened the door smartly and bathed my face in cold water as the old woman eyed me suspiciously before handing me a thick white towel with which I dried my hands, my face and my eyes.

'I have to pull myself together,' I thought and I dragged myself back to the table and tried my best to be charming to the wide-faced Taiwanese guy. Later, in his suite, we drank champagne and I remember making a conscious effort to laugh a lot and to gasp as if I was pleased when he kissed my neck and pulled my blouse open with his thick-fingered grasp, and after that I just concentrated on breathing hard. It was a contrast to the last conference I'd worked when Rosie and I had between us totalled thirty-four men in a little over twenty-four hours. And we were joyous. On a high. At two in the morning and two more men down, I couldn't stay any longer and I crept out of the room, pulling my jacket closely around me as I took the lift downstairs. The hotel lobby was almost deserted as I crossed it and I could hear the air-conditioning fan overhead swooping around and around. It gave me the shivers and I caught sight of myself in one of the huge mirrored walls: a thin white-skinned blonde girl in a loose well-cut dress of thick black silk. I felt helpless. Hopeless. Small.

I just wanted to get out of there, to make a break for freedom. I had it in mind that I would be able to catch a cab home at least for a few hours to touch base before having to return, when all of a sudden I heard a jolly voice across the lobby. I guess it was probably only late afternoon in London and Professor Stimson was wide awake in the bar, downing a drink or two because he couldn't seem to get to sleep.

'Come and join me,' he grinned.

I almost hesitated. That's how low I felt. It was the first time in my life that I hadn't just taken a day of strange men fucking me silly in my stride. It's kind of a crude way to put it I suppose, but well, it's the truth. I was so out of it that I almost turned the old guy down, but then, my professional instincts kicked in, and I knew that I had to be polite. He ordered me a Bloody Mary and we chatted amiably away really for what must have been quite a while. The professor, it turned out, wasn't only an expert on ancient ceramic techniques, but also on modern production. He was fascinated by large-scale factory processing which seemed at odds with his main field of expertise. A couple of whiskies in, and he started to talk about polymer resins which allow clay to be moulded in shapes which were previously impossible and then he carried on for a while, telling me about working guns made out of clay, which, he explained, terrorists could use for tricky, dangerous sniper attacks because they were easy to smuggle through customs. Easy to get in, easy to get out.

'They can smash them up afterwards too,' he said, eagerly, 'destroy the evidence entirely if they have to. Clay is the medium of the future, you know. You can use polymers to mould it and then burn them out in the firing.'

It was then I think that I clicked. It was then that I realized Rosie's easiest way out. Not that clay-gun stuff – I would have to have had a hefty dose of Serge and Arthur's brand of twisted realism to go for that. No, it was the *in and out* idea which really grabbed me. I could have kissed Professor Stimson. I mean, I could have kissed him for real. What Rosie needed to do was to go into China all right, but she needed to go in there as an assassin. Get in, knock the old guy off, and then get out again. It had to be possible. Even if it took her a couple of years, I figured, even if she would have to be careful that it wasn't obvious that she was involved in the old general's death, at least if it came off she'd be back pretty soon, relatively speaking and she wouldn't have to just sit there waiting for him to die of natural causes. The more I thought about it, the more it seemed a really good alternative. Of course I had no idea how to do it. I've never murdered anyone in my life. Goes without saying. But that didn't matter. The only thing that mattered was that the idea I'd been waiting for had finally come to me and I was so excited that I just wanted to run all the way back to the house and shake Rosie awake and tell her all about it. I could hardly wait. I had gone into the bar dragging my feet. I came out walking on air.

Luckily for me, Professor Stimson tired after a while and I got myself out of the hotel and into a cab, and I bobbed eagerly up and down in my seat as we headed northwards. The streets were pretty quiet, it was late and most of the nightclubs were closed for business, and as we pulled up the slope to the sleepy, dark-windowed street I was so keen to get inside that I almost threw the fare money at the driver. I bolted into the house and hammered up the stairway like an excited teenager. I wasn't even tired any more. I crept into Rosie's room, holding myself back from jumping on the bed to wake her up, and instead tiptoeing across the carpet. She was lying on the mattress, looking different from when I'd left. Her hair was in a long plait down her back, she wasn't wearing any make-up and her clothes were uncharacteristically dowdy. There was a free-standing full-length mirror to one side of the bed and a pair of wire-framed round spectacles in her good hand. Rosie, in a blue liberty jacket, had been dressing up as a Communist. She looked like a student. Like one of those kids on telly protesting over Tiananmen Square.

'He'll hate this,' I smiled, and gently tugged on her sleeve.

'Rosie,' I whispered, 'wake up, wake up. I've got it.'

And she had barely come to as I began babbling. I suppose I had drunk a lot and I was excited.

Rosie's eyes widened. She laid her hand on mine to stop me talking for a second.

'Yes,' she said, 'I thought of that too. I'm going to kill him. I'm going to do it.'

She sounded really strong and determined. She looked it as well, sitting there in her Communist gear, all dolled down and off to Canton.

'I hate him so much,' she said, and I fell down next to her on the bed.

'Me too,' I replied with venom. And I did. I hated him more than anything for trying to take her away.

Chapter Twenty-one
Chieh: Limitation

The next day, of course, I had to go back to work. I set
my alarm for eight in the morning and after my first
night's deep sleep in ages, made my way back over to
Tsim Sha Tsui East, straight-backed in a cab to give
some old man in a luxury suite the wake-up call of his
life. I did eight different punters and then, as evening
drew in, I togged myself out in a slinky black dress
and caught a cab to a reception at the China Club over
the river at Admiralty. It was pretty swanky really and
even Conrad Beckett deigned to put in an appearance.
He emerged from the ornate antique lift, and came out
on to the thirteenth floor of the old building which
housed the low-lit plush reception hallway of the
China Club, with its tiny flame-feathered caged birds
on their beautiful intricate enamel stands, and its
discreet valets in pristine white jackets, waiting to see
to the guests. I always think that black-and-white
photographs of parties at the China Club must look
like the grainy sepia shots of the colony at the
beginning of the century which you see so often in
history books.

I was waiting for Beckett when he made his
entrance. I sat perched on an antique needlepoint and

ebony chair, as I had been instructed. He took me by the arm and escorted me in. On the next floor up, we danced together, he and I, out on to the balcony, away from the crush of people – all the experts I'd been entertaining and luminaries of the Hong Kong business community with their wives and, of course, a good dozen or so hookers, there to work the crowd. I was nervous of him. It felt like my heart was quivering in my chest.

'You look very beautiful, Kate,' Conrad said.

And I babbled something about the food smelling nice and about me being hungry so he took me indoors again and we picked up plates from the buffet table and piled them up with the most delicious food at which I picked half-heartedly. People were high on cocaine that night. One middle-aged Welsh woman, with peroxide blonde hair was wearing a fringed gold dress, and had that madness in her eyes that you only get from too much of the stuff when you aren't accustomed to it. Her mascara had run and she was dancing like a dervish, the tasselled fringing on her outfit giving her a two-inch aura of sparkling gold in all directions while her stiffly lacquered hair hardly moved at all. It was a jazz band, I think, playing in the background. The shimmy. And I remember thinking to myself that she was going to get into trouble like that. Not my kind of trouble of course. My kind turned out to be quite different.

Conrad was watching me. Whenever I looked up his eyes were on me. I hadn't been this afraid with the crazy mercenary plan on my conscience but I began to imagine all sorts – bugs in Rosie's bedroom, maids out on the balcony. Our plans laid bare and Bobby only a phone call away. I tried to smile a lot and laugh at the bad jokes of the ceramics experts.

Professor Stimson must have asked for me, I guess, because Conrad came to get me at about midnight, and he told me to go downstairs and wait for the professor to come down after me. I jumped as he put his hand on my arm and helped me pull my wrap around my shoulders. There would, he said, be a car waiting outside the front door.

'Busy day, Kate?' he asked.

I nodded. 'But I love my work,' I smiled, 'you know that.'

Just the smell of Conrad's aftershave made me feel queasy.

'Well, you're good at it. Go and look after Stimson,' he said.

And I thought to myself that Conrad didn't have a clue after all. He didn't know.

'Maybe we're going to get one over on him,' I thought. And why not?

I swept out through the dark wood and tapestry of the hallway into the small mirrored lift, safe in the knowledge that this job would be finished soon enough. I was keen to get home. To get on with things. To get back to Kadoorie Hill and Rosie.

After a few minutes Stimson joined me, slipping surreptitiously into the back seat of the shiny black car and as the driver pulled out into the traffic, towards the tunnel under the estuary, I stared out at the half dark of the night-time city, trying to make out the heavy smog that hangs down low and obliterates the stars.

'What do you think will happen when the British hand the place back?' I asked.

The professor looked at me very earnestly. 'I imagine that the Chinese will behave very badly,' he said.

And that gave me the shivers and I longed even more to be back at Kadoorie Hill in the tropical green of the garden with the red splashes of the open flowers. I wanted to be with Rosie so much that the muscles in my body became quite tense and I knew that I had to calm myself down because there was no getting away. I felt as trapped as she was. It made me panic and I laid my forehead on the cool glass of the window and watched the streetlights zooming past one by one to collect my thoughts. At least he was old. He'd sleep, I told myself. I felt very resentful.

'Communism,' I observed, 'is a pile of wank.'

And the professor laughed and began to stroke my hair.

Chapter Twenty-two

Wu Wang: Innocence (The Unexpected)

The next morning, quite early, I met Rosie at the Star Ferry terminal on the Hong Kong side of the estuary and we hopped on to a boat out to Lamma Island from pier six. The feelings I'd had the night before, the midnight horrors of bugged rooms and overheard conversations hadn't left me. I wanted to get away. It was just after ten o'clock in the morning by the time I could escape from Stimson, and the hotel had almost emptied out. I'd slept for a good six hours and woken up quite refreshed. I sat on the end of the professor's empty bed and checked with Conrad before leaving.

'Where are you going?' he asked.

'Lamma,' I told him. There didn't seem to be any point in lying. 'Rosie wants to.'

'You're working again tonight, you know,' he said.

And I told him that would be fine and then I gathered together my things and left the building.

Lamma Island is only forty minutes on the ferry and you can wander around the little village in the bay, and enjoy the bright flowers and the easy open spaces of the countryside. It has a reputation in town for being sort of arty and the *gweilohs* who live there smoke a lot of dope and go home early because the last ferry is around midnight. A bit of a contrast to the coked-up, frantic, packed-out pavements of the big city. Yang Shue Wan is the only settlement on the island, a cluster of ramshackle modern apartment buildings, and a few shops and restaurants. Further up in the hills there are gardens which people have actually cut into the side of the slopes, and of course there are lots of grave mounds, burial plots. Pretty well every time I've been there I've seen relatives tending those remote hillside graves in among the purple orchids. They burn hell money or leave offerings. There's nothing much up there but nature, so Rosie and I knew we'd be alone.

When we got off the boat, we climbed the mountain pathway, dodging between the fuchsia dragonflies and the wild green trailing plants, and every now and again we would take a seat and rest on the rough stone path shaded from the heat by the overhanging trees. Rosie looked very small indeed that morning, in her thin white silk dress and her low-heeled sandals. Her wrist looked so fragile in the heavy white dressing which Dr Harry had bound around it for support.

'I think it's getting better,' she said.

And I started to smile until I realized exactly what that meant. Time was marching on. Time was running out. Rosie leaned against a low piece of wall and cast her eyes downwards.

'So how did it go?' she asked me.

And I told her about the conference delegates and the party at the China Club and my call to Conrad Beckett and how we would have to leave in the middle of the afternoon and catch the ferry home again so that I would be ready for the evening. But I didn't tell her I'd cried the night before when I went to sleep, that I'd lost all sense of time because I didn't want to lose her.

It all seemed too serious. Perhaps we'd dulled too many of our instincts for admissions of our feelings to come easy.

Rosie stared out to sea, gazing at the almost surreal blue of Lamma Bay. We'd come here once with Serge and Arthur and had a laid-back day. The four of us. A picnic on the hillside. The odd white cloud in the brilliant blue sky and all afternoon just to daydream. Serge had said, 'We should buy grave plots out here,' and I remember a blush passing across Rosie's cheeks because we were going to be lifelong friends.

I lay back, the feeling of the warmth of the sun and the rough-hewn stone of the pathway behind my head as I stretched out like a cat. It felt good just lying there, my mind empty for a minute, my worries dissipated by the heat, but Rosie was twitchy and wanted to go on. She had scrambled up a pile of old stones beside the road to give herself a vantage point from which she could navigate our route.

'I think there is a garden along here somewhere. It has a pond,' she said.

I was perfectly happy just where I was but I hauled myself up and tramped up the hill after her anyway. My mind was on murder, though you'd never have guessed it to look at me. And I was finding it difficult to bring the matter up.

I suppose my parents must have instilled some morals in me after all. Useless bloody morals. But in the broad light of day I didn't seem quite able to make the plan I'd intended. Letting a man climb on top of you and stick himself inside is one thing. Snuffing the bastard is quite another, no matter what he's done. I was having second thoughts.

'You could give him a heart attack,' I said after some deliberation. 'That would be the best thing.'

A wry smile crossed Rosie's lips. 'Heart attack,' she mused. 'Good way to go.'

I laughed, kind of surprised at myself but at least we'd started. Rosie just looked worried and shook her head.

'Young wife though,' she continued as if we were discussing a hypothetical case, 'they would blame her, you know. Not so clever.'

Murder in China is a capital offence. They're pretty cut and dried about it. The state even sends a bill to the murderer's family for executing him, which is supposed to bring the responsibility for antisocial behaviour right back to the family. It's a mindset thing. Convictions are notoriously unsafe and executions run at a rate of well over a couple of thousand a year. It's a lot of people, and more than a few are probably innocent. The stuff considered admissible in court, the kind of evidence – well, Rosie wasn't being paranoid, let's put it that way. Just about anything goes. It wasn't as completely crazy as it should be that a young wife inducing a heart attack in her older husband might not be put on trial. Especially a concubine. We would have to make a plan which made Rosie look completely blameless no matter what.

'I dunno,' I said. 'Maybe we'd better get the boys on to it. Maybe they could help.'

'Yeah,' Rosie replied and I guess she was developing an appetite for sarcasm. 'Yeah, and they'll send me in there with two Uzis and a bazooka gun. No, you and I are going to deal with this one on our own.'

Rosie was standing with her back to me and as I got slowly to my feet I could see that she was looking at her hands. Her fingers were stretched out wide and the sinews were so tense that the tips of her fingers were arched upwards, back towards her body. She was right of course, the boys were out of the game now. They were out of it for good. It was Rosie and I against everyone else, and that scared the hell out of me because I couldn't control it. It began to look to me like you could take the girl out of Coatross, but you couldn't take Coatross out of the girl. Not completely. And I really couldn't face the seriousness of it. I just didn't have the bravery to do it. Killing a person. Killing something alive. Plotting. Rosie must have been thinking the same.

'How do you hurt someone like that?' she asked. 'How will I kill him? I don't think I can.'

I suppose there has always been violence which has gone on around us. And I suppose that, for me certainly, it's always been something which I have for the most part ignored. In the face of violence I just freeze. There was one time in London when this guy had done Eddie over. I think he was an undercover cop. Maybe he was vice squad or something. Maybe it was drugs. I'm kind of vague about it all, and that really proves my point. I never bothered to find out. Eddie and I had stood back while Elton had done the business, his strong black fists contorting the cop's body. I remember thinking that it was like some kind of cartoon. It was like Popeye. As Elton laid the punches in, the guy's body became more and more angular. The blood leaked from his nose and after a while he didn't even try to hit back.

'I'm sorry you had to see that,' Eddie had said, as if he was a gentleman and I was some kind of lady.

Elton had disappeared and Eddie and I had gone to a pub around the corner. I think we were somewhere near Kensington, just off the High Street. It was an upmarket kind of pub, anyway and I'd ordered a soft drink – a soda water with a dash of lime. Maybe that was why Eddie had thought I was shocked.

'It's OK,' I had shrugged. 'I'm fine.'

And I was. But I've never hurt anyone myself. Not personally. And Rosie hadn't either, whatever we might have seen. Doing it yourself, that's quite different and we were both beginning to realize where the defining lines of our morality were drawn, just how far we could go and still be ourselves. You think you know people, but you don't know someone until you've seen them under pressure, until you've seen them dealing with the difficult and the dangerous. You don't even know yourself.

I reached out and laid my palm on Rosie's, pulling the tension right out of her hand and curling my fingers down between hers.

'Maybe not,' I said. 'Maybe it isn't the right thing to do. Maybe we shouldn't plan for you to hurt him.'

There are some places too low to go. Some things even someone who sucks strange men's cocks for a living won't do.

Rosie shrugged. Her fingers had relaxed again and she squeezed my hand tightly.

'But I want to do it,' she said, her eyes bright and hard. 'I want to kill him. How dare he? I just don't know how.'

And I realized just how different Rosie and I could be. Just how different we really were. An uncrossable gulf was opening up and I felt stranded. Her eyes were unblinking and I knew, looking into them, that she'd do anything she had to. In that moment Rosie would have strangled me if she'd thought it was for the best. I'm sure of it. For the first time ever her face looked ugly to me, her tiny nose and wide mouth set hard in concentration. It was as if she wasn't Rosie any more at all. It scared the hell out of me.

Chapter Twenty-three

Ku: Work on what has been spoiled

The next few days or so were weird. I was working most of the time, and Rosie just got on with her own business. That afternoon on Lamma had freaked me out a bit and so for a few days we didn't really discuss things in any kind of detail and we both backed off. Rosie didn't trust me completely any more. That much was clear. Her bedroom door remained resolutely closed in the morning and any questions were greeted with hard-eyed indifference. I felt very rejected, but I couldn't help the way I was or what I'd said. I couldn't cross the halfway line which had been marked out between us.

Around us the world carried on, like a funfair roundabout. Serge rang twice with updates on his progress, or rather the lack of it. It seemed (much to our relief) that mercenaries for work inside mainland China or even in Hong Kong were hard to find. No-one wanted to cause trouble on triad territory. Serge said he was having more luck hiring helicopters and finding the necessary equipment. I sounded deliberately unimpressed on the phone and in our only real conversation that week Rosie and I both agreed that she should speak to Serge soon. We couldn't let it go on much longer.

'You do it,' I said, 'he'll take it from you,' and I skulked off into the garden and stuck my nose in a magazine. I tried not to think about how ashamed I felt at my lack of involvement. I shut it out of my mind.

That week, while I spent my time resolutely avoiding things, Rosie spent her time facing them. She found some crooked doctor who worked out of his own flat in Mong Kok and was prepared to get her a few years' supplies of contraceptives for a pretty good price. Rosie, rather dramatically, ordered herself a vanity case which came with false sides and a false bottom, so that she could stow the pills away. She also came home with power of attorney forms for me to sign and details of her bank accounts and investments to go through with me. We had no time, though, and I think, really, that I didn't want to make time for it, so I just signed the forms and then pleaded exhaustion whenever we might have to discuss anything.

Lying on my bed, when I got in each morning, I found it hard to sleep, hard to even close my eyes, and I threw myself into my work instead, which netted me the sum total of seven hundred pounds in tips and three bottles of Chanel perfume. I found for the first time in my working life that I didn't want to go home when the job was done. Once I made it back to Kadoorie Hill I either tried to sleep or I crouched in the open space of the living room, rocking on my haunches like a mad person in the night. Trying, I suppose, to make myself small. I was at once fascinated and repulsed and I skirted round the edges of Rosie, reading the books she was reading, watching her make her arrangements. Murder does not make an appearance in *The New Macmillan Guide to Family Health* but I gleaned plenty from its pages. Arsenic and aconite were poisons easily found in the body after death. Digitalis, however, given in high doses, could produce heart failure and was less easy to trace. Strychnine poisoning, similarly, was difficult to diagnose post mortem. All the time I kept thinking that it was the wrong thing to do, but I didn't stop looking. I thought about it constantly.

Rosie for the most part seemed to ignore me. She stayed very deliberately on her side of the halfway line. A book on the subject of wild mushrooms was hidden in the drawer of her bedside table and I noticed that the pages of the chapter on death caps had been particularly well thumbed. She also began smoking temple balls, which Bobby seemed to bring her almost every day. There was a clay pipe on the table out on the balcony where she used to sit and a gold-leaf ashtray which was always full of the burnt-out scrapings from the pipe. I can't blame her for wanting to get out of it, though. It was one way at least of escaping from the claustrophobic, awful atmosphere of the house and from the wordless chasm which had opened up between us.

One afternoon we tried to rekindle the life we'd both known and loved by taking a taxi downtown to do some shopping. It wasn't a big hit, I have to admit, and we didn't quite manage the sea of Armani bags which had so often undulated around us as we walked up Nathan Road looking for a ride home at the end of an afternoon in town. We didn't buy any clothes. Rosie bought a knife though. I guess we were both well beyond the frivolous. It was a six-inch hunting knife with a heavy leather handle and a rubber sheath. My eyes must have questioned her because, absolutely calm and determined, she just said, 'in case' to me as she handed over her credit card to pay. She was scaring the shit out of me.

Afterwards, and for no reason at all, we decided to go down to the front and have our hair done. We used to go from time to time to this salon on the third floor of one of the new buildings. The way things had turned out, though, it didn't seem to make any sense to be there because both Rosie and I had vital matters on our minds. Matters of life and death. But we persisted, Rosie with her knife stowed away both safely and stylishly in her Gucci handbag, and me hardly able to take my eyes off it. As one hairdresser massaged oil into my scalp I heard another trying to make casual conversation with Rosie.

'This is going to look really good on you,' he was saying, with his scissors poised.

Rosie gave him a stare which said quite clearly, 'Of course it's going to look good on me. Why else would I ask you to do it?' The glamorous frivolity was well and truly over.

It's hard in my position to talk at all about morality. I know that. But killing someone, even a wicked bastard like Ho, that's way down on the moral scale. It's a low thing to do. You can laugh. I know how most people see my job. But I don't think there's anything wrong with what I do. It always pisses me off when they show those awful, violent movies at home and they're rated so that fifteen-year-old kids can see them. You can blow someone up right in front of the camera and they'll all chat about it at school the next day, but those same kids can't legally watch a real sex scene. That's over eighteens only, and censored entirely if it shows anything worth seeing. I don't get it. Public morality. Proper values. I was shocked at Rosie. I hadn't known she had it in her, not really. I didn't want her to go. I wanted to save her. Desperately. I just wanted the problem to go away. Serge had been right.

In a cab on the way home afterwards, lonely and scared, I knew I had to speak to her. I wanted more than anything to make it all right.

'Rosie,' I said, 'we have to talk about this. It's freaking me out.'

But she didn't even turn around to face me. She only slid her hand across the back seat of the car and squeezed my arm. The new, decisive Rosie walked alone. She took all the responsibility herself, in the end, and maybe her silence was an act of kindness. When the chips were down, she'd learnt a lot about me too.

That night when I came home after work the living room was in disarray. One of the sofas had been upended and a couple of ginger jars lay smashed on the carpet. The glass doors that led out to the garden were open and I could hear shouting. I ran outside and saw Rosie, Serge and Arthur sitting down by the pool. Arthur had a fresh bruise on his eye and was nursing it with an ice pack, and Rosie and Serge were shouting at each other very fast in Cantonese. I picked up some swear words before they noticed me standing there and fell abruptly silent.

'There you are,' said Arthur.

'What's going on?' I asked, as I walked down the lawn towards them.

Serge rounded on me, his eyes fiery. They seemed to glow into the humid darkness, like hot black coals.

'She is ridiculous,' he snapped. 'How could you encourage her in this? It will never work.'

'That,' Rosie pointed out coolly, 'is not up to you, Serge.'

I sighed and sat down next to Arthur, laying my head on my open palms. 'God,' I murmured, 'this is awful,' and when I pulled my head up again Serge had stormed off and was kicking the shit out of a tree at the bottom of the garden.

'He wrecked the living room,' Arthur said. 'I kind of got in the way.' And I leaned over to see more closely how pink and swollen the skin around his eye was.

We sat there feeling useless for a minute and then Rosie set off down the garden to fix things. She stood right in front of the tree trunk as if she was daring Serge to take it out on her instead. He stood still for a moment and then he cracked. He reached out and pulled her close to his body and they stood like that for ages. It was like he couldn't let her go. And of course that was the problem.

'How long have you been at this?' I asked Arthur.

He checked his watch. 'All fucking night,' he calculated. 'It was mad. Serge just lost it. We got chucked out of the restaurant. He won't give up.'

I let my head fall forward again, to rest on my hands. Rosie was being amazing. This was happening to her, after all, and we were all flailing around. Serge still hadn't let her go.

'Can't you talk to him?' I asked Arthur, but he only shrugged.

Behind him I could see insects like little specks moving in the light cast by the street lamp over the wall. The air was heavy.

'Just let it alone,' I heard Rosie say to Serge behind me. She was begging him.

Up in the house I could hear movement. Someone was putting the furniture back into place.

'I'll get them to bring us something to drink,' I offered. I suppose I wanted to do something. I smoothed my skirt down as I rose and began to make my way towards the house. In the shadows of the living room, though, I didn't see the outline of the maids. Bobby was beside the drinks cabinet mixing himself a Scotch and soda. I hesitated for a moment, hardly able to breathe. Then as I turned I think Rosie saw it in my eyes, because she pulled herself back. And as Rosie backed off, Serge following her like a little lapdog, Bobby walked out on to the verandah with his drink in his hand.

'Oh fuck,' I heard Arthur whisper, almost silently.

Rosie walked purposefully up the lawn towards the house. She pulled on my arm, her stiff fingers digging into my flesh so that I moved, dreamlike, behind her. We lined up behind Bobby. In solidarity. As I passed him I thought I saw Bobby smirk. Arthur and Serge must have been bricking it. For a second or two I was bricking it myself, but Rosie was right. Closing ranks was our best chance for leniency. Bobby took a sip of his drink. He looked at the glass as though he was appreciating the quality of the whisky and then he looked up.

'Get out,' he spat.

And Serge and Arthur walked out of the back gate and Bobby finished what was in the glass, stared at us both for a full minute without blinking, and then he just left. Rosie and I sat down on the living-room carpet.

'Too close,' she said. 'We can't see them again.'

And I nodded, my stomach turning over.

The next day, when I came downstairs at lunchtime Conrad was sitting in the high white lounge playing checkers. Rosie was still upstairs and her door was closed. Conrad's checkers opponent was a Chinese girl wearing a baby blue catsuit and a pair of Gucci shoes.

'Ah, Kate,' Conrad smiled. 'This is Nancy.'

I shook her hand. It didn't feel right. I hated myself. I felt like a traitor, but I was getting used to that.

Beckett said, 'Nancy will be your new tutor for Cantonese.'

He had engaged her two evenings a week as it turned out. Recruited from the sales department of one of his hotels and anxious to take on anything for a little extra pin money.

'I was thinking of giving up,' I mumbled uselessly and Nancy looked crestfallen.

'Well, perhaps just today,' Beckett said. 'Just for an hour,' and he pushed the checkerboard away and got up.

'How did you know?' I asked, but he didn't reply. I shrugged my shoulders as he left the room and then I slouched into a chair, in contrast to Nancy who was perched eagerly on the edge of her seat. I felt like a kid being made to have extra Latin lessons or something. I felt horrible. But after the previous night I'd have done anything Beckett said.

'You don't want to learn?' Nancy asked. 'What happened to your last teacher?'

'He got promoted,' I lied on Max's behalf and I took a cigarette out of the amber marble box on the coffee table and lit it up.

'Nice place here,' Nancy said.

And I said to her, 'I'm a prostitute. That's why I live here. I'm a whore.'

But she didn't walk out. I expected her to, but she didn't. She just sauntered over to the table and picked up a cigarette of her own, her light eyes completely placid.

'Conrad told me,' she said in Cantonese as she lit up.

She stayed for nearly an hour. We talked about nothing in particular. It wasn't too bad I suppose. It passed the time and when Nancy left I noticed that the stone of desperation in my stomach had gone at least temporarily. I had been distracted and, I thought, maybe Conrad was right. Maybe it was OK. Rosie was leaving. Maybe I just had to let her go.

'Next week?' I asked Nancy, and her mouth widened into a beautiful smile.

That night I took a cab over to Arthur's place after work. It was the best thing I could think of doing without going home, and I decided it should be safe to see him as long as we weren't at Kadoorie Hill. He had a flat in one of those skyscrapers at the bottom of Nathan Road, near Chungking Mansions with its Indian gold merchants and thin-faced smack addicts. Arthur had taken the place when he'd first arrived and then once he'd got a good job and was earning a packet he'd got used to it so he just never moved out. He said he liked it there – that side of town gives maximum density a whole new meaning with eighty thousand people living in every square kilometre of the district. The hustle and bustle of it was just his style. It was two or so in the morning when I finished working and the taxi dropped me off, and I stared straight up at the bars high on the vertical rows of windowpanes rising thirty storeys into the sky.

'Why do they need bars that high up?' I thought to myself, and then I giggled, trying to make out behind which of the windows Arthur was safely stowed. I was drunk I guess, and I wanted some company. I had been at the Heavenly again, and had taken some miniature bottles out of the fridge in some guy's suite and I pulled one from my handbag and slugged it down in one and then stared upwards again in amazement, just like a tourist. I wanted to go back to my first moments in Hong Kong. I wanted to forget all the feelings I'd had. I was hiding.

It took Arthur a while to answer his doorbell but I was prepared to wait. Eventually he buzzed the main entrance open and I stumbled through the dimly lit hallway and into the lift. As the electric doors closed on me I thought I made out a figure sleeping on the floor at the back of the entrance hall. Perhaps it was the caretaker. I don't know. That's where caretakers often sleep as I understand it. It's part of their job. When the lift brought me up to his floor Arthur was waiting at the doorway of his flat wearing only a T-shirt and a pair of rather tight, dark red underpants. He had been asleep and his hair was all tousled.

'Hello,' I said sheepishly. 'I needed some company.'

'Come on in,' he offered kindly and stepped backwards into the room to let me pass. It was pretty grimy over at Arthur's place, really. The rubbish bin was piled up with empty beer cans and apart from one big leather chair there wasn't really any furniture in the main living area. Through the door to the bedroom I could see a single mattress laid out on the floor and a filing cabinet where Arthur kept his clothes. 'S' for Shirts, Socks and Suits, 'T' for Ties, T-shirts and Trousers and 'U' for Underwear. Arthur pulled a pair of tracksuit bottoms out of the 'T' drawer and motioned for me to sit in the chair. I pulled what was left of the contents of the raided minibar out of my handbag and offered him a small bottle of rum, but he pointed instead to a rather violently green bottle of crème de menthe.

'Poor taste,' he observed, 'is my favourite flavour.'

And we toasted each other, clicking the thin glass of the tiny bottles before we drank.

'What's up?' he asked me.

'Oh God,' I keeled over sideways for comic effect. 'This thing is really getting to me, Arthur. I just didn't want to go back to the house. Being around Rosie. It's really hard.'

'Serge has chartered a helicopter,' Arthur said with a wry glint in his eye. 'He thinks we're going to burn the stuff out. He's buying equipment off some dodgy Irish guy who deals arms in the Middle East. By fucking computer.'

I began to laugh. It was a low kind of giggle and it was contagious because after a few seconds Arthur started laughing too. His hair flopped down over his face and he smiled as he knocked back the last of the crème de menthe and reached out for another of the small bottles. It was chartreuse that time, I think. I don't know why they stock all those revolting liqueurs in minibars. No-one ever drinks that stuff. Well, that's what I'd always thought anyway though Arthur did seem to be knocking it back good style right enough.

'He's going to get us all killed, isn't he?' Arthur said. 'I mean, either before, but hopefully afterwards, they're going to find out, and Serge is going to go down with the ship. Noble and doomed. I think maybe that's what he really wants.'

'We're not going to get killed,' I replied. 'We're survivors. There is no way that that is going to happen. You two shouldn't be involved at all. Arthur, you have to talk Serge round. You have to stop him. I don't want anyone to get killed.'

There was an awkward silence then, during which I realized for some reason that I had never seen a dead body. I mean, it's not something people normally do see much. When my grandfather died I'd seen him in his coffin, but somehow, I decided, that was quite different and I had been very, very young in any case. In fact, it's not even the body that I remember, well, certainly not very clearly, although it must have been there, I guess. What I really remember is that my granny cried through the whole of the funeral service, clinging on to my mother's arm, and afterwards Mum had had bruises the shape of my grandmother's fingers.

What have you got if you haven't got friends and freedom? Eh?

I got up and walked the length of the room. Then I paced my way back until I was standing right in front of Arthur again. I put my hands on his shoulders and rested my forehead on the top of his head. I think he stopped breathing. For a few seconds neither of us moved and then he shuddered.

'You got laid tonight, then?' he asked.

I think I blushed. My cheeks burned anyway and I shrugged my shoulders and backed away. I was suddenly very aware that I might smell of it. That somewhere about me the scent of an old man's tight kisses on my skin might still linger. I couldn't bear it.

'Don't,' I begged.

Arthur apologized. 'Sorry,' he said, 'it's just that I always wonder.'

And that made me blush some more. I ran my hand through my hair.

'Oh God,' I said again. 'What the hell am I doing?'

I stumbled towards the door, trying to leave. Arthur was pulling on his shoes.

'I'm OK. I'm OK,' I said.

'What is it with you?' he muttered. And followed me.

Some nights they race cars along Princes Road. It's illegal but it's never been stopped and the boy racers of Hong Kong bring their MR2s and TVRs and MGs and put them through their paces and people gather to watch. I figured that it would be a good place to go with Arthur in tow. He wouldn't leave me on my own. The night wasn't cool, but at least the air wasn't too heavy and there was a mobile snackbar selling noodles and cans of Coke to the crowd. Arthur wore a baseball cap which he pulled right down over his face, and he bought us some fizzy drinks into which we poured two miniature bottles of brandy and half a shot of whisky each and then we marked out a place for ourselves where the pavement meets the concrete slope and we watched the black and red paintwork of the cars zoom past us in the deep, dark night. It seemed kind of quiet and Arthur was standing so close to me that I could feel him. He kept his eyes on the cars and when there was a lull on the track he cast his eyes to the tarmac.

'He's in love with her, you know,' he said. 'If she leaves I'm not sure what he'll do. He's desperate.'

'We all love her,' I replied, deliberately ignoring what he meant. 'We're all desperate.' And then there were six cars all roaring past at once and the crowd cheered from time to time at the antics of a trick driver. We didn't let our eyes meet. We stood stock still. After a few minutes Arthur began to strike up a conversation with the guy next to him and laid a couple of casual hundred-dollar bets which I think he lost. I moved back, leant against the streetlight and swigged on my drink.

'I'm paralysed,' I thought, 'I don't know what to do.' Everything seemed so serious, every conversation laden with difficulties I just wasn't equipped for, or silences I couldn't bear. Things were too intense. There are some feelings I just turn my back on, and I guess in the face of danger I usually do just freeze. Look at what had happened when Elton had beaten the shit out of that cop in London.

And now I was frozen again. Frozen in the face of a drugs baron who would put Howard Marks to shame and arguably the most dangerous organized-crime racketeers on the planet. Frozen in the face of my closest friends and the feelings we all had for each other, which hung on us like ill-fitting clothes. Uncomfortably. I couldn't believe it was spoiling. I couldn't believe that things had gone wrong in Hong Kong. That my dream was turning bad.

But as I watched the cars zoom past, as I stood there, insulated from my surroundings by the drinks-cabinet miniatures, I decided that I had to face up to things. That stamping my foot and saying it wasn't fair just wasn't going to cut the mustard. The last few days I'd lost my bottle, I realized. And well, that would never do, because there was Rosie to consider as well. She was my best friend, and even if she'd changed, even if she'd gone hard, cold, tough, I had to back her up no matter what. I had to do the right thing. I'd never be able to live with myself otherwise.

I had to decide to help her murder the old guy. Of course I did. There was nothing else for it. You can't just want things not to happen. You can't expect other people to take on responsibility for you. You have to be there, to do it yourself. It had taken a long time but I was back on track.

'Arthur,' I said, finishing off my drink and breathing a sigh of relief, 'let's get a cab.'

And Arthur paid off his debts and then he hailed a red and white and dropped me off at home.

'You stop Serge,' I said, 'it's all you have to do. OK? You do it. Promise.'

'I'll try,' Arthur nodded.

And I kissed him on the cheek and got out, ready to face everything, so high on my first ever decision not to just look after myself but to really go over the halfway line for a friend, that I hardly slept a wink.

Chapter Twenty-four

Yu: Enthusiasm

When Rosie got up the next morning she came out on to the balcony as usual. I watched her from the garden as she automatically lit herself a cigarette before she even focused on the view. I hadn't slept much but I wasn't tired so I had decided to go down to the garden and make a rather dramatic apology. I had taken red crêpe paper from the study and cut out the words 'I'm sorry' in letters as long as my legs, and laid them out on the grass. It was a beautiful blue-skied morning and the sunshine was beating down. I picked white flowers and placed them all around, then I arranged breakfast on the verandah and waited.

Rosie laughed and leant over the balustrade.

'Will you come down?' I shouted up, and she nodded and disappeared back into her room to search out sunglasses and a robe before walking barefoot out on to the grass. I stirred the tea in the pot and poured out two cups. Rosie popped a sugar cube into her mouth and drank her tea through it. As it dissolved she popped another between her teeth. I was back. The noonday sun was dazzling.

Upstairs, in the shady bedroom, Rosie's suitcases were lying open on the floor. She had already started to pack, slipping forbidden books behind the pale green silk lining of her heavy leather cases and sewing them up again one-handed. There were less than two weeks to go. On the side in the bathroom bottles of Clinique toner had been poured down the sink and refilled with an arsenal of poisonous tinctures.

Rosie drained her teacup and rolled herself a joint between slim, elegant fingers, lighting it with a 1930s Dunhill lighter which Arthur had bought for her as a going-away present. She breathed in deeply.

'Good,' she said.

I was nervous. I didn't want to say the wrong thing. It was going so well. She asked me to help her pack and I agreed. It must have been difficult, right enough, with her hand all bandaged up. Slowly, conspiratorially, we began to talk about her return. As Rosie blew the smoke over in my direction I felt on top of the world. But it wasn't just the grass that did that for me. It was Rosie. Whether she was an assassin or not, I had overcome my problem. I had committed myself well and truly to my friend.

In my fitful sleep the night before I dreamt I stood in the middle of a circle of men. Men I had slept with. Punters. One by one they fell face down into the circle as a dark sky bore down, until I was the only person left standing, surrounded by pale corpses. In my waking life however, I had no reservations. Rosie would, by our calculations, be back in Hong Kong in eighteen months, and I was right behind her. She would be coming back a widow.

Up in the bedroom I lay out on the bed, watching Rosie dress. She came and sat down next to me, pulling her top up to reveal a Chinese figure which she had painted on to her skin.

'It means a bird about to take off in flight,' she smiled.

'Like me.'

Rosie was so defiant. The painting on her skin would only last for a few days, but that didn't matter. What mattered was that she had done it at all. Suddenly I felt I wanted to make a gesture too. I took a safety pin from Rosie's dressing table and pricked my finger, squeezing the blood out in perfect ruby drops.

'At home if we mixed our blood we would be sisters,' I said.

Rosie looked wary for an instant.

'Blood sisters?' she asked and I nodded before she took the safety pin from my hand and pierced her pale skin.

'Now we are bound together no matter what,' I said.

Looking back, it's strange really. I had pushed myself to the limit to back her up, but what I didn't know was that Rosie was prepared to go further than I could imagine. She was ebullient. High on the thrill. And whatever endpoint I thought I had come to, for Rosie there was always another step up the ladder.

We hit Victoria Park at about six that evening. We wanted to go out, but I was booked to do hospitality in one of the private boxes at the racecourse at Happy Valley later. It was some big, corporate do and I wasn't looking forward to it. Myself, I prefer milling around in the crowd at the races, watching the old Chinese men up at the back placing their bets and taking my own chances on the odd flutter from time to time. You can just pay in at the turnstile that way. But it was a private box for me that evening and a host of equities dealers and property speculators. Rosie and I had reckoned to wander around the park for a while before I had to go. We were, I suppose, just trying to chill out.

The grass in Victoria Park is really manicured. It's perfect. But we stuck to the tarmac and walked around the whole circuit steadily, taking our time. Back together.

'The only thing,' Rosie said, 'is that I'd like to see Serge again.'

'Better not to,' I thought out loud.

Despite what she had suggested I think Rosie had a healthy respect for Bobby as far as that could go. He had let us off the hook twice already and we knew we shouldn't push him. She nodded and I felt relieved, but well, Rosie was pretty unpredictable. She kicked out against the boundaries. Two joggers passed us and Rosie pulled me off the path.

'One last adventure,' she whispered.

She must have felt invincible. It was tantalizing.

'Just think. We could sit out in the dark on the Peak and stare at the bay together. The four of us. Just for an hour. We could lie and look at the stars and have things the way we really wanted them one last time,' she said.

That was the thing. Rosie was so romantic, and it was very appealing. It's difficult to keep a good girl down.

'No,' I shook my head. 'It's too serious.'

Rosie stared, disappointed, up at the Peak, which was just ahead of us.

'One last time,' she said again.

But I stuck firm.

'No risks,' I insisted. 'When you get back, we can sit up there all day and all night if you like. But we mustn't do anything else with the boys now. It's too risky.'

'You're right, I suppose,' she said sadly.

And as we walked out of the park I hailed a cab to take me over to Happy Valley and Rosie disappeared into the crowd.

Chapter Twenty-five

K'uei: Opposition

When I got back to Kadoorie Hill later on Conrad Beckett was waiting for me. The races had finished around ten but the party in the private box had continued for another couple of hours, so I had completely missed the crawling, jammed-up streets after the main event and had made it back to Kowloon in record time with a virtually clear stretch of road ahead of me. It was only one in the morning. Conrad was smoking a cigarette slowly and not smiling at all, even when I gave him my most charming grin. He was wearing a very expensive-looking understated grey suit and his eyes had taken on its colour.

'Sit down,' he said.

I flopped down on to the sofa. There was a strange atmosphere in the house. Conrad wasn't drinking and it felt as if he was listening all the time. As if he was expecting something to happen. I was uneasy. Upstairs there was a crash from Rosie's room and I jumped, unnerved. Beckett didn't start. He didn't move at all. He just sat, drawing on his cigarette from time to time with his usual air of cultivated calm.

'Conrad,' I said. 'What's going on?'

But he only smiled and then, with a sinking feeling

in the pit of my stomach, I knew that it was very, very bad news. My temples were tingling and my mouth quivered.

'Fuck,' I thought, 'they know.'

And I waited, staying as still as I possibly could, feeling the weight of my fear. Wishing that I'd been firmer with Rosie all along. Wishing I'd stopped her picking out that knife or buying poison from the herbalist in Yau Ma Tei, whatever it was they were on to. I was relieved when Rosie came downstairs, even though she was white as a sheet and her fingers were trembling.

Outside Bobby and Conrad wanted to bundle us into the back of a black van. Rosie wouldn't look me in the eye.

'What's going on?' I asked again but no-one replied.

The sinking feeling inside me got worse and I felt sick. Suddenly I couldn't believe what was happening. What had we been thinking of? Our pagers could have been bugged. They could have heard anything. They obviously had. We were, I was sure, going to die, and my breath was caught in the back of my throat. As we walked quietly out of the house I thought about making a run for it, breaking away and legging it down the street, straight into the back of a taxi and over to the airport. It was a momentary thing, a stupid impulse, and as Bobby opened the back door of the van my heart sank some more and I knew that I wouldn't be leaving. Serge and Arthur were laid out on the floor. Their arms were bound up with tape and they were unconscious, although, my first thought was that they were perhaps dead. Ron, the policeman, was standing over them and he turned to help Rosie and me up into the back.

I shouted 'Let them go,' and Ron hit me in the mouth, and then as the doors closed he bound our forearms together and we sat down. I heard snatches of conversation. Odd words in Cantonese from outside. Bobby's voice saying 'rice for brains' and Conrad Beckett laughing and then the engine of the van started up and we drove off.

'Less bruising this way,' Ron said, cutting the tape from the roll as he finished tying me up.

'I'm sorry,' Rosie whispered to me without looking up.

They had found everything, of course. Bobby had torn apart her luggage and laughed as he took away the pills and the poison and the rubber-sheathed knife. We had been so stupid. Amateurish in the face of world-class professionals, though it had been Serge's fruitless forays searching out mercenaries which had got back to Bobby. Ironic really, since that hadn't even been our real plan. We hadn't had a chance all along. You can't trust anyone you have to buy, can you?

'Don't worry,' I said to Rosie, but she still didn't look up, and then I felt something heavy and hard come down on to my skull and I toppled over, unconscious.

When I woke up again it was dark and we were still moving but I guessed from the rocking motion of the floor that we were in the hold of a boat rather than still in the back of the van. I began to struggle, and as I did so I realized that I was naked, and then, as my eyes got accustomed to the dimness of the light I could make out Rosie, Arthur and Serge, and I realized that they were naked too. My stomach began to feel queasy in the swell. I hadn't eaten for hours and the blows to my skull and my mouth had left me light-headed and sickened.

'Shit,' I mumbled to myself in frustration and then the voice spoke to me out of the dark.

'We are going back to Hong Kong. Twenty minutes I think.'

There was a sudden phosphorescent burst of flame and I caught a photo quick image of a Chinese man all in black, lighting himself a cigarette before the match was extinguished. He was crouched down on his haunches, squatting in a corner beside some old ropes. I'd never seen him before.

'Isn't there a light in here?' I asked.

'Sure,' the voice replied slowly, as if he was laughing at me, 'I just don't want to switch it on.'

The others were still out cold. The end of the cigarette glowed orange and somehow the slight, amber light made it more difficult for me to see. I struggled fruitlessly against the tapes which tied me, striking my ribs on the linoleum floor as I did so.

'No point to struggle,' said the voice. 'No way out of that.'

I laid my head back.

'You very good friends, you people?' asked the voice.

I squinted over at him. 'Yes,' I said because I wasn't going to deny it. 'Yes we are.'

'Bobby is gonna kill you. I hear you're pretty stupid.'

'Yes,' I agreed.

'Too late. He gonna kill you now. He's really mad.'

I tried to sit up. It took me a while, but in the end I managed it. I wished one of the others would wake up, but they didn't seem to be close to that. As I hauled my body erect I brushed my leg against Rosie, hoping that she might come to, but she didn't. The guy was further down the hold. I could see him. He was watching me.

'Can I have a cigarette?' I asked.

The figure moved slowly towards me and I pursed my lips as the soft felt of a cigarette filter pressed up against my mouth. I'd have hit him if I could. If there had been any point. Then the guy lit me a match. I drew my breath in deeply. My head was pounding with a dull ache and my legs were cramped. I smoked the cigarette to one side because I didn't want the hot ash falling on to my skin. I figured that I needed it, though. The nicotine. The tapes around my arms cut into my skin.

'It's too tight,' I said, 'I think it's cutting the blood off.'

'No it's not,' replied the voice. 'I did it lots of times to people. It leaves no marks. There is fat there. It's very fleshy.'

I breathed in deeply and felt the smoke go way down into my lungs and then I sighed because it was hitting my bloodstream.

'Will you go and ask Bobby if I can speak to him?' I said. 'Will you go and tell him that I'm sorry and that I want to explain? These guys,' I started, but he cut me off.

'No point. He gonna kill you now. It's too late. He's decided.'

'Well,' I pressed the point. 'Could you just tell him anyhow? Ask him if I can speak to him?'

'You'll speak to him pretty soon. When we get there. Not long now, pretty lady. Your friends will wake up soon. You must have pretty strong skull bones. You woke up early.'

I pressed the back of my head against the wooden panelling behind me and then slowly I turned towards the guy's face as if I had something else to say, but instead I spat the lit cigarette towards him, aiming for the eyes. The guy was quick. He dodged out of the way. Then he walked over and stamped the cigarette out with his foot.

'I'm not gonna hit you again. It'd leave too many bruises,' he explained and then he backed off towards the door and squatted down again and we didn't say anything else to each other until the engine wound down and the door opened and we were hauled up one by one, into the light.

Arthur came to first. Almost as soon as we got upstairs. The light was hurting my eyes and I had to squint to make out how many people were there. There seemed to be half a dozen men, some of whom I recognized. Bobby, Ron and in the background like a kind of blurred shadow I could see Beckett. All the Chinese guys were dressed in black.

'Give them a drink,' Bobby said sharply, barking the command, and a man brought over a carton of cold lemon tea and held it to my lips first and then to Arthur's. I gulped deeply. It was sweet, cold and refreshing. This, I thought to myself, was a good sign, an act of kindness. Then Bobby knelt down behind me and he cut the tapes and one of the other men threw me a towel, which I wrapped around myself. Arthur wasn't so lucky, though. They left him bound up and naked. I could see his hands quivering. I could see the muscles in his shoulders tensing up, to try to stop the shaking. I could see the terror in his eyes and it made my stomach turn. I was fucking terrified. I've never felt like that before. I mean, there was absolutely nothing I could do but stand there and feel helpless. It didn't matter how brave I was. It wasn't going to matter what I said. It didn't even matter if I totally broke down. Bobby was going to go ahead with whatever he wanted to and all I knew was that we were fucked.

Someone poured cold water on to Rosie's face and she opened her eyes and so did Serge, who started, immediately, to struggle. Without saying a word Bobby pulled his gun from its holster and fitted the barrel into Serge's mouth, and then, of course, Serge became very still. I stopped breathing. When Bobby

214

backed off, I think I whimpered. Then they pushed Rosie and me into a corner and we just stood there and held hands, terrified. I remember reading somewhere that it is really possible to die of fright. Your heart can just seize up, you know, and I think that it has something to do with calcium production. You make a lot of calcium all at once and then you just keel over. Well, I thought that was going to happen to me. Probably the only reason I didn't just die there and then was that I wanted to see what was going to happen. I was expecting an explanation. A long discussion. Beatings. Blood. I was praying it wasn't going to be as bad as I thought.

'Tough guys, eh?' Bobby said to Arthur and Serge. 'Big, hard men.'

He flipped Arthur over like a piece of meat and eyed him. 'Not so big and hard now?' he said, poking Arthur's limp cock with his foot, and all the men laughed.

Arthur just stared without lowering his eyes or softening his gaze. I couldn't bear it. I couldn't bear him being so brave, allowing the silence without trying to explain or to ask for leniency. It was a strain.

'Please Bobby,' I stuttered from behind him. 'Please. We weren't going to let them. It was us. It was me.'

But I didn't get a chance to finish whatever it was that I wanted to say because without any warning Bobby pulled the trigger on his gun, and Arthur screamed and there was blood everywhere and Arthur had been shot in the leg and he was making this awful, wounded sound which I will never, ever forget. He was just wailing and wailing. And then Bobby, and I swear he smiled as he did this, shot Arthur's other kneecap off as well. I didn't hear the shot though, just the sickening sound of the bullet hitting Arthur's flesh and then his screams and I pulled back, thumping my whole body against the wall in shock and terror. I think I maybe shouted out. I think I screamed. I don't know. I can't really remember.

'Throw him out,' Bobby said. 'If he makes it to the beach, he lives.'

And Rosie and I started pleading for him hysterically. We were sobbing, 'No, no, no,' over and over again.

'This is your fault,' Bobby sneered in our direction. 'This is because of you.'

Rosie reached out to him. She fell on her knees in desperation. 'Bobby, please,' she begged. 'Please. We wouldn't have let them.' But he just ignored her and a couple of the men hitched Arthur up, ready to carry him out.

Serge was whimpering. He had been sprayed by Arthur's blood and it was clear that he was next. Arthur was just crying, quietly, and his body jerked from time to time as the men pulled on his arms and hitched him up on their shoulders. I'm surprised that he didn't pass out. There was blood everywhere.

'Kneecaps,' Bobby said, like he was trying out the sound of the word in English. 'Kneecaps,' as if there weren't pieces of kneecap all over the floor, as if it was hypothetical.

As Arthur was hauled out of the cabin and we heard a muffled splash and the sound of his screams I was sick on the floor and when I raised my eyes again I couldn't see any lights through the door of the cabin as it opened and closed. Wherever we were it seemed that it was isolated and dark. I wondered how far we were from the shore. I wondered if Bobby had given Arthur any semblance of a fighting chance, though I doubted it.

I was clutching at straws. There are sharks in the South China Sea, and quite apart from that it's sea water, it's salty, and Arthur's wounds were mortal. I was sure of it.

'Let me help him,' Rosie begged. She was still on her knees. 'Throw me in after. Let me help, please.'

'No,' Bobby snapped and then, like a kid, he began to sing under his breath in English. 'Hands, knees and boompsidaisy. Tra la la la la la la,' and he moved his gun up and down Serge's body. 'You like him, Rosie. He loves you,' he sneered. 'We heard all about it,' he said and he put one hand up to his head as if he had an earpiece in. As if he was tuning into a conversation there and then.

And Rosie turned her face away. She couldn't bear it.

'We give him a better chance I think,' Bobby grinned, 'just for you,' and for one tiny moment I felt relieved and Rosie looked up pleadingly and Serge breathed out audibly and then very, very quickly and entirely without warning again, almost as if it was a casual thing to do, Bobby shot off both of Serge's feet at close, close range.

'Oh sweet Jesus,' I said and I fell to my knees. One of the men was holding Rosie back now. And then they hauled Serge off the same way as they had done with Arthur and flung him, bleeding and footless, into the sea.

'Please, please, please let them make it. Please let them be all right,' I thought and then I realized that it wasn't them I should be praying for because Rosie and I were next.

Chapter Twenty-six
Pi: Holding Together (Union)

It's not that triads don't hurt women. Of course they do. But Rosie was bought and paid for and well, there wasn't really a lot they could do to her. Not physically anyway. That, I suppose, had been the point of hurting Arthur and Serge so badly. Of shooting them like that. It was the worst thing Bobby could do to Rosie without actually laying his hands on her. When Bobby turned his attention to us he had a couple of the guys hold us roughly by the arms.

'See what you did?' he said. 'See what you made me do? Trouble. Trouble.'

I began to cry.

'Get them their clothes,' Bobby said. And then the engines started and what we had been wearing before was brought in in a bundle and Rosie and I were thrust into a corner and we began to get dressed. There was blood spattered everywhere. Ironically, everyone but us was covered in it. Bobby and Conrad disappeared out of the room and then, once we had pulled our clothes on, Rosie and I were led in to a smaller cabin with comfortable chairs and a few rugs and even a window. The officers' mess if you like. Bobby and Beckett were nursing crystal beakers of whisky. Rosie and I sat down.

'You're going to Canton next week,' Bobby said to Rosie as if he was discussing normal travel plans, as if he was making the opening gambit in a conversation which could be in any way two sided.

Rosie lowered her eyes in submission. 'Yes,' she said.

'And you're going back to work,' he said to me without even looking and I did just what Rosie did. I said 'Yes,' and I said it with my teeth clenched, but the fact I said it at all, well, I was ashamed of that. I felt a little glimmer of guilt turn over inside me. Perhaps the helpless always feel guilty. Perhaps that's normal. Bobby continued.

'Little lesson today,' he said. 'Little lesson for both of you. I can't believe you thought that we wouldn't know. Silly, silly. Soldiers. Secret firearms. Ha. You think we're stupid.' And then, suddenly, I'm not sure why, I wasn't scared any more. I was just outraged because Bobby was so casual about the whole thing and because it had been so pointless. My fear disappeared and all that was left was that feeling of guilt and well, I've never been good at guilt. So right at that moment I just got really furious and I hated Bobby more than anything. I hated him so much that I had to take him on despite the fact that he had a gun, despite the fact that we were at sea, that no-one would miss me if I just disappeared. I knew all of that and I wasn't afraid, not really. I was just red-cheeked in my rage. I was mad, both in the American sense and the English.

'You think you can do anything, don't you?' I sneered under my breath in contempt. 'You think that you can do anything.'

Bobby stopped for a second and then he laughed. I wouldn't have thought that there would be that kind of fight in me, I have to admit. It's not like me to challenge someone like that, but well, the chips were down and that was what I ended up doing, with Rosie clutching my arm, squeezing it to try to get me to stop, and Bobby surprised, grinning and happy to take me on.

'You maybe want me to shoot you too?' he asked slowly, his eyes absolutely cold and hard.

'You're a bad person,' I told him. 'You're evil. You don't have to do that.'

Slowly and deliberately Bobby took his gun out of its holster and laid it to one side.

'Evil?' he said, as if he was considering it. Then he walked over and crouched down right in front of me and almost playfully he pushed me off my chair and Rosie sprang back in fright. After the shootings before, I guess she thought that any second there would be blood everywhere and I would be dead, but that wasn't what Bobby had in mind. He wasn't very big, but he was strong. He knocked me right off my seat and held me down on the floor with the violence growing in his eyes and his lips rigid.

'You're just a hooker,' he spat. 'You're nothing. No-one.'

And he slid one hand down my body and stuck it between my legs while he held me down with the other.

'You're just a hooker,' he kept repeating. 'That's all you are. You're not worth anything. You're trash.'

I must have had sex with hundreds of men. I lost count after my first two weeks on the job. And as I've said before I can't remember doing it with any of them, not really. Except Bobby that night of course. I'll never forget that – every thrust, every twitch of it. Being held down like that and Rosie and Beckett just sitting there and Bobby's hands rough as he leant down hard on me and he pulled his cock out and pushed it inside.

'Hooker, hooker, hooker,' he said and he pushed hard and it hurt a bit. I turned my head to one side because I didn't want to look at his face. There were spots of blood around his eyes and the memory of that hurt a lot more than anything he could push inside me. Eventually he came.

'You're nothing,' he spat as he did up his trousers. 'You're nothing at all. Cheap woman. You're a whore.'

I wasn't any less angry though, after that. I don't know what he thought he was going to fuck out of me, what he was trying to demonstrate, but I was still furious. I sat up.

'You pay me,' I shouted. 'If I'm a whore you pay me for that. You owe me it. I don't do that for free.'

And Bobby laughed and he slapped me hard across the face and then hit me with the butt of his gun and I must have blacked out again.

When I woke up I was at home. I was in Rosie's room and she was beside me. For a second I didn't remember and then I felt sick. Rosie was sitting up in the bed, absolutely rigid against the headboard and she was staring straight ahead. This was where it had started for her. Bobby had ripped the room apart but the mess had been cleared up by the maids. They'd made everything as perfect as usual, cleaning and tidying anything which was disturbed. Making everything all right. Cleaning blood from the pale carpets on their hands and knees, wrapping the broken bottles in dusters before throwing them away, hoovering the little pills up in broad sweeps until everything was perfect. I was going over what had happened in my mind and it felt like something was jammed in my heart. I couldn't quite believe it.

'I phoned the police,' Rosie said without turning

around. 'They are going to look for the bodies. We were somewhere near Aberdeen. Bobby said. They're going to look anyway.'

'Bobby fucked me,' I said. I don't know why. She'd been there, after all. She knew. Perhaps I was only just remembering it properly then.

'Me too,' Rosie said, 'after you were out.'

'What were we thinking of?' I asked her with tears in my eyes as what had happened came back to me bit by bit. The violence. All the blood. 'What were we trying to do?'

'We were trying to stay safe,' Rosie said. 'That's all.'

And I realized as she said it that Rosie had changed again. She even smelled different.

We stayed up all night waiting for phone calls. The first thing we learned was that Arthur had survived. No-one seemed to know how, but he'd swum and swum and made it to the shore and when they'd found him he was unconscious and he'd lost a lot of blood, but he was still breathing. When the call had come to the house both of us had cried with joy, and afterwards Rosie had felt very guilty. She said she didn't think she'd be able to see him. I was just the opposite. I wanted to go straight to the hospital. But they didn't allow anyone to visit for two days.

Serge was dead. There seemed to be a bit of an argument about what exactly he died of. They'd found salt water and seaweed in his lungs, but he too had lost a lot of blood and there was some kind of professional wrangling over whether or not he'd drowned before he actually bled to death because his lungs weren't full enough, or something. But that wasn't really the point. He was dead. That was all. As the sun came up we sat out on the balcony together and Rosie burned a big pile of hell money to help him on his way through the afterlife and I threw a square or two of hash on to the pile and we talked. Serge's mother was flying in from Taipei to organize the funeral and we weren't sure if she would even let us go to the grave.

It was a nightmarish few days, but part of me relished being there for every second of it. I wanted to see it all. To feel all the emotions running through me. I wanted to visit Arthur in hospital as soon as I could and I wanted to lay orange flowers on Serge's grave. To be there for everything as my beautiful life lay shattered around me, blasted to pieces and rotting in the thick, heavy Hong Kong heat.

But Rosie just wanted revenge.

If Bobby thought he'd got rid of his problem he was wrong. He'd made it far worse. If he hadn't shot them, well, we might have given up. A little shock, nothing too vicious, and Rosie might have trotted off to Canton like a lamb. But as it was she went in as a Trojan horse. While we sat up all night Rosie was thinking and in the end she came to the conclusion that it was all about fucking. Whatever happened to Rosie and me, it was always going to be about that. And Rosie came up with a plan. One which would work this time no matter what. We'd seen Serge and Arthur have holes blown in them. We'd seen the blood and the flesh and the horror. And Rosie wasn't scared any more. These were dire circumstances and they required an extreme response. And Rosie, as it turned out, was more than up to the job.

Chapter Twenty-seven

Kuei Mei: The Marrying Maiden

Town was busy as usual. Rosie sat on a bench in front of the Chanel shop and finished off her cigarette with satisfaction, regarding the gold evening dress in the window with unaccustomed disdain. Then she got up and walked across the road to the tram stop, carefully avoiding the metal tramlines laid into the tarmac. I followed her. We'd discussed it all the night before and together we'd come to a decision and now we were focused. We knew what Rosie had to do and I had offered to come along as well. I'd have done anything I could to help.

We realized straight away that we weren't being watched. I suppose when people are forced to witness summary executions they tend to fall into line. Besides, we could have just been out shopping. But we weren't. At eleven o'clock we switched our mobile phones off and taped them to the underside of the wooden first-class seats on the Star Ferry. Then we got off on Hong Kong Island.

We'd both deliberately dressed down for the occasion. Just jeans and cheap cotton shirts because we didn't want to attract any attention. We looked like tourists as we mounted the tramcar in Des Vouex Street and slid on to the green plastic seats at the back. I laid my head gently on the wooden-effect Formica wall of the tram and stared upwards at the old wooden ceiling, fingering the coins in my palm for the whole of the journey, ready to pay as we got off at the end of the line in Kennedy Town. We were on our way to revenge, and I was nervous.

As the sharp city buildings disappeared and the docks began to peep through on the right-hand side, I watched Rosie staring out of the window next to me and counted carefully as people got on and off and the passengers changed over, until I was sure that no-one had been on as long as we had and it was certain that we weren't being followed. There were a row of builders' supply shops, just cubicles really, with bricks pouring out on to the pavement. Outside there was a woman just sitting on a multicoloured deckchair while her kids played lazily in the cement dust on the floor. White faces disappeared and there were no shop signs or advertisements in English. Rosie smiled.

'Are you sure about this?' I asked her, but she didn't even bother to answer me.

At long last the tram reached the terminus and everyone piled off, paying as we went. One dollar sixty cents flat fare – no change given. I laid four dollars into the driver's hand for both of us together, and then we stepped out into the heat and I followed Rosie down towards the dockside. It was wasteland really and we struggled a bit over the rough ground. A fresh, salty breeze blew in from the harbour, tinged slightly now and again with the smell of dead fish and effluent. Further up they were unloading crates of live animals – pigs or sheep or something – from a rickety old boat on to some blue lorries. I turned around and stared back at the first row of shops. I could just make out that there was a garage up there. The car repairs spread out haphazardly all over the pavement. Behind that, up the hill, there were high-rises.

'Is it near here?' I asked Rosie.

It had been a long time ago. Or at least it seemed that way, but when she described it to me it was still vivid in her memory. The shooting gallery. The opium den. A place of grimy floorboards and dusty windows and desperation. The place where Conrad Beckett had brought her to make her afraid, right at the very beginning.

'It's near,' Rosie said. 'I can't remember just where, but it's near. There is a hardware shop directly opposite the entrance and some bushes outside. It has a green door.'

We began to walk towards the steep hill, past a couple of open-fronted bars where we could hear old men playing frantic games of mah-jong in the background. My legs ached but we kept on climbing right up the hill.

We cut down an alleyway, following Rosie's instinct, although the last time she had been there, she had arrived by car. I was getting hot and nervous. I had never been in a shooting gallery before. The way Rosie described it was as a desperate place. Cutting through the shady alleyway we rounded a corner on to a main street and Rosie nodded slightly so I knew that this was it. She rang the buzzer apprehensively and the door clicked open before us.

'Stairs,' Rosie said as she turned towards me and I just nodded. It was a precaution. Two reasonably well-to-do girls would give you anything if you stopped the lift halfway between floors. We'd heard all the horror stories, so instead of taking the easy way up we climbed the five flights of stairs. The door to the apartment swung on its hinges. Number seventeen. Whoever had opened it for us had long since returned to their activities rather than wait for some fool to climb up to the fifth floor of the building. Rosie pushed the door open and went inside. It was just as she had described it to me. The long shadows on the bare floorboards, the dirt and the smell of burning sugar. As we entered the main room there were men lying against the walls with their unfocused eyes cast to heaven. Rosie spoke to a thin man sitting at a grubby, ash-covered desk. He was the only guy in the room who was fully conscious.

'I came to get a hit,' she said in Cantonese. 'I came from town.'

The man sat still at the desk but his eyes were eager. He seemed, I thought, too young. He shouldn't have been there.

'You brought your own gear?' he asked her as he sized her up. I suppose we were patently not policemen. We just didn't have that air about us. But then, we didn't seem like addicts either. We didn't have our own gear.

'I don't care what I use,' Rosie told him.

'You're a nice girl, you should be careful,' he said.

'That's none of your fucking business,' she snapped back. 'Just give me the stuff. Set me up.'

And she gave him a couple of notes.

In return he gingerly passed her a small packet between his outstretched fingers, just a little too far away so that Rosie had to reach over to whip it away from him.

'Over there,' he said, nodding at some used syringes. 'You can use those if you want.'

Rosie took a deep breath. She knew, I suppose, that this was her last chance to get away, to change her mind. To run. She flexed her toes. Neither of us had ever taken smack before. No heroin. That had always been the rule and we had both prided ourselves on being good girls in that respect. On doing the right thing wherever we could. We had looked on our arrival at Kadoorie Hill as some kind of smart career move. We each had a vested interest in not messing it up. Neither of us had ever thought we would end up in a place like this. Not willingly anyway.

Rosie looked at me and I shrugged my shoulders slightly. It really was her own choice whether or not to continue. I mean, it wasn't up to me.

'Perhaps,' she said in a whisper, 'I could sleep with his eldest son. That would be the more traditional way to revenge.' And then she laughed and split the little packet open and poured the powder carefully into the bowl of the spoon. We'd both seen it done before. In countless movies. On TV. In the five-star hotel rooms of American film stars who called cocaine 'toot', and who were never terribly sure about what continent they were on or whether or not they had met you before. Behind us the guy got up from his desk and came over to watch. Rosie became quite self-conscious.

'You've never done this before, have you?' he teased her.

Rosie didn't reply. She just carried on. I shifted uneasily, trying to block his view slightly, but he moved forward towards her.

'Here,' he said, reaching out a hand to try to help but Rosie kicked him away.

'Fucking leave me alone,' she snapped, so he sat back and watched with an amused look on his face as she kicked off her sandals. I wasn't sure that I was going to be able to watch. My eyes narrowed, but the guy was enjoying it. He looked delighted.

'Between your toes, eh?' he asked. 'And not a mark

on your skin anywhere I'd bet.'

Rosie pulled the liquid up the syringe and tapped it carefully. She took a deep breath.

'You got more used stuff? Different needles? Dirty?' she asked.

The guy shrugged his shoulders. 'Anyone here will sell you their needles. Anyone. I don't advise it.'

'Later,' Rosie said to me. 'Make sure we do it later, Kate. Before we go.' And she plunged the syringe into the white skin between her toes and pushed the plug down, lying back on the floor almost straight away with a blank smile on her face. I felt sick, but I held her hand and I waited. Anything could have happened to her in that state. I knew I had to look out.

I've read that it's quite difficult to actually contract AIDS. Rosie had less than a week to pull it off. But if you're determined enough, there's nothing you can't do. They hadn't left a lot else open to her. We knew, of course, that they couldn't take the virus away, not once it was in her bloodstream, and anyway, they'd never have known in time to be able to check. We'd cocked a snook at the triads. Done something so outrageous, so dangerous that they couldn't have suspected it. It was a good plan. The best available. But then, we were after the ultimate revenge. If you're going to take on the brotherhood you have to be just as cold and determined and vengeful as they are. You have to fly under radar. And Rosie had it in her. She was prepared to die to get what she wanted, to make her point. Even though I didn't realize just how far she would be prepared to go. Dying is one thing, but how many people you take with you, well, that's quite another.

Chapter Twenty-eight
K'un: Oppression (Exhaustion)

The hospital seemed very big, and once I was inside it felt like there was no natural light at all, only the long neon strips mounted on the low false ceiling. When I looked down at my hands they seemed slightly swollen. They looked like someone else's hands. I walked up to the ward, the soles of my shoes clicking on the green-and-orange patterned linoleum, and then I asked a plump nurse in a peach uniform where he was.

'Mr Arthur is sleep, I think,' she said. 'In that room. Number 147.'

And so I waited there, beside his bed, watching him breathe. He looked quite normal, really. Quite healthy, if a little pale. You couldn't see his legs under all the covers. He could have been in there for anything, I thought. He could have been in to have his tonsils out, he could just be recuperating in this small private room away from the rest of the ward.

After a couple of minutes Arthur turned over and winced. He drew in a deep breath and opened his eyes and I realized that I hadn't taken my gaze away from him once.

'Kate,' he said, his voice weak as he came to, 'they

said that you'd phoned,' and I wrapped my arms around him and started to cry.

'I'm sorry,' I said and drew my palm across my face to get rid of the tears. 'I'm sorry. How are you feeling?'

Arthur shrugged. 'I won't be able to walk again,' he said. 'I'm going home. I'm a cripple.' I didn't know what to say to that. I knew, more than anything, just how much going home was what Arthur didn't want to do, so I squeezed his arm and didn't say a word and then I began stroking his hair and slowly, out of the silence, Arthur began to talk. He had been alone for two days – not a single person he could confide in around him. He hadn't told anyone what had happened.

'I've been having nightmares about it,' he said. 'Not during the day, but once it's dark. They have these low orange lights on at night. It's like having night vision. It scares me. I just keep seeing Serge's face.'

I nodded and just kept on ruffling his hair with my hand, gently, like he was a pet, or something. His hair was very soft. It smelled of medicated shampoo and reminded me of when I used to go swimming as a kid and we all washed our hair with Vosene afterwards. Arthur cast his eyes back. My hand on his head was therapeutic for both of us, I realized, and then, after he'd taken a deep breath, Arthur continued in a whisper.

'I didn't tell them, Kate. Not anything. I didn't want to risk it. Just said I was picked up off the street and when I woke up they did this to me, and I didn't know who they were.'

'You think the police will go for that?' I asked him.

'What are they going to do to me?' he shrugged. 'Blow me away from the hips this time?'

I nodded slowly. He was right. Whatever the police thought, whatever the rights and wrongs of it all, if

Arthur told them what had happened he'd be a target for revenge. He was lucky to be alive at all. Bobby had given him long odds on survival, and Arthur had cashed in. I was grateful. Sounds weird, I know, but I was really bloody grateful. He was alive.

'Rosie is going soon,' I said. 'But it's going to be OK.'

'OK?' Arthur questioned me, taken aback. Offended. 'Kate, I'm going back to my mum and dad's poxy house in the middle of fucking nowhere. I'm never going to walk again. Nothing is going to be OK.' And he turned his face away from me and his whole body shook.

'I'm sorry, Arthur. I'm sorry,' I said and he gripped my hand so tightly I thought my bones would crumble. I don't know why I'd said it. It was just stupid. I got up from the chair and sat sideways on the bed next to him to try to bring him round.

'Oh baby,' I whispered, lying down next to him. 'Arthur.'

And we rocked. Just the motion you make to calm a little child. Just like that, although when I moved my leg over a bit I realized that the sheets fell flat just below his knee and they'd taken the bottom part of his leg off and he hadn't been able to tell me. I began to cry. 'Sweetheart,' I whispered. 'Sweetheart.' I thought of a million things. All the times we'd been together. All the things we'd done. Our adventures. I thought of telling him I'd go back home with him. That I'd look after him. That things wouldn't change as much as he thought. I had this vision of a cottage in the country. Of snow-bound winters and summer picnics.

Arthur stopped crying. He sniffed a bit. I wanted desperately to do something for him and then I hit on it. The only thing I knew how. The thing which got me into the mess in the first place. I kissed his neck gently, smelling his skin. Arthur's beautiful golden skin. He didn't push me away so I carried on, slipping my arm under the covers and down inside his pyjama bottoms, letting him get hard in my hand as I hung on firmly at the very base of his cock. 'Kate,' he murmured and he began to breathe shallow, panting breaths, stroking me through my clothes. I think that was what he'd wanted all along.

'Shhh,' I whispered and I carried on pulling on him until I felt him shudder and come all over his stomach and he squeezed me very close and stroked my face and kissed me. It was, I figured, the least I could do. I cleaned my hand off on a damp tissue beside the bed and I sat up to talk to him, kissing him lightly on the cheek, but there wasn't any time for that.

Somewhere behind us we heard the door open and close. I assumed, I suppose, that it was just a nurse. That it was perhaps lunchtime or something. And then I heard this cough. The kind of cough that only English people can really do. A cough which announces someone's presence in a totally unapologetic way. Not an 'I'm terribly sorry to disturb you' cough, but an 'I'm here and what on earth are you doing?' cough. I turned round.

It was Arthur's mother, I knew that straight away. She was older than I'd expected. Well into her late sixties anyway. Arthur looked down, awkward and sullen. She'd only left him for a little while and when she returned there was a blonde girl on his bed, sitting beside him, their fingers entwined.

'Mum,' he murmured, 'Mum, this is Kate.'

I hopped off the bed.

'Don't any of your friends have last names?' she said.

'Kate Thompson,' I smiled, not giving up, but she passed right around the bed and sat down on the other side from me.

'Oh, how nice,' she said, 'you brought flowers.'

And I looked puzzled, I suppose, because I hadn't. There weren't any flowers in the room. Not a single bloom. It was weird. And Arthur didn't say anything. He didn't take a shot at it at all.

'I'd better go,' I said. Well, I could hardly stay. I leant on the mattress and took his hand in my own once more. 'I want you to have this,' I whispered and I took the key of the safety-deposit box out of my purse and put it on to his palm, curling his fingers around it, then I wrote the name and address of the bank down on the pad of paper next to the bed while his mother stared straight ahead, her eyes like some kind of painting, focused on nothing in particular, but somehow able to follow you right around the room.

'Come back and see me later,' Arthur asked.

The old lady looked at me like, well, like I was some kind of hooker. She just hated me on sight. Like she knew.

'Sure,' I lied. 'You know what that is?' I asked him. I had to check.

'Yeah,' Arthur replied. 'I know.'

And I kissed him on the cheek and walked away from the scene of my only ever freebie.

Chapter Twenty-nine
Po: Splitting Apart

The day that Rosie left there were eight cases downstairs in the hall piled up near the door. It was a Friday and she had spent the whole of the night before lying on her bed sweating, her limbs shaking and her stomach sore.

'A few days is too short a time to develop a habit,' she said crossly and it occurred to me that I had seemed to spend a lot of my time that week looking after everyone else. Giving, one way or another. I had nursed Rosie right through the night and when dawn came she was a lot better, although her eyes were still quite bloodshot and her skin had a cold, unaccustomed pallor like the paint on the face of a porcelain doll. I had drawn a bath and poured in some sandalwood oil, so that the whole room smelled of it, rising up on the steam. As she stepped into the water, Bobby came hammering on the door to tell her that it was an hour until she had to leave and I laid my head back on the tiles and breathed in deeply, wondering whether that hour would feel short or long. I felt there was a lot I wanted to fit into it.

'I'll miss you,' I said.

And Rosie smiled a kind of mysterious smile but she didn't reply and I felt suddenly very lonely because it was so silent, with only the sound of her legs slooshing the bathwater from side to side, and I felt that I wanted to talk to her because I thought it would be my last chance to do so, whether she had things to say or not. It was quite selfish of me really, but then whatever happened I knew that Rosie would be able to make the best of it. I wanted her to leave me something just for me. The last shared secrets, a time of intimacy, the hour before she left.

'Do you think it worked then, Rosie?' I tried.

Rosie opened her eyes and shrugged her shoulders. 'I don't know,' she said.

And then there wasn't really anything more I could say. I mean, 'Well, how long do you think it will be before you can tell that you have it?' wasn't really something that I could say out loud, although that was what I was thinking. The Chinese government doesn't recognize AIDS. Hell, the Chinese government doesn't even recognize homosexuality. It is a country of a billion very straight people, you know. There aren't many statistics anyhow. Doctors put other diseases on the death certificate of people who die HIV positive. But among Hong Kong's down-and-out junkies, like with any down-and-out junkie, I suppose, the odds are high.

Rosie soaked for a long time and then she got out of the bath and dressed slowly and carefully while I lolled around on the unmade bed thinking of all the things I wanted to say, but staying silent nonetheless, because there wasn't anything left, really. Everything had been done. We had organized a lot over that last week. Dr Harry had removed the bandages from Rosie's wrist and we had played in the garden, daring each other to do handstands for longer and longer, the blood rushing into our cheeks and both of us squealing as we toppled over, her newly healed wrist stronger than ever and taking the strain. I think she liked the pain, you know. It meant at least she could feel something. I had all the money. I was to keep it until she could return. We had signed an agreement to that.

Serge had been buried two days earlier. We had both attended the funeral, keeping to the back of the crowd of mourners so as to be out of the way, burning incense late at night on his grave up in a New Territories burial lot once everyone had gone. His mother had chosen it despite the note we had sent her to let her know that he had once voiced an intention to be laid to rest among the hillside orchids on the island of Lamma. Arthur had been too ill to go with us. He was due to go back to England in the coming days, accompanied by his own unsmiling mother.

It seemed so strange. It was over. All over. We had cried a lot that week, both of us, and after all the drama I was just going to stay there and work. I was the one who had got off scot-free apart from a ticking-off from Conrad which I couldn't even take that seriously because it had taken place the afternoon we got home from Kennedy Town. It seemed all I had to do was to carry on earning my keep on my back and hope one day for a phone call from Rosie to tell me what flight she'd be arriving on. I was the banker, the custodian of Serge's grave, the one who would keep the home fires burning. I was the lucky one.

Rosie had gone to her fate joyously. She had been so defiant. There was, I suppose, a sense of freedom for her because she just wasn't afraid any more. Not of anything. There wasn't any point.

She took my hand silently, leading me out of the room and across the hall into one of the spare bedrooms to the side of the house, closing the door quietly behind us. She brought her finger up to her lips, so that I wouldn't say anything out loud, and there was a sparkle in her eye. It reminded me of the way she was before. There was a rustling in the corner of the room, but I couldn't really see what was over there. The blinds were half drawn and the room was shady. Rosie made straight for the source of the noise, picking up a bamboo cage hidden behind an armchair. Inside was a little brown monkey.

'Where did you get him?' I asked.

'Bird market,' Rosie giggled. 'Yesterday.'

'But why?'

And then I noticed that in her other hand Rosie was holding her pager suspended on a piece of thick elastic.

'Never say die,' she whispered and she opened the door of the cage and petted the creature, slipping the pager over its shoulder.

'Rosie,' I started, 'I don't think we should.'

But Rosie was grinning as she opened the window and sat the little monkey down on the sill. She'd nothing left to lose, and they'd have a hard time proving anything.

'Watch,' she said, and the monkey leaped away from us, agile in the tall trees, disappearing over the garden wall and down the street. It took all of five seconds for the front door to open and two of the triads to run out. They had been well and truly on their guard and they thought it was Rosie making her way down the road at a rate of knots. There was a hammering on the stairs as another man rushed up to check the bedrooms.

'Fuck,' I said.

My palms were sweating. Rosie pulled a comb out of her pocket and handed it to me quickly as she sat down at the dressing table.

'Do my hair,' she said, switching on a table lamp with the assurance of someone who has planned everything.

I started just in time. The door burst open and we both turned round and stared as if we had no idea what had been going on. When it closed again we burst into giggles.

'I will come back,' Rosie said as our laughter subsided and I knew then, of course, that it was true.

She wore white that day. The colour of Chinese mourning clothes. A Katherine Hamnett linen dress and white kitten-heeled shoes.

'You won't forget, ever?' she made me promise.

And I swore.

I think, you know, that was the only time Rosie ever played a practical joke. The only time. The day she left. And I think she did it for me.

We walked down together. Beside the pile of trunks and suitcases laid out in the hallway there were two green nylon bags which hadn't been there before and as we came down the stairs I realized that there was a girl out on the verandah. She was lying on one of the loungers in her sunglasses, sipping some iced tea. A replacement. Conrad Beckett was out there with her. We could hear his voice, but he didn't come through. I don't know if Rosie realized that. She didn't flinch though. She didn't mention it. I suppose it didn't matter. She only smiled at Bobby politely and told him that she was ready.

Seeing Rosie leave that day, clinging to her in the doorway and watching her slip smoothly into the back seat of the car, I thought it was like seeing the sun set for the last time. It felt like I'd lost everything, and it would never get light ever again. I was totally alone. That day – it hangs over everything, even now, like a dark, dark cloud. I'll never forget it. My hands quivered and my stomach jumped, and I closed the front door and leaned back against the wall. I felt like I was going to faint. Maybe I would have, only Beckett strolled casually past me and invited me to join him in the garden.

'You've met Nancy,' he said. 'She'll be moving in.'

And I felt so betrayed. I felt like I'd helped him pull her. I felt guilty.

'What did you tell her?' I asked.

And the whisper of a grimace passed over Conrad's face like an old ghost.

'About the money of course,' he smiled.

I laughed. The stupid, pointless, empty money. What use was that when Rosie was gone?

'Was it that easy with me?' I wondered out loud, knowing the answer already, but still wanting to hear it for myself.

'It's always that easy,' Conrad replied.

And I didn't take a gun and shoot him, I didn't push him over and pummel my fists into his ribs, I didn't do anything like that. Anything that I should have done. Instead I survived. I followed him outside into the sunny, fragrant garden and I sat there for a long time. They might have tried to give me a new Rosie straight away, but Nancy and I, well we never really clicked. Nancy's young and she's simple. She'd never pull the monkey trick, she'd never race me to the most men on a busy day, she'd never sleep all night on the pale, fine sand. 'You should get out now, if you can,' I told her that very first day after Beckett had left us alone, but she turned her back on me and that was that.

It's hard to believe that things could have gone on. But they did. That was the weirdest thing. They really did, just the same as ever, and I resigned myself to it. As long as it took. Day by day. Hotel room by hotel room.

Fuck by casual fuck. I found myself even thinking of Coatross in a favourable light from time to time. It got that bad. I thought of my fresh-faced mother, frying up frozen food. Of my father reading the paper in his pyjamas. I suppose that they were all I had left, Mum and Dad. The one constant certainty. It was all that kept me going, those faces conjured up out of memories long gone. And every day for months as I climbed the stairs and caught a glimpse of the door to Rosie's room, for just one second I'd forget. I'd wonder if she was in there, though by the time I reached my own door the feeling had gone and I was empty again.

'Will you come and visit me, Kate?' Arthur pleaded, before he boarded his plane for London. 'Come over for a week or two in old Blighty.'

And I promised, although I knew I wouldn't and so did he. My vital organs were turning slowly to stone inside me. We were in the departures hall for a long time that day at Kai Tek. We didn't drink a thing, but I suppose we weren't really ourselves. Arthur's face had aged. The doctor said it was the pain that had done it. But that wasn't all. His mother stood beside us, like a cold grey statue. Like fucking Britannia. I hugged him tightly before she wheeled him away and then I just stood there with the whole airport teeming around me and I realized that I was alone. Completely alone. Everyone else had gone.

Chapter Thirty

Shih Ho: Biting Through

I didn't hear a word for what seemed like forever, though really it was less than a year. High summer once more with the clammy hot weather we all hated so much, and overcast, thick clouds endless in the sky and the whole town heavy with people because of the end of the Empire. For weeks before there were TV crews on every street corner and elegant European ladies sporting Shanghai Tang bags wherever they went. I worked and I worked. Professional. Miserable. Always wanting to be somewhere else. I just worked.

And then like magic the call came through on my mobile phone a week before the big day. I was jogging. I had taken to running two or three times a week in the early morning while it was still quite cool. I'd do it when I first came in at four or five in the morning after a night of hard work. It was the closest I ever got to running away, I suppose. Pounding the pavements on a three- or four-mile track which I mapped out between the house on Kadoorie Hill and the park at Kowloon City.

When my phone rang I sat sweat-drenched and panting on the grass, fished it out of my backpack and when I heard Rosie's voice I screamed. The park was all but deserted.

'Rosie,' I shouted. 'Oh my God, it's you. Are you OK?'

'Coming back next week,' she told me, and I could hear from her accent that her English had lapsed a little. She had been speaking only Cantonese for so long.

I started to cry. My lip quivered and my heart pounded hard.

'I will arrange everything,' she said.

'Yes. I can't wait. I just can't wait. It'll be just like old times. Just like before,' I babbled in my excitement and I lay back on the damp grass smiling like an idiot.

'Better,' Rosie assured me. 'It's going to be better.'

And then she hung up and I sprang to my feet, dancing and leaping all around the grass before running to the main road and hailing a taxi to take me home. I was so excited.

The day the British handed over Hong Kong it pissed down with rain, which is kind of ironic. In Chinese mythology they say that dragons control rain and flood. And the dragons were taking over the whole show that hot, dull afternoon as Prince Charles turned up at the harbour at Tamar for the farewell show, the Brits speaking only English and the Chinese speaking only Chinese, each incomprehensible to the other under a sea of black umbrellas. Earlier on when they'd lowered the Governor's standard it had been just as wet and Chris Patten had stood there looking painfully glum as they played God Save the Queen and Auld Lang Syne. With all those politicians in town, all the diplomats, every hooker in the city was on call. Except me. I had been booked, you see. I had been paid for. Twenty-four hours. One punter. Rosie had seen to everything, just like she said.

When she arrived she had gone straight to her hotel and I had been summoned. I guessed she paid a fortune for me. Bobby drove me over himself and watched without smiling as I skipped light-footed up to the room, hugging Rosie in the doorway. Hugging and crying. Both of us. Bobby stood there right behind me, but I hardly noticed him at all. He just didn't seem important and as we broke away from each other Rosie stepped backwards, pulling me inside and shutting the door, leaving him outside in the hall, alone. Together again. It felt good.

We toasted each other with ice-cold brandy and danced around the floor. It was already getting late and we decided to go out straight away. The whole city was celebrating. There were parties in the street, flamboyantly spreading the carnival atmosphere so that complete strangers tried to grab your hand and kiss your cheek and wrap themselves around you. We disappeared into the back seat of a limo, trying to keep away from the heaving, happy crowds. It was too overwhelming. Too intrusive.

'Where to, ladies?' the driver asked and Rosie directed him away from the main drag while I fiddled with the air conditioning. My arms and legs were covered in goosebumps, my skin wet from its brief exposure to the rain, and my initial joy subsiding. Rosie wasn't smiling enough, I realized. And she didn't seem to want to talk. Now that I had time to study her there were subtle, tiny differences in her appearance. The colour of her skin, the way she smelled of hairspray. She looked older, her red lipstick one shade darker than before, her hair bobbed shorter and eyes which seemed to know everything.

'Do you know?' I asked her. 'Did you take the test?'

Rosie hung her head. She sucked on her lower lip, transferring some of the glossy lip colour on to her front teeth.

'HIV positive,' she said. 'I have about ten years.'

That, for some reason, didn't really chill me. Ten years is an eternity. Well, that's the way it seemed.

'And Ho died?' I prompted her. But Rosie only nodded and then she pressed the intercom button on the arm beside her and told the driver to stop the car. We clambered out into the rain through the industrial machinery and boxes down on the docks. There were a few people nearby, like us, avoiding the crowds. It was very dark.

'Nearly time,' Rosie said and I followed her.

From the roof of a shipping container we stood watching the royal yacht *Britannia* set off while thousands of cameras flashed in the windows of the nearby high-rises. Everyone with any kind of vantage point was taking photos of the last Governor sailing out of the Pearl River Estuary, and I hung on to the fact that Rosie was beside me. Not just in my mind. Not in my imagination. She was really there. Rosie was back.

As we stood on the dockside she pulled her jade ring off her wedding finger and threw it into the dark water of the harbour. I couldn't quite make out where it landed and I strained up on my tiptoes to see. It was a lot of money to throw into the sea. Rosie didn't even look. I suppose she'd given up trying to second guess where things might be heading. She'd learnt a lesson in life.

'I wanted to watch him waste away,' she said sadly, as we climbed down and walked over to the limousine which was waiting for us. I didn't answer her. I mean, the old guy was dead, and for me, that was enough. Though not, it seemed, for Rosie. The driver jumped up eagerly out of his seat and opened the door and we both slid into the back of the car. 'What a waste,' she sighed, and I had to agree with her there.

We had, between us, tickets for fourteen private parties. The whole world was out drinking champagne to the end of the Empire and neither of us could face it. The initial delight had dissipated and Rosie seemed to be carrying a great burden with her. She had something to get off her chest. From time to time a barely audible sigh would escape from her glossy lips.

'Rosie, what is it?' I asked. 'You're home. You're home.'

'And I have a plan,' she said, 'I know what to do, but you aren't going to like it. You're too good.'

I had to laugh at that. 'We could go back to the hotel,' I offered. 'We could talk there.'

Rosie shrugged her shoulders. The hotels were all so busy. All over the place there were comfy chairs set up so that leading statesmen and politicians could be interviewed for TV about what was going on, though as far as I could make out the British were interviewing the British, and the Chinese were interviewing the Chinese, which seemed to me to be strange, but then it fitted with the way it had been all along. One way or another just walking through the lobby was an effort.

'Let's go to sit on a beach,' Rosie said, and without waiting for a reply she snapped something I didn't catch to the driver, who started up the engine and pulled away.

I knew of course that Rosie would have changed. The moment she rang I knew big changes were on the cards and I wanted to hear about it, to soak it in, like that day I had lain next to her on the bed. She didn't tell me all at once but she did start then to give me some small details.

Ho's mansion had been golden and ornate. The gardens had smelled of fruit trees. There was a mango grove. His children played on expanses of lush green grass which it took three men to maintain. Ho came to her bedroom every second night and slept there with her. Rosie had smugly thought to herself, as he laboured, 'I'm a time bomb. I could go off at any minute,' and she put up with it. He would tell her to rub his feet, he would bore her with tiresome stories about the adventures of his youth. His mother's pet name for him. His cousin who had died. How he had denounced his dead father during the Cultural Revolution. His first big break. During the day she walked with him past the household gardens to the farm where the fields of poppies were almost ready for their red harvest and where acres of cannabis plants swayed in the southern breezes. A mile and a half from the house there was a warehouse made of rusting corrugated iron.

'How much was I worth?' she asked him.

And the old man smiled, his marked yellow teeth protruding slightly.

'More than the sky. They undersold you,' he replied.

And Rosie hated him. He made her shudder. The way he laboured over her as if he expected her to enjoy it. The way he would stare into her eyes. She wished on him a thousand tortures and knew that she would be there to watch them.

'Old man,' she would say over him as he slept, 'you are weak. I am strong. I will last longer.'

And she wondered to herself just how long it would take.

In the third month after Rosie arrived he had gone to Beijing. There were no newspapers, no television, no radio in the house. Rosie wandered the gardens alone. She watched as Ho's wife showed her how she ran the household. Bottling plums. Playing mah-jong all the hot afternoon. Taking tea in the summer house. She had longed, she said, to walk free. She had longed for paved streets and excitement. Music. Even music. There had been nothing there for her. Nothing which made her life her own.

When Ho returned, turgid weeks later, he brought other men with him. The planes landed on the lawns early in the morning. They had flown through the night. The household was in chaos. All twenty bedrooms in use, and Ho's wife bustling up and down the hallways giving orders. Ho had disappeared into his private rooms with the men, and they worked all day in his study, meals brought to them at the table there. In the evening the men ate alone. From her bed, Rosie had heard the laughter and knew they would finish late. The old man spent the first night with his other wife and early the next day he disappeared into his study once more. Rosie knew he would spend the second night with her. It would seem that he was scrupulously, excruciatingly fair if absolutely nothing else. Near midnight the knock came on her door. He started by kissing her neck, murmuring to her, wanting to take her slowly, but Rosie couldn't bear it. She pushed him back on to the bed and climbed on top of him, pulling the sheets around her as she did so.

'Watch me,' she whispered and his tired eyes lit up as she moved.

The next day the planes had left in the afternoon. But Ho worked hard with extra secretaries flown in from Canton and junior officers arriving from time to time by helicopter, their wrists shackled to boxes of papers. Six weeks, Rosie said, of late nights and exhaustion. He ate special meals prescribed by his doctor. He ate them at his desk and some afternoons he'd call for Rosie, pushing her to her knees, demanding a blow job and then working right on as soon as he'd come. At long last when the work was over he had prepared for another trip to the north. That day he had eaten with his family for the first time in weeks and then he had called his wife into his study and they had spent all evening together. Rosie had gone to bed alone. In the morning, when she awoke, the study light had still been on. It was too early. Rosie had knocked lightly on the door to the room and had heard nothing. She had pushed it open and in the yellow light she saw him there. Stiff and cold. The old man had died in his chair and his wife was kneeling before him, her head in his lap. She had been crying there, quietly, all night. Alone. And Rosie cried too. 'Such devotion,' she had heard the servants whisper among themselves. After Ho's death Rosie hadn't been able to eat for days. They left trays of food outside her bedroom door. And she grieved. Mourning for herself and her decisions. Trying to make sense of what she'd done.

'I'm a time bomb,' she laughed at herself in her gilded mirror. And there were dark patches under her eyes and her skin had a grey pallor from the lack of sleep and the lack of air. She couldn't have known what was going to happen, that it was all to be wasted. That he'd die of a heart attack. That he'd die so suddenly in his sleep.

She was silent when she finished the story. We had walked right along the beach, right around the bay, and come to rest together on the sand.

I leant my head back and closed my eyes.

'Fuck,' I said.

My left hand was shaking. I didn't want Rosie to see.

'Come on,' she said. 'Let's go back to the car.'

Outside Shek-O there is a quarry surrounded by a wire fence and signs telling you to keep out. We knew it would be deserted. It's a huge area, the earth piled up high in between deep valleys. Sometimes when it rains heavily lakes form in the dips. We had the limo park up in a bus stop on the main road and then we scaled the fence, nimble even in evening dress, vaulting over the top. It wasn't that high. Rosie lit up a cigarette and we headed into the darkness, climbing the red muddy hills, moving away from the bright lights of the village down in the cove.

We shared the cigarette as if it was a toke, passed hand to hand, and when we got up to the top of the incline I stubbed it out, threw back my head and screamed. The sound seemed to undulate. Maybe it was the landscape we were in. After a second or two, Rosie joined me and we howled together out into the blackness open-mouthed, and somehow I felt a surge of freedom. A tantalizing rush of what it used to be like when Rosie and I were together. And then it was gone and I could feel the tiny spit of raindrops on my tongue, my skin flushed in the warm evening air. And I felt low again because we were together but I knew it couldn't be for long.

'You're back,' I said sadly.

'And I have a proposition for you,' Rosie replied, suddenly serious. But before she could tell me we heard panting in the darkness and we tensed, only breathing out when we realized it was the driver of the car running towards us up the hill.

'OK?' he asked, panic in his eyes and a heavy-looking stick in his hand in case he had to take on some adversary. 'I heard screaming.'

And Rosie and I laughed together. 'Letting off steam,' we said, and the poor guy looked almost disappointed and I shouted out again just to demonstrate, and then we followed him back down to the road and told him to take us to Rosie's hotel. After all, there was no point in torturing him, and besides, we really did just want to be on our own.

Chapter Thirty-one

Pi: Grace

Rosie had taken the penthouse suite. We emptied the minibar on to the bedclothes and sat cross-legged behind the pile of little bottles as if we were teenagers at a sleepover party. Rosie chose first. She clicked open a tiny bottle of Bailey's and necked it back. Rosie's never been a great drinker. Her cheeks glow pink after two or three shots and she starts to dance no matter what after about five. I picked up one of the vodkas and downed it in one. This, I decided, was going to be fun.

'Proposition me then,' I smiled.

And by way of proposition, Rosie continued her story.

After Ho's funeral his eldest son, Lee, had asked to see her. He had inherited his father's estates and was the new head of the household. His father had procured him a commission in the Red Army some years before. Rosie hadn't even met him until the day of the funeral. He had come home, though, for several weeks to see to his affairs and comfort his mother. Rosie had swept her hair up into a bun and wore black Western mourning clothes. He came to her room. A kid of twenty-six, older than both of us in years, but younger in experience by far. Rosie said that she had liked him. There was something honest about him. Something innocent.

'You may do whatever you wish,' he said to her. 'You are free to go. Free to stay.'

It was a strange encounter. I suppose neither of us are used to people who don't want anything. We're accustomed to being currency. Rosie's room had lacquered walls and ornately carved furniture and heavy drapes through which the light filtered obliquely. She knew she couldn't go back to her old life, she had burnt her bridges there. Lee had been gentle and naive. He'd never presume to lay a hand on her. He didn't want to. She had felt motherly. Protective. His eyes were wide and young, a heavy responsibility falling on his shoulders after Ho's death, for which, it seemed, he wasn't prepared.

'What will you do?' she asked him. 'What are your plans?'

And Lee had smiled the smile of the innocent. He hadn't formed his thoughts fully, he said, but he would stay on in the army to be sure. Keep the estate going. Plan to retire there when he had been promoted highly enough.

'I want to be a great general for the Chinese people,' he had told her.

'A great general,' Rosie had repeated, a smirk playing on her face.

'Yes. Like my father,' he had replied in earnest.

Rosie thought about it. This man, it seemed to her, was not like his father at all.

'You will need money then,' she started. 'Money is a great insurance in these matters.'

'Insurance,' Lee smiled at her. 'Yes, insurance is important.'

And they both knew that they were talking about money for bribes. Rosie remembered crossing her legs as she thought about this. It was pretty clear that the kid wouldn't last five minutes with the likes of Bobby, she knew that much straight away. She glanced out of the window at the open blue sky. At her freedom. And then she took a deep breath.

'Your father made a lot of money,' she said simply. 'He sold pharmaceutical products to the triads in Hong Kong. Where he found me.'

'I know. I know.'

'Will you still do that?' she asked him.

Lee had got up and moved around the room. He laid his hot palms on a cool marble table against the wall and then ran his fingers through his short soldier's haircut and gazed out of the window. He hadn't anticipated this conversation at all. She was too young, he had thought, she was too pretty.

'Big business,' he murmured, obviously out of his depth.

And Rosie had realized all at once what she was going to do. In the event of it being impossible to go back, she was going to go forward instead. Onwards and upwards. Survival.

'I can help you,' she had told him. 'I can help you a lot,' she had said.

I frowned. 'You're going to be become a drug dealer?' I asked her.

'Big time,' Rosie nodded, and she picked up a miniature bottle of whisky, and without really looking at it she knocked it back, grimacing at its sourness. 'I make the deals. I organize everything. I get 20 per cent commission,' she smiled serenely. 'Sales job and Bobby has to deal with me now,' Rosie nodded with satisfaction. 'He has to deal with me.'

And I realized that Rosie had moved up the ladder. She had made a leap. She'd had to.

'So, you want a job?' she asked me.

And I didn't know what to say. I mean, I'm no drug pusher. Drug pushers have guns. Drug pushers blow off people's kneecaps. People I know. It was a big step to take. Even to be with Rosie, who seemed almost oblivious to exactly what she was asking me to become.

'Gonna make a lot of money here,' she continued. 'A fifth off the top. That's the deal. Pretty good, huh? I'll split it with you. Fifty-fifty.'

My head felt dizzy. More money than ever. A golden paved highway to an early death. The room swam so much that I could only see the colours – dark wood and muted beige and a navy throw-over in the direction of the bed. Everything I ever wanted – Rosie and untold riches. Little black suits and cases of dollars in cash. An air-conditioned Daimler of our own at the airport, rather than one which someone else had sent. A sleek little gun hidden in my handbag, which I'd have to learn to use. All these things, I have to say, were not unappealing. We could have hung out as much as we liked.

But maybe what happened with Arthur and Serge had made me grow up a bit. Maybe I'd drawn lines more distinct than ever around what was and what wasn't acceptable behaviour for me. Places I wanted to go and places to avoid. I'd been close enough to drug deals and money to know perfectly well just how the whole thing really works when it comes right down to it.

'You sure that you want to do this?' I asked Rosie in disbelief.

And she didn't reply, but her face, without moving very much, seemed to say 'what the hell else am I going to do, Kate?' I suppose that the alternative was probably just to wait. To do nothing. Eventually, to die.

'I can't come back,' she whispered, at last.

'Just live here, Rosie. Just stay here. I'll work till the end of my contract and then we'll think of something to do. We can buy the apartment. Live together. Like we planned before.'

But Rosie shook her head, her eyebrows knitted very slightly together and I just lay there on the mattress and stared at the white smooth ceiling, knowing I'd lost her. Rosie hadn't had enough yet. She still wanted her revenge.

Later she sat with me as I was driven home in a mirror-windowed car from the hotel's VIP fleet. It was awkward between us, the elation gone, the rush subsided and both of us left in silence in a difficult position and on a sea of emotions. Love and revulsion. Jealousy and insecurity. Horror. We didn't say a thing. I didn't want to leave it that way, but I didn't know what else to do so I sat to the left and looked out of my window and Rosie sat to the right and looked out of hers. There was two feet of leather upholstery between us which neither of us seemed able to cross. It had all been for nothing.

As the car pulled up to Kadoorie Hill I noticed that the lights were on upstairs, and we just sat there for a while. Rosie rolled down the electric window to catch the scent of the flowers which were hanging over the wall of the garden.

'You want to come in?' I asked her.

She seemed nostalgic but she shook her head. 'No point,' she said, and then scrambled to put her window up again as the front door of the house opened and the soft glow of the hallway lights tumbled down the driveway. It wasn't quite dawn. Bobby was walking alone after a long night of parties, swinging the keys of his shiny black car in his strong-fingered grasp. He grinned at us parked there and although he couldn't see, he knew perfectly well who was inside the black windows of the limo. Rosie nodded at me, and I got up and opened the door, hopping out on to the pavement. She obviously wanted to leave.

'Hi,' I said as he walked towards me.

'Had fun?' Bobby asked. When I nodded he said, 'Well, she paid a lot for you.'

'You enjoy your girl?' he continued, leaning into the back of the car, where Rosie was sitting up straight, stiff and over-dignified. 'We can put her back to work now, if you're finished. What you want to do – let her off early?'

Rosie leant forward. 'I was just sitting here looking at a nice house, Bobby. I've got no plans in particular. It's a nice place you've got here,' she said, 'but where I live now, it's nicer.'

Bobby laughed. 'You've gone up in the world. That's good. But if you make this too difficult, Rosie, you'll have to do business with someone else. Hard feelings are tough to make a deal over.'

Rosie paused for a second. I could see her thinking it over. 'Oh no,' she grinned amiably. 'Bobby, I want to deal with you,' and then she slipped elegantly along the seat. 'I've thought about you a lot,' she said.

I stepped backwards, to move towards the house. It was turning my stomach.

Bobby was falling for it though. 'Old friends?' he smiled and Rosie obligingly patted the seat next to her.

'Old friends,' Rosie repeated as he climbed in. 'You and Beckett. Old friends are the best,' she agreed, compliant and deadly, her glossy hair shining, and her arms long and thin, I thought, like a black widow spider. She was so beautiful, you see, she'd have been hard to resist, and Bobby, well, he'd had a thing for her all along.

And as he closed the door of the car she was smiling with the low light of revenge in her eyes, knowing exactly what she was doing, and I walked back into the house alone as the car pulled away.

Epilogue

Hsaio Ch'u: The taming power of the small

Getting back to my old, normal life wasn't easy. I missed all of them. I missed the way that it was, the beautiful, brilliant illusion I thought was my life. I stayed in Hong Kong for another two years and watched the city change. The market exploded and property prices tumbled and on the street you could feel it, just the quiver of a monumental difference, economic reality kicking in. Six months before I left I went dancing in Lan Kwai Fong and in the corners of the nightclub there were loads of people smoking temple balls, a humid cloud of opium hanging around them. I was dancing on my own, but it didn't feel that way, because there in the corner was a little part of Rosie. A sign. At weekends I watched Bobby and Beckett. For them tiring too quickly or feeling unwell. Rosie's a worker and I knew that she'd get them in the end. She was a miracle, really. The power of her was everywhere, like a mighty mountain goddess. I'd see the flowers she left on Serge's grave when I went to visit it myself. Those fuchsia orchids she always loved, that grow on the hillsides in Lamma.

It worries me, I suppose, that I tried so hard. That I really believed in all of us and look how it ended. We were the goodies, I'm sure of it, but we didn't finish up like goodies are supposed to. Maybe it was Rosie's story all along. Maybe from her point of view she reckons it's OK. When I think of everything she did I'm amazed by her bravery. She was the one who called the shots. I only watched. I bottled out and walked away from everything I thought I ever wanted. I stood in the shadows and I stayed alive. I surprised myself in my very ordinariness, but in the end I wasn't cut out for it. Not at all.

I couldn't imagine leaving the big city, the fast cars and the endless lights and the excitement. The truth is that two years later when my contract was up, even as I packed my bags I didn't know where I was going to go. In the car when he came to pick me up Conrad told the driver to take a detour, and we drove through Mong Kok one last time and took the tunnel under the estuary over to Hong Kong Island and up on to the Peak to savour the view over China's most recent acquisition.

'Who'd have thought it, of all of us, I survived the best of all?' I thought to myself.

That day Conrad reminded me of the way he had been in London, a charming, well-turned-out business-man. A stranger.

'I know someone in New York,' he said. 'I've heard it's amazing to live there. Pay's not bad either. Do you want the number?'

I almost ended myself laughing.

In London I booked into an hotel to get over my jet lag and I took stock. There were girls my age coming out of college and what the hell had they learned? In Hong Kong where my sell-by date had been well and truly reached I had felt as if everything was over. Walking in Hyde Park in the fresh morning air I began to see that maybe it was only a beginning I was coming to and not an end at all. I was twenty-one and I had made my first million. They do say that the first one is the most difficult, don't they? And there I was back in London again and not excited about it at all.

I slept for days on end and dreamt of nothing, slowly emerging from my hibernation, coming alive again bit by bit to a new reality. The possibility of a fresh start. Each day was a time for remembering, a time for reflection, until gradually I stopped looking behind me and started looking to the future.

I bought myself a flat in Notting Hill and began to look around for something to do. It surprised me that no-one knew. No-one suspected a thing. People just couldn't see it. I got a couple of modelling jobs and helped out on a documentary this guy I met was making about street girls in Paddington. And he didn't say 'how the hell do you know?' when I wrote a list of the perfect questions to ask them. He didn't seem to wonder at all. One project led to another and I worked hard. The money was lousy, but that didn't seem to matter any more. The point was that I had got away with it. I had got off the train. I had quit the pleasure express.

Kate Thompson was born in 1975 in Coatross. She tells people that she worked for some time as an investigative journalist. Recently she founded The Underbelly Guide to the World, *the definitive guide to the world's brothels, strip clubs and drug dens, which she researches and writes herself. She lives alone.*

Also by Sara Sheridan and available in Arrow:

TRUTH OR DARE

Crime is easy once you get started you know. It's the initial break with respectability which is difficult.

Libby and Becka are two ordinary girls. They've both got things in their lives they'd like to forget. But when the owner of the flat they're borrowing (without her permission) goes missing, things start to spiral and the girls take to the road on what might be the trip (the last trip) of a lifetime.

They break the rules. They make up their own. They lie, cheat and panic in equal measure. It's a story about London, Glasgow, Belfast and Dublin. Drink, drugs, bleached hair and bad disguises. Idle fun, stolen millions and running for your life.

Truth or Dare is a rollicking road movie of a book, an exhilarating, funny and poignant novel of female friendship, family . . . and premeditated murder.

'A thriller for a new generation . . . Sara Sheridan will go far'
Harpers & Queen

'Darkly comic and compassionate'
Mike Ripley, *Daily Telegraph*

'A revenger's tragedy crossed with a blithe and black picaresque road comedy . . . so well written you never notice the writing' *Glasgow Herald*

'A story of friendship, bad money and lies . . . it made me laugh out loud, but it also nearly reduced me to tears'
Sunday Express

MA POLINSKI'S POCKETS

Intrigue, adventure and a stack load of cash!

When Rachel White is summoned to an Edinburgh lawyer's office, nothing could have prepared her for the news that she's inherited a fortune. A very big fortune. Eight million pounds, to be precise.

Just why would Ma Polinski, an old antiques dealer Rachel knew as a child, leave her everything?

It's not enough to take the money and run. Rachel wants answers. With the help of her best friend Nina, she sets out to dig into the past. But the secrets which are unearthed rock her previously stable existence and raise long-buried ghosts.

'A thoughtful, passionate novel' *Daily Telegraph*

CORDIAL AND CORROSIVE

Sophie Hannah

Life isn't fair . . . so why play by the rules?

Sebastian Nunn's surname reflects the number of jobs he's been offered. He has applied for twenty-two, been interviewed for eleven and got none. So when he is shortlisted for the best job in the world, his wife Kate, driving instructor and crusader against the injustices perpetrated by appointment committees, takes matters into her own hands.

And no sooner has she started poking her nose in than she discovers this prestigious position is not what it seems. Not only does the chair of the interview panel turn out to be the mother-in-law of the favourite candidate, but the last person to hold the post disappeared in mysterious circumstances. And when Kate takes on a depressive new driving pupil, things go from strange to stranger . . .

'Sophie Hannah's books define originality . . . [she] has put "You must read this!" back into books and we love her for it' B

'[*Cordial and Corrosive* has] an edge and precision its rivals in the twentysomething lifestyle genre often lack' *The Times*

'Enjoyable and pacey' *Cosmopolitan*

'An entertaining fast-paced farce' *Sunday Mirror*

ALSO AVAILABLE IN ARROW